"Laci's father knew you'd make it."

Brant turned to stare at the other man in surprise. "He didn't like me."

"That's where you're wrong," Charley said. "He liked you well enough. He just didn't want his daughter traipsing all over the countryside after you. All you could think about was the rodeo."

"I love her," Brant said.

"But not enough to quit."

Brant couldn't argue with that, because his love for Laci and his need to win the world championship had nothing to do with one another. But no one had ever understood that. If it had been his own choice, if his promise to his brother hadn't existed, he would have quit the rodeo and done anything Laci had wanted him to do rather than lose her.

But he didn't have a choice then—and he didn't have one now.

MARRY ME,
Cowboy

THE RETURN
OF THE COWBOY

Cheryl Biggs

Secrets!

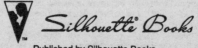

Silhouette Books

Published by Silhouette Books
America's Publisher of Contemporary Romance

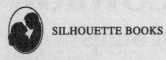 SILHOUETTE BOOKS

ISBN 0-373-65357-3

THE RETURN OF THE COWBOY

CHERYL BIGGS

was never really a reader while growing up, but got hooked on Gothics, then romances, when her three children were little. While they napped, she read. Finally she decided to write a romance. That manuscript went into the closet, with the next four or five. Years later, after selling her personnel agency, she pulled out her first manuscript and went to an RWA conference, which garnered her an agent and several good friends. A year later that first book was sold, and a dream came true.

Cheryl lives in the San Francisco Bay Area, in a sunny suburb at the foot of Mount Diablo with her husband, five cats and blue-eyed dog. Her children are now grown, and in her spare time she loves to travel, shop, read and try to talk her husband, Jack, into adopting "just one more animal."

Please address questions and book requests to:
Silhouette Reader Service
U.S.: 3010 Walden Ave., P.O. Box 1325, Buffalo, NY 14269
Canadian: P.O. Box 609, Fort Erie, Ont. L2A 5X3

This book is dedicated to my family: my dad, who handed down to me a love of Westerns; my mom, who passed on to me her love of books; my children, who are always encouraging and supportive; and my husband, my one and only hero.

Chapter 1

"Looks like Garrison's in trouble," the rodeo announcer declared over the PA system.

The woman watching felt her breath catch in her throat and shuddered as long-ago memories fought to resurface. She struggled to ward them off, and in spite of herself, leaned closer to the window of her office that overlooked the arena. The last thing in the world she wanted to do was watch Brant ride, but she couldn't look away. Tension seized her and the old memories that refused to be vanquished once again became reality.

Brant struggled to free his hand from the grip rope that held it tightly to the bull's back. At that same moment the huge Brahma bucked and Brant was thrown, his arm nearly jerked from its socket as his gloved hand remained imprisoned beneath the rope. He slammed into the bull's shoulder and fought off a wave of dizziness.

"Please," she prayed softly, old fears instantly overwhelming her, "get him out of there." Her hands curled into fists at her sides, flashbacks of a long-ago tragedy filling her mind as terror for Brant's safety threatened to stop the beat of her heart.

A clown ran past Brant, yelling and waving a flag to draw the bull's attention.

Nightmare roared in fury, spun and charged.

Brant was jerked forward, stumbled, and his left leg tangled with the bull's. He cursed as pain shot through his knee. Simultaneously the girth rope snapped and his hand broke free. He slammed into the ground, rolled instinctively and jumped to his feet as several more rodeo clowns ran into the arena, yelling and waving arms and flags at Nightmare to draw his attention away from Brant and head him back toward the pens.

The woman released the breath she'd held pent up in her lungs. Feelings of relief, the likes of which she hadn't felt for more than seven years, washed over her, leaving her weak and momentarily drained. She sighed, but continued to stare down at the man she had never expected to see again.

Brant snatched his black Stetson from the ground where it had fallen earlier, slapped it against his thigh to rid it of dust and glanced up at the lighted scoreboard. He tried to ignore the dull throb of pain nagging at his left leg. A second later the board lit up with the score for his ride. The crowd cheered and Brant smiled. He'd made his points. Hopefully he hadn't reinjured his leg in the process. But he was still in the lead. Brushing back a curl of black hair that had fallen forward to dangle over his forehead, he resettled the Stetson in place, waved to the spectators, and turned toward the chutes located beneath the raised arena office.

A cloud drifted in front of the sun and a faint image beyond the glass window of the office caught Brant's eye.

The PA system crackled to life again. "Well, folks, that was a close one for Garrison, but a good score, and a terrific wrap-up for today's bull riding. Now the Reno Rodeo, hosting the World Championships for the first time ever, is proud to present a special exhibition ride by our flag girls."

Brant heard the announcement, but didn't move. He stared at the huge window that spread across the front of the office, uncertain whether the light was playing tricks on him, or he'd really seen Laci standing behind the silvered glass and looking down at him, her long blond hair flowing over her shoulders. Before he had time to decide, the cloud slowly drifted onward, and once again the mirrored window became a near blinding reflection of golden light. Still, Brant didn't turn away. The thought of her being this close, looking down at him, meeting his gaze and watching him ride, caused a knot of need to form in his gut, twisting and burning like a branding iron set to tender flesh.

Even now, after all this time, he could still remember the satinlike texture of her skin beneath his touch, the sun-kissed landscape of each curve and line of her body, and the hot, scorching heat that had always enveloped him whenever he'd held her in his arms and pressed her length to his. Years later, and the gnawing ache for her was still there. A jumble of mixed emotions coursed through him, not the least of which was anger at himself. In spite of what had happened between them, or more accurately, what had not happened, he'd learned over the years that it was useless to try to deny that a part of him still loved Laci. It was a reality that he lived with, but he didn't have to like it.

Out of the corner of his eye he saw the parade gates open and the exhibition riders enter the arena, their flashy sequin-trimmed shirts and the silk flags they carried a blaze of color. The crowd cheered them on as they began to circle the area in single file.

Brant ripped his gaze from the office window and stalked toward the rails. With each step he cursed beneath his breath, disgusted that a memory better left forgotten had kept him standing like a fool in the middle of the arena, his body hardening with desire for a woman he should have gotten out of his system a long time ago.

High above the rodeo arena, safe and comfortable in the air-conditioned office that had once belonged to her father, Laci James-McCandrick tried to quell the trembling that was rippling through her body. She knew it was impossible for Brant to see her through the mirrored glass, nevertheless she had the feeling he had been looking right at her.

A faint sigh escaped her lips. He was back. Brant Garrison had finally returned to Reno, and while she'd stood there looking down at him, the years had quietly slipped from her mind as if they'd never existed.

Despite her reservations, and all the years that had

passed since the last time she'd seen him, a shiver of excitement skipped its way up her spine. Laci hugged herself against the unwelcome sensation, surprised at it, and afraid of it.

Had it really only been seven and a half years since she'd felt so safe and secure within his embrace? Felt the passion that had always sparked within her whenever Brant's lips had claimed hers? Tears stung Laci's eyes and chagrined, she hurriedly blinked them back. But her memories were not to be banished as easily as her tears. She could still remember the feel and smell of him, the taste and passion of him, as if she had been in his arms only yesterday, yet in other ways it seemed more like an eternity. A lot of things had changed since he'd left, though in some respects nothing had changed at all.

"He's still crazy," she said softly. "Secures his grip rope too tight. Takes dangerous chances. Risks it all." The last tremors of the fear that had held her in its clutches only moments before swept through her in a mild shudder. She'd watched dozens of men ride since the last time she'd seen Brant, but the terror and anxiety that was so near blood chilling came only when he was on top of a bull, only when it was his life at stake.

"Yeah, but he's on top," Charley Brownning replied, setting down the PRCA's Rodeo Media book he'd been flipping through. He removed a brown cowboy hat from his head and swiped a hand through his thick gray hair. "This time he's gonna make it, Laci," he said. "I can feel it in my bones. And winning that World Championship buckle is what counts to them boys. It's their dream."

She didn't look at the old man—she didn't have to. Laci knew his expressions, voice and thoughts as well as she knew her own. She also knew he thought she and Brant belonged together, but he was wrong. Brant belonged to the rodeo.

"Yeah, that's what counts," she said softly, absently echoing Charley's words and a little surprised at how much they still stung. "Their dream."

Once, years ago, Laci had also thought she and Brant belonged together. That had been her dream. She'd loved him with all her heart. When he left her she'd resented and nearly hated him, and finally, with the passing of time, she'd come to accept the fact that they merely weren't right for each other.

The anger, resentment and hatred had eventually subsided, but there was still a part of her heart that loved him and always would. She'd secretly followed Brant's career over the years, aching for him whenever he lost, filled with joy for him when he won and she'd saved whatever news articles about him she could find and had tucked them away.

She'd called herself a fool more than a million times, but it didn't matter, and neither did the fact that he'd finally come back to Reno. He was only in town because of the World Championships, not because of her, and she'd do best to remember that.

"He's off to a good start," Charley said, invading her thoughts. "Made his points today. Starting off right up there in the lead." He clucked his tongue and nodded. "Damned good ride, I'd say, considering he nearly ended up shining that bull's hooves with his face."

Charley chuckled at his own words.

Laci nodded absently, but her thoughts were else-where, dredging up yet another memory. Before his unexpected death, her father had organized and produced the Reno Rodeo for over thirty years, and Charley had been Ed James's assistant and best friend that entire time. Now Charley worked for her, but he was much more than her assistant. Since the day she'd been born he'd been like a second father to her, and she thanked the heavens every night for that, especially now when she needed his help with the rodeo.

The World Championships were normally held in Las Vegas, but a union strike by southern Nevada garbage collectors had nearly crippled that city, so the Pro Rodeo Cowboys Association had voted to hold this year's World Championships in Reno. Because of the abruptness of the strike and the hasty vote of the PRCA to relocate rather than cancel the event, to say nothing of the problems Laci was still encountering as a result of her recent divorce, there hadn't been a lot of advance preparation time.

She continued to stare down into the arena as Brant walked toward the rails and out of her line of sight. Laci knew all too well how much winning the title meant to Brant. How much it had always meant. She could still hear the words he'd said to her that night, just before he had walked out of her life.

"Sorry, I guess I'm just not the settling-down kind."

She'd never forgotten the look that had been on his face, in his eyes that night, just before he'd turned away from her. It had said he was lying, that part of him wanted desperately to stay with her, but there was something inside of him, some restlessness, that wouldn't let him put down roots, wouldn't let him consider anything permanent in his life if it interfered with his career on the rodeo circuit. Yet whenever she'd tried to talk to him about it, she'd met with denial, or stone-cold silence.

Laci sighed softly, not even aware of having done it.

Earlier that same night, before they'd argued and he'd left, Brant had asked her to go with him on the circuit, but he hadn't wanted to get married. He'd done that twice already, and he'd said twice was enough, at least for a while.

But Laci did want marriage, and a home, a family and a normal everyday life. She hadn't wanted to live out of motel rooms or trailers, never putting down roots, never in any one town for more than a few days. But that hadn't been the real reason she'd said no to him; it had been her excuse. She'd loved him so much she would have followed him across the universe and lived in the back of his pickup truck if it had meant they'd be together. But she couldn't set aside the terror that filled her every time he climbed onto the back of a bull or wild bronc. Every time she watched him ride she remembered Sonny and her heart froze in fear, waiting for the disaster she felt certain was sure to come.

Brant hadn't understood her refusal, and she'd never been able to explain. She'd dated Sonny for almost a year and thought she was in love with him. Then on the night of their high school graduation they and several of their friends had driven out to the old Ranch Road to celebrate. The boys had raced their cars and motorcycles against one another while the girls stood on the sidelines and cheered. It should have been a night she remembered with fond memories—instead it was a nightmare that she would live with for the rest of her life.

Sonny had been racing two other boys when the front tire of his cycle blew. Sometimes, even now, when she heard a car skid around a turn, its tires screeching, she would still cringe and wait for the crash, and the deadly silence that followed. Sonny had died instantly.

Two years later, while home from college for the summer, Laci had met Brant and fallen head over heels in love with him. She'd thought life was perfect, until the day she watched him ride a bull and he'd been thrown. Laci had found herself suddenly paralyzed with terror, the scene before her meshing with the memory of watching Sonny being hurled from his motorcycle. After that she couldn't watch Brant ride, so she'd made up excuses.

Laci closed her eyes, remembering all too well the night he'd left, and wishing she didn't. Letting Brant Garrison walk out of her life might have been a mistake, but marrying Judd McCandrick had been worse.

Absently twisting a long lock of blond hair around her finger, she shook off the memories and feelings they stirred and forced her thoughts back to the present. But it wasn't any more pleasant than her regrets of the past. One thing she was certain of, however, was that no matter what happened, no matter what was said or done, she would never go back to Judd. Turning away from the window she straightened and looked down at Charley, still seated behind his desk. ''I've got to get back to the hospital and pick up Kit.''

"You need to go down and talk to Brant." He leaned back in his chair, the old wooden seat creaking loudly, and looked toward the window. "Set things right between you two, Laci. It's been too long."

She stiffened. "I need you to help me run the rodeo, Charley, not my life." His old brown eyes met hers and she instantly regretted the harsh words. "Sorry," she mumbled.

He smiled. "Yeah, I know."

"Look, you don't need me around here anymore, do you, Charley? I really should go. Kit's probably already wondering where I am."

"Nah, I can handle things. The ladies will be doing some barrel racing after the exhibition, then we got some amateur cutters coming on."

"You sure you won't need my help later?"

He smiled, the gesture causing his already generously full cheeks to puff and the ends of his thick, gray mustache to turn up at each corner. "Piece of cake. I'll have Lester take the day's receipts to the bank and Bobby can help me close and lock the place up when we're done."

She nodded. "Oh, and what about that young cowboy who got hurt earlier? Rawlins? Did the doctor in the Justin Medical Trailer take care of him?"

Charley waved her toward the door. "He's fine. Looked worse than it was. Doc said he just had a broken nose. Now go on, and make sure you get yourself to Hank's Corral tonight for the party."

Laci paused while reaching for the door. She'd forgotten about the opening night kickoff celebration she had arranged to welcome everyone connected with the rodeo. All of the contestants would be at Hank's, which meant Brant would be there. A flutter of apprehension swept over her. She wasn't ready to face him. Laci looked back at Charley and shook her head. "Charley, I don't know about coming to the party. You'll be there to represent James Enterprises and I really should stay home and spend some time with K—"

"You can't," he said, cutting her off and eyeing her pointedly. He tilted back in his chair, which caused his generous mound of stomach to protrude all the more. "Your old man always welcomed the rodeo contestants personally and they expect you to do the same now that you've taken over. Anyway, it'll make good press, and we can use that. Good press brings in more spectators, and more spectators brings in more money."

Laci sighed. "And we need that, don't we?"

Charley pulled his gaze from hers and swiveled around to stare through the window. "Well, we're not sold out yet, which ain't usual, especially considering this is the World Championships. And without having any idea what's in the books..." he shrugged "...who knows what we need."

The offhanded comment was statement enough of how little he trusted Judd McCandrick. But Charley had his reasons for distrusting Laci's ex-husband, and she had begun to form a few reasons of her own. After the unexpected death of her parents several years ago Judd had taken over the management of James Enterprises. At the time Laci had been struck with grief and happy to let him handle everything. But now that she and Judd were divorced, the company her father had founded was Laci's responsibility, and one Judd didn't want to lose. He hadn't wanted the divorce, or to give up control of James Enterprises, but she'd given him no choice in either matter.

There was no doubt in her mind that Judd wanted her to fail so she'd need him again, and he'd done everything he could in the last few months since their divorce to ensure that would happen. He had even, up until two days ago, ignored the court order she'd obtained that directed him to hand over all the company's records, bank statements and logbooks. By the time he'd finally done it, trucks, trailers, livestock and cowboys had already started to arrive for the Championship rodeo and Laci and the arena hadn't been anywhere near ready for them.

Charley swiveled about to face her again. When Judd had taken over James Enterprises, Charley had promptly retired, five years ahead of schedule, and he'd only come back because she needed him. "How's Kit doing?"

She pulled her mind from the unpleasant thoughts of Judd McCandrick. "The doctor assured me that he's as good as new. The concussion was a slight one."

"Just make sure you get him back on a horse right away, Laci." He threw her a serious look, then chuckled again and pulled at one end of his mustache. "We don't need any ground-stuck cowboys around here."

She smiled and said, "Right," which was far from the way she was truly feeling. But if she told Charley that the last thing she wanted to do was put her son back up on a horse, she knew she'd get a lecture and she didn't want that, either. But whether or not Kit got back up on a horse wasn't really her choice. He loved to ride, and she didn't have the heart to refuse him that, even after his fall had usurped a few years from her life and left her sporting several gray hairs. Laci slung the leather strap of her oversize handbag across her shoulder and pulled open the door. "Okay, I'm off. See you later, Charley."

Stepping from the office onto the staircase landing and letting the door close behind her, Laci was instantly assaulted by both the brightness of outside and its accompanying ninety-four degree dry heat. She took a deep breath in an effort to reenergize herself. With everything that had happened lately it wasn't surprising that she'd begun to feel ninety instead of twenty-seven. She was just thankful she hadn't started to look it, too. Or, she hoped she hadn't.

Throwing a last glance toward the arena and flag girls circling it, Laci turned and began to descend the stairs while rummaging through her handbag in search of her keys.

Since the bull-riding competition was over for the day the chutes below the raised office were empty, the animals having been taken back to their permanent pens beyond the Reno Rodeo Association's office. The immediate area was quiet since most of the contestants and workers had finished up and left for the afternoon. Laci's steps echoed hollowly on the metal stairs as she descended. She felt the back of her fingers graze against her car keys and twisted her hand around to grasp them and pull them from her bag.

"Yeah, I still drive, don't like flying too much. Long way down if something goes wrong, you know?"

Laci stopped, one foot still on the last step, the other on the ground. She clutched at the railing. That voice was one she had never forgotten. She looked up and felt her heart somersault wildly, then threaten to stop beating altogether. "Brant." His name left her lips before she had a chance to stop it, and even though the sound of her own voice had been little more than the whisper of a hummingbird's wings on the wind, it had been enough to interrupt the conversation he'd been having, cause his head to turn and his eyes to meet hers.

Laci stared at him, suddenly feeling as if unable to breath or move. She knew she should say something more, but her mind was a jumble of confusion. Part of her knew she should offer him some kind of witty welcome back to Reno, and congratulate him on making it to the Championships, while another part of her mind demanded that she damn him for leaving her and having the audacity to come back now, when her life was already one big mess.

Brant and the cowboy he'd been talking with stood beside the bull chute pens, less than three feet from Laci, but as her eyes met Brant's her world tilted. Suddenly all of the loneliness and the few remaining shreds of resentment that she had secretly harbored disappeared. She wanted to run to him, and she wanted to run from him. Seconds ticked by as neither moved or spoke. The other man seemed to fade away, though whether he actually left or Laci just stopped noticing that he was there, she wasn't sure.

For one brief second, one millisecond of time, she tore her gaze from Brant's and let it travel the length of him. The thought she'd had earlier, when she'd first seen him enter the arena, echoed in her mind. *He hadn't changed at all.* His body was still a sinewy length of force, the white shirt he wore doing little to conceal the shape of his broad shoulders or the muscular arms that had once held her in the safety of their embrace. Nor did the black leather chaps, fringed and adorned with silver conchos, hide from her the well-remembered shape of the long, lean legs that had once entwined with hers as she and Brant made love.

Her gaze moved back up to his face. His hair was still as black as night and lay in ragged curls over the back of his shirt collar.

A smiled tugged at the corners of Laci's lips as she remembered that once, long ago, she had enjoyed nothing more than sliding her hands through the thick, wavy layers of those ebony strands and feeling their silkiness slip through her fingers. But that was before she'd discovered the soft sprinkling of black curls that covered his chest, and how enjoyable it could be, for both of them, to bury her fingers there instead.

Memories drew her back in time, while his presence held her rooted to the moment.

His jawline was a slash of strength, his cheekbones sharply cut like ragged cliffs hovering over deep, dimpled hollows. Separately they were merely handsome features, but together, and combined with a straight, long nose, they gave him an air of rugged defiance and poised arrogance. Laci felt her pulse accelerate as old yearnings surged forth and threatened to overwhelm her. His hat rode low on his forehead, the small silver conchos attached to its leather band reflecting the sunlight and sparkling brilliantly, while its brim cast a shadow over eyes that were still the deepest blue she had ever seen, like a storm-swept sea that could turn black without a moment's notice.

How many times in the past had she looked into those eyes and felt herself propelled into a maelstrom of emotion? Felt almost as if she were drowning in her love for him? Her want of him? She fought to squelch the memories and regain control of her composure.

"Hello, Laci."

The sound of her name on his lips, hearing it spoken in that slow, deep drawl she remembered so well, and had missed so much, was like a caress to both her skin and her senses, just as much as if he'd actually reached out and touched her. She'd had plenty of time to forget and heal…but she suddenly knew beyond question that it hadn't been enough.

"Hello, Brant." Her tone was cool and crisp, and in total contrast to the heated flush racing through her veins.

"You look good."

"So do you." She instantly wished she could call back the softly spoken words that had sounded all too tender and *nice,* and replace them with something sharp and cutting. But the anger she'd felt toward him years ago was long gone. There was still a little resentment, but not much. What had happened between them, or what hadn't happened, had been as much her fault as his…maybe more. "I didn't expect to see you here…in Reno, I mean."

He nodded and cocked one hip, slipping his thumbs beneath the leather edging of the black, fringed chaps. Cocking his head slightly, Brant rolled his wide shoulders in a shrug, espousing a nonchalance his eyes said was a lie. ''Yeah, well, didn't have a lot of choice, what with the Championships being held in Reno this year.''

Laci nodded. She'd known he hadn't come back to see her, that he'd only come because of the Championships, but it still hurt to hear him say it. Over the years Brant had gathered his points in other states and cities. He'd nearly taken the World Champion All-Around Cowboy title twice in spite of steering clear of Reno, which was one of the nation's ''big three'' rodeos, and usually a must for anyone planning on trying for the championships.

She'd thought maybe he wouldn't come. Had even convinced herself of that, but she should have known better. This wasn't just the Reno Rodeo, this was the Championships. The world titles would be determined here this time, and winning that title had always been Brant's dream. He'd been doing well all year; it would have been foolish for him to stay away.

''So, where's McCandrick?'' he asked when she didn't respond. Brant glanced past her as if looking for Judd. ''I heard you two got married a few years back.''

''He's…we're…not together anymore.'' We should never have been together, she added silently and watched Brant, afraid of what she might see in his eyes at her words…and just as afraid of what she might not see. Her fingers squeezed down on the car keys in her hand, but she disregarded the ragged metal edges cutting into her palm. Did it matter at all to Brant that she'd married Judd? Or that she wasn't married to him any longer? Or had she ever *really* mattered to Brant Garrison at all? He'd already been married and divorced twice when she'd first met him, and he'd sported a reputation as a real ladies' man. Maybe she'd just been one of a long string of women who'd fallen into his arms, and in love with him, only to be left behind.

"You're not together anymore?" Brant echoed.

"No." She saw surprise in his eyes, but nothing more.

Disappointed, and angry with herself for being so, Laci pulled her gaze from his, but before she could think of a graceful way to excuse herself, a woman exited the registration trailer a few yards away and called to Brant.

"Hey, Brant, have you seen Chuck Worsall?"

Brant turned toward the woman whose skintight white jeans and form-fitting silk shirt with its red sequined trim and fringe, left little to the imagination. "I think he went to his trailer, Roxie."

The woman smiled as her gaze raked over Brant, invitation in her eyes, if not on her lips.

A flash of jealousy burned within Laci's breast, startling her and plunging her thoughts further into the past. For weeks after he'd left her, she'd cried her eyes out. A month later she'd come to realize that Brant had walked out on more than just her, and for a while she'd cursed him endlessly, coming close to actually hating him. Finally she'd accepted that they had just each wanted something different out of life and that, maybe foolishly, she'd loved him a little too much. Definitely more than he'd loved her, if he had loved her at all.

"You're divorced?" Brant asked, turning back and

breaking into her thoughts to jerk her back to the moment.

Laci looked at him, into that storm-swept sea of midnight blue, but his eyes revealed little of whatever he was feeling or thinking. Frustration stoked her temper. He'd always had the ability to somewhat hide his emotions behind a veneer of nonchalance, as if, no matter what was happening around him, he didn't care. Now she saw that he'd honed that ability to perfection. There was no readable emotion in his eyes whatsoever, or in the set of his features.

An instinct for self-preservation warned her that the best thing she could do for herself now was to react in kind, excuse herself, and stay as far away from Brant Garrison as she could while he was in town. The Championships would only last a little over a week, then he'd be gone. She could avoid him for that long. She had to.

Laci forced a smile to her lips. "I...I really have to go, Brant. It was nice seeing you again." Her mouth felt dry with the lie. It was wonderful seeing him again—and it was horrible. She'd thought of a hundred things she would say to him, things she should say to him, but at the moment her mind was as blank of thought as the desert was of water. She brushed past him. "Good luck with the rest of your rides, Brant. I hope you win." She walked toward the sea of cars, but the Cyclone fence that separated the rodeo grounds from the parking lot had never looked so distant. Laci hastened her steps, afraid that he might follow, but he didn't. She unlocked her car door, swung it open and practically fell onto the driver's seat.

"What is the matter with me?" She lay her head against the back of the car seat and closed her eyes. The urge to cry almost overwhelmed her, along with the urge to scream. Her heart was pounding a thousand beats a minute. She cursed silently and ordered her body to calm, but it refused to heed. It was in the throes of turmoil, caught within a multitude of conflicting emotions struggling for control, all battling one another, and calm was the furthest from victory. She sat up and gripped the steering wheel—hard, her knuckles turning white from the pressure; but it didn't help, her hands continued to tremble.

"Stop it, Laci," she snapped at herself. "There's no need for this insane panic." She turned the ignition key, then flipped on the air conditioner. Cold air immediately flowed forth from the dash vents and gave her respite from the near stifling heat the car's interior had accumulated while sitting in the sun. But it did little to cool the fervor that had invaded her veins upon her encounter with Brant.

Laci inhaled deeply, filling her lungs with the chilled air. What she'd had with Brant, what they'd had together, was long over. Dead...buried... *forgotten.* She had to remember that. It had been seven and a half years. She was over him, and had been for a long time. Laci moved her hands to the top of the steering wheel and leaned forward to rest her forehead on them. So if she was over him, if the past was the past, buried and forgotten, why was she so nervous now?

A sinking feeling filled her breast. She opened her

eyes, and sat up, turning to look back toward the chutes. Brant was nowhere in sight, but the answer to the question echoing through her mind was all too obvious, and very unwelcome.

Chapter 2

Laci stepped from the hospital elevator and walked down the corridor of the children's ward. Its white walls were covered with colorful posters and decals of cartoon figures, obviously an effort by the hospital staff to brighten what could be, for some youngsters, a very somber and scary place. Just before reaching the door to Kit's room Laci smiled and waved to a nurse who stood at the end of the hall pinning a chart to a bulletin board. Her features bore a faint resemblance to Laci's.

Trish Lawrence waved back. "Hey, cuz, how's everything going?"

"So far so good. Why don't you and Jeff bring the boys down to the rodeo this weekend?"

"Sounds good to me," she started to walk toward Laci, "but my mom just got back in town and is staying with us for a few weeks, so I'll have to see what she's got planned."

"Aunt Vi's in town? How is she?" Laci asked.

"Fine, except I doubt she'll…"

"Come to the rodeo," Laci said, finishing Trish's sentence when her pause seemed endless. Laci's father had been Violet McKenna's older brother, and they'd been extremely close, but ever since his death she'd refused to come to the rodeo, insisting it reminded her too much of Ed James.

"So come without her," Laci said, "and I'll stop by the house sometime next weekend and visit with Aunt Vi." She pointed toward the open door of Kit's room and raised her brows in question.

Trish smiled. "The doctor was here earlier. Kit's release papers are on my desk, all signed and finalized. And I'm sure he's more than eager to go home, though he isn't dressed yet. Rules, you know."

Laci nodded and walked into Kit's room. He was lying with his head propped up by a mound of pillows and the entire surface of the bed was covered with comic books.

Laci smiled. Riding his horse was Kit's first passion in life. Reading comic books was his second. At the moment he was thoroughly engrossed in the book he held and hadn't heard her entry.

She glanced at the little boy in the next bed, saw that he was asleep, and paused at the foot of Kit's bed. Her breast filled with pride and love as she looked down at her son. Had he really been in her life for almost seven years? It seemed like only yesterday she was lying in the delivery room of this very same hospital cursing the nurses and glowering through spread-eagled legs at her family doctor as he told her to push. As if she would have been able to do anything else. A swell of nostalgia filled her as she recalled the nurses saying they'd never seen a baby born with so much thick, wavy hair, and all of it coal black.

Just like his father's she remembered having thought that day, and almost every day since whenever she looked at Kit. He bore the McCandrick name, but since the death of Laci's parents, she and Judd were the only ones who knew that Kit wasn't truly a McCandrick. And that was the way it was going to stay.

Laci absently brushed a lock of blond hair past her shoulder. Kit had his father's eyes, too: that same blue that could be as sparkling as sapphires one moment and as dark as a midnight sea the next. But he had her nose. Or at least she thought he did; short, straight and slightly turned up at the end. Of course, as he grew she knew that could change.

A flash of sentiment gripped her at the memory of the tiny baby she'd held in her arms and she wished the years hadn't flown by quite so quickly. Laci moved to the side of his bed. "Hey, cowboy, I'm back. How about a kiss for your old mom?" She leaned over, laughing softly as she did, and gave him a peck on the cheek.

Kit's nose wrinkled in feigned distaste and he quickly rubbed the back of his pajama-clad arm over his cheek, as if to wipe away her kiss. "Ah, jeez Mom," he groaned, screwing up his nose. "You did that just a couple of hours ago."

"Sorry," she said, and tried to look contrite. "I guess I just can't help getting all mushy when I'm around such a handsome cowboy. But I promise," she held up her hand to mock a Boy Scout salute, "I'll do my best from now on to limit myself to just one smooch a morning. Okay?"

"Yeah, right." Kit rolled his eyes then scrambled up onto his knees. "Can we go home now, Mom? I want to see Buster. He's probably missed me, huh? Is he okay? Can I ride him this afternoon? Please?"

Laci shook her head and laughed. "Slow down, cowboy, we haven't even left the hospital yet and you've got what little of the day is left all planned out."

Kit jumped to his feet and began to pull his pajama top off. "Auntie Trish said I couldn't get dressed to leave until you came."

"Okay, I'm here." Laci pulled a pair of clean jeans and a shirt, along with underwear, from a canvas satchel she'd brought in from the car and tossed them on the bed beside Kit. "Where's Mrs. Dabney?" She glanced around in search of some evidence that their housekeeper, who was also Kit's nanny, had only left the room for a minute. They'd ridden into town together that morning and Mrs. Dabney had planned to run some errands, then stay at the hospital and visit Kit while Laci went to the arena to make sure everything was running smoothly and on schedule.

"Oh, she left. She said she knew you'd be coming and she wanted to go to the market and would get a ride home with Mrs. Holmes." He grinned and kicked his pajama bottoms off. "She said she was going to get broccoli, but I think she really went to the store to get me some new comics."

Laci faked a glare and lowered her face before

Kit's. "Comics, huh? It couldn't be that you asked her to do that, now could it, young man?"

Kit shook his head and his brows shot skyward. "Uh-uh, Mom, really. I didn't. I just think that's what she's doing cause I told her I was done reading all these." He pointed to the books strewn over the bed.

Laci shoved several comic books aside and settled a hip on the edge of his mattress. "Okay, so, it seems you've had quite a day already, what with visiting with Mrs. Dabney, reading all these comic books, and I would guess, keeping your Aunt Trish and the other nurses hopping. So, maybe you're too pooped to come home."

Kit pulled his T-shirt over his head. "No, Mom, really, I'm fine."

Laci laughed, then gave Kit a mockingly suspicious scowl. "Are you sure, young man? Once we get home you know, you won't have all these nurses waiting on you anymore. It's back to picking up your own stuff, cleaning up your messes, and doing your chores."

Kit's nose wrinkled. "Yuck."

Laci tried to keep from smiling. "So, does that mean you'd rather stay here?"

His eyes widened in alarm. "Heck, no." He flopped down on the bed and thrust one leg hurriedly into his jeans. "I wanna go home and see Buster and Bear. They don't have any animals here." He glanced across the room at the stuffed animals lying in a pile on his roommate's bed. "Well, not any real ones anyway."

Laci walked to the closet and retrieved Kit's boots.

"Is Buster okay, Mom?"

She pulled a pair of clean socks from her bag and handed them to him. "Buster is just fine. He wasn't the one who had to go to the hospital, remember?"

"Did you give him a carrot this morning? You know he likes to get a carrot for breakfast every morning."

Laci helped Kit tug on his boots and tapped a finger on the end of his nose. "I remembered, big guy. I had a horse when I was growing up, too, you know. Buster got his carrot, and I even gave him a sugar cube for dessert. And Bear got his doggy cookie."

Kit stood and zipped up his pants while Laci gathered his comic books from the bed. It gave her something to do with her hands, which had begun to tremble at just the thought of Kit climbing onto a horse's back again. Buster was the gentlest horse she'd ever known, and it wasn't his fault a snake had appeared on the trail and spooked him. Nevertheless, Kit had been thrown from the saddle and sustained a concussion, and Laci had been scared witless.

Kit slid from the bed to the floor. "So, can we go home now, Mom?"

She checked the drawers of the table next to his bed to make certain nothing was being left behind. "Okay, but what's the hurry, you order a pizza?"

"Can we? Lunch was yucky."

Trish suddenly appeared at the door. "Hold on a minute there, mister," she said, her tone a teasing snarl and a frown creasing her brows. "What do you mean lunch was yucky? And just where do you think you're going?"

Kit's eyes widened. "The doctor said I could go home, Aunt Trish. Really, he said…"

"I know, I know, don't panic." She laughed, glanced behind her and waved at one of the other nurses, then stepped aside as the woman pushed a wheelchair into the room.

"Does he really need that?" Laci asked, alarmed.

Trish shook her head. "No, but it's hospital rules."

"Oh."

A few minutes later the elevator doors slid open and the nurse pushed Kit's wheelchair into the lobby. Laci followed, but as they neared the center of the spacious room she suddenly stopped dead in her tracks as her heart slammed against her chest. Brant. His name echoed in her mind, each replay creating a new sense of fear within her, a new wave of anxiety, a new onslaught of confusion and indecision. Her gaze darted from Brant to Kit and back to Brant.

Had he seen Kit? Had Kit seen him?

The nurse didn't notice Laci's pause, but Kit did. He leaned over the arm of the chair and looked back at her. "Come on, Mom, what are you doing?"

Laci stared at Brant, who was standing just in front of the sliding glass doors that gave entry to the hospital lobby, while he talked to an intern.

"Mom?"

She tore her gaze from Brant and looked down at Kit. Reason failed her, so instinct took over, spurred on by an abrupt flash of panic. She grabbed the nurse's arm to make her stop. "I'm sorry, really, but I have to dash into the gift shop."

The woman frowned. Laci knew why, but at the moment she didn't care. People didn't usually visit the gift shop on their way *out* of a hospital. But it had been the only thing she could think of.

"Please, I can take Kit from here." She tried to sidle her way between the woman and the wheelchair, but the nurse, built like Elsa the Warrior Viking, maintained her grip on the chair's handlebars. "Please," Laci insisted, "I wouldn't want to keep you from your duties."

"It's hospital regulations," the woman argued stiffly, and practically glared at Laci. "I'm supposed to see him to the car and help him into it."

"Well, it's not necessary, really," Laci retorted. "I'll take him and he'll be fine. Thank you." She yanked the chair from the woman's grasp, whipped it around as if doing a wheelie, and headed for the gift shop.

Brant thanked the orderly who'd given him directions to the emergency room and turned to enter the lobby. A series of curses stomped their way through his head. He'd gone to the Justin Medical Trailer at the arena to make sure that the break he'd sustained in his leg last year hadn't fractured from his tangle with Nightmare that afternoon, but they'd been too busy to even take an X ray. Everyone in the trailer was working over a guy who'd suffered a heart attack.

Normally Brant wouldn't have even bothered having the leg checked, but he was too close to winning this year to take any unnecessary chances. He was thirty-three now and his body was getting too old and too tired for him to even contemplate going on the circuit for another season. His bones didn't heal as fast as they once had after being broken, and his muscles ached like hell's own fury for days after a fall. If he was going to win and fulfill his vow to Brett, he had to win the World Championship this year. He just didn't have the energy or the desire to go another year. But it wasn't about just winning the title and buckle anymore. Now he needed the money, too, for the ranch and the school.

Brant took a step and winced at the dull throb of pain in his leg. If it was fractured, he'd have it taped up, because nothing was going to stop him from getting the Championship this time.

Across the lobby a nurse and another woman were standing beside a reception desk, talking, when the nurse noticed Brant and threw him a flirtatious smile. Not blatantly, just coyly. Brant smiled back, though the gesture was pure reflex rather than interest. Most likely, he surmised, the two women were talking about which of the hospital's doctors was the most eligible catch. He nodded casually and was about to pass them when his gaze was caught by a woman hastily pushing a kid in a wheelchair toward the gift shop.

Brant paused and stared after her, his eyes moving over her long hair. It was dark and shimmery, like old gold, and held just the slightest hint of a red blush, the way Laci's did. How he used to love to let her hair slip through his fingers. It had been an erotic tease to his senses he'd never experienced with any other woman, before or since. But then, he'd never loved any other woman either, not like he'd loved Laci James.

At the thought of her, Brant felt the warming of desire that still unsettled his insides every time he allowed himself to indulge in memories, which for the sake of his own sanity, wasn't often. He watched the woman maneuver the wheelchair through the open doorway of the gift shop. His gaze moved over her subtle curves and lines. Her legs were long and lean, as he remembered Laci's had been, and were encased in a pair of tight-fitting, faded blue jeans, which had always been Laci's favorite mode of attire. Her waist was encircled by a tooled western belt....

Brant tried to steel himself against the memories, but he couldn't force his gaze away from the woman, even though he knew he was merely torturing himself. Her dark blue chambray shirt accentuated the silky gold-red tresses that cascaded down over her shoulders and back in flowing waves.

He pulled a deep breath into his lungs. He'd lost track of how many times over the years he'd thought he'd seen Laci, only to be enveloped in disappointment at finding out it wasn't her. How many women with long blond hair and sun-kissed skin...with slender legs that seemed to go on for an eternity...with sultry voices and narrow waists, had he spotted and thought were her? And he'd always been wrong. But this time was different. This time he was back in Reno where she lived, and this time he knew it could really be her.

He opened his mouth to call to her, and as abruptly closed it. There was no point to encouraging any kind of relationship between them. Friendship wouldn't work, and anything else was out of the question. He had purposely not kept up on what she'd done with her life since he'd heard that only three months after they'd argued and he'd left her in Reno, she had married Judd McCandrick. Obviously her love hadn't run all that deep.

Brant felt a flash of the anger, resentment and jealousy that had almost consumed him all those years ago. He'd convinced himself then that if she had really loved him as much as he'd loved her, things would have worked out differently. She would have been with him, or she'd have waited for him to come back.

He'd hoped the anger and hurt would fade away as the years passed, but they hadn't. In spite of the other women he'd known, the concentration it took to compete, and even his investment in the ranch and the planning of the school and camp, nothing had taken the anger and pain away. It had remained, deep inside of him like a wounded animal, hiding, waiting, ready to overtake him any time he dwelt too much in the past, within his memories, and his dreams of what might have been.

The blond woman disappeared into the gift shop, and the nurse at the reception desk behind him laughed softly at something her companion said. Brant was aware of everything and everyone around him, yet he didn't move, he was too lost within his thoughts. He could still remember the night he'd heard the news that Laci had gotten married. The date was imprinted in his memory, like his own birth date. He'd been in Mesquite, Oklahoma and had garnered a pretty good purse for himself after drawing one mean bull. Several of the guys had gone out afterward and one of them mentioned Laci's marrying Judd McCandrick.

Later that night Brant had thoroughly trashed the motel room he was staying in, breaking everything in sight, even the bed. After that he'd gone to a bar with every intention of getting drunk, but hadn't. He'd sworn off liquor a long time ago, after it had helped make him stupid enough to marry for a second time, and he didn't need that kind of grief ever again. Anyway, he had a promise to keep, so he'd resolved to forget Laci, the dreams he'd imagined for them, and the life he'd planned. After all, she obviously hadn't spent a whole lot of time pining after him.

Brant jerked his gaze from the direction of the gift shop. He didn't need to stand in the middle of a hospital lobby playing the fool like he'd done in the arena earlier.

Laci looked past the fluffy pink ears of a stuffed rabbit and felt her heart jump into her throat. Brant was standing beside the reception desk and staring in her direction. Her hands began to shake and she nibbled on her bottom lip. He'd seen her. She hadn't moved fast enough.

He began to walk toward the gift shop.

Oh, Lord, he was coming to talk to her. She glanced at Kit. Brant was coming to confront her. Fear settled over Laci like a paralyzing blanket of ice, wrapping her in its frosty shroud and squeezing the breath from her lungs.

"Mom, what are you doing?"

Laci felt Kit's wheelchair brush against the side of her leg and jerked around to look down at him again. He was trying to glance past the clutter of merchandise that lined the glass shelves of the gift shop's window and see what she was looking at.

He'd see Brant. The thought nearly sent Laci into a faint and turned her blood to a current of ice water.

She grabbed the handles of Kit's wheelchair and turned him to face her. "I was just thinking of buying you this cute little stuffed rabbit, sweetie." She grabbed the toy from the shelf, then immediately put it back. "But you don't like stuffed animals anymore, do you? I still do. They're so cute. Lots of people collect them you know." Kit had always loved stuffed animals, but that was before Judd had accused him of being a sissy. "Everyone loves stuffed animals, Kit." She was babbling. How close was Brant?

Laci glanced over her shoulder hurriedly and pushed Kit toward the magazine rack. She looked again but didn't see Brant. Had he reached the door of the gift shop yet? Panic threatened to close her throat altogether and stop her heart.

"Stuffed rabbit?" Kit echoed. "Mom." He twisted around and gave her a look of disdain.

She looked into the lobby again and this time caught sight of Brant. He was well past the reception desk and still coming in her direction, though she could see now that he was limping slightly. He must have injured his leg when he'd been thrown off that bull. She frowned. Was it the same leg she had read he'd broken last year?

Laci nearly groaned aloud, frustrated with herself. What did it matter at the moment which leg he'd hurt, or if it was the same one he'd hurt before? He was coming right toward them and he'd see Kit—*that's* what mattered. She looked for another way out of the gift shop. There had to be a back door—but there wasn't. Laci whirled and grabbed several magazines from the rack and thrust them at Kit. "How about these, big guy?'' She looked down at him, letting her hair fall forward so that it hid her face.

He stared at the magazines. *''Pop-u-lar Mec-han-ics?''* Kit looked up at her. ''Why would I want to read about some guys who fix engines and stuff?''

Rats. Why did Kit have to be one of those children who'd started reading only minutes after he'd gotten out of diapers? Sometimes having a bright child was more of a hindrance than a gift. Like now. She forced a smile. ''It's about building things, which I thought you might like to do. Like, maybe you could, ah, build a chest to store all your comics in, or a...a model airplane to hang from the ceiling, or something.'' She threw a quick glance over her shoulder again. Brant was almost at the door to the gift shop.

''Travel Time?'' Kit said.

Laci looked back at her son. ''Ah, what? Oh, ah...I thought maybe we'd do a little traveling next summer? Go on a trip. You know.''

He held up another magazine. The male cover model looked like nothing but a mass of shining, well-tanned muscle.

Laci smiled weakly. ''Build up those old biceps?'' She snapped his shoulder with a fake punch. ''Make you into one of those he-man types.''

Kit frowned. ''I don't think so, Mom.''

Another look toward the lobby. It was empty except for two nurses who were standing and talking near the elevators. Laci sighed and felt like sagging to the floor in relief. Brant was gone. Thank heavens. She grabbed the magazines from Kit and stuffed them back onto the rack.

He looked up at her.

"Okay, fine. Forget those. Let's go home." Laci sighed. She had always thought it was wonderful having a child who seemed far more intelligent and mature than his age should have allowed. But she'd long ago also discovered that when she needed to fool him and didn't have time to be cleverly creative, like now, it was frustratingly difficult.

"Well, yeah, okay," Kit said, "but since we're in here, Mom, how about buying me a candy bar?"

Laci smiled. "Okay, hotshot, but just one, and you can't eat it until after dinner."

Kit nodded, but she didn't miss the way one corner of his mouth turned down at her words. Kit was a genuine die-hard chocoholic, most likely willing to eat the stuff for breakfast, lunch and dinner if she'd let him.

Just like his father, a little voice said in the back of her mind.

And a hundred thousand other kids, she argued with herself silently, angry at the direction her thoughts had been turning ever since she'd run into Brant Garrison earlier.

Laci paid for the candy bar, dropped it into her handbag, and pushed Kit's wheelchair back into the hospital lobby.

"Giddy up," Kit said, and giggled.

"Laci?"

She stopped in the center of the spacious lobby, every nerve and cell in her body suddenly frozen, every muscle rigidly tense. Her heart felt as if it were going to explode from her breast. She'd thought he was gone, but she would have known that voice anywhere, even if she hadn't only heard it less than an hour ago. It had haunted her for years. A deep Texas drawl that was as smooth as honey, as dark as night, and as seductive as promises of forever murmured on satin sheets. She didn't want to turn and face him, yet there was nothing else she could do.

Her fingers tightened their hold on the handles of Kit's wheelchair, as if the death grip could provide her both the strength and courage she needed to get past this moment.

The instant her name left his lips Brant wanted to bite his tongue off. First of all he should never have called out to her. It was stupid. And he hadn't meant to do it. They'd said their polite hellos back at the arena and there was nothing more to say. Better to leave things dead and buried in the past where they belonged. That logic was sound; it was what he'd planned ever since realizing if he wanted to win the title he'd have to return to Reno. So why wasn't he following it?

"Hey, Mom, why are we stopping?"

Brant watched as Laci leaned down and whispered something to the child in the wheelchair.

Mom. Brant swallowed—hard. The boy had called Laci Mom.

"Okay," Kit said, "but don't forget, you promised we'd stop for pizza and get some more carrots for Buster."

He was her son. Brant stared at the child. He was Laci's son. Hers and Judd's. A dull ache, like that of loss, or for what could have been, tore through his gut. He pushed the sensation and the thoughts aside. They weren't important. And he had no room in his life for any more regrets. He had enough as it was. Brant's gaze swept over Laci hungrily as she straightened and he waited for her to turn toward him or move away.

Ever since hearing that the Championships would be in Reno rather than Vegas, Brant had worked on preparing himself to see her again. He thought he'd been ready—but he'd been wrong. An hour ago that fact had hit him between the eyes like an angry bull and it had been all he could do to keep from dragging her into his arms. The moment he'd seen her back at the arena, desire—swift, hot and unexpected, had filled him, sweeping over him like fire dancing across the dry fields of a Texas prairie, the same as it always had when they'd been together all those years ago. And it was no less searing this time.

He knew he should say something else to break the silence but polite pleasantries had been exchanged at the arena, and if he really faced facts, polite pleasantries were really all that was left between them except for maybe a few shared memories, and on his part, a few fruitless dreams.

She finally turned and her gaze met his, hesitantly at first, then more steadily, the blue of a spring sky melding with the blue of a midnight sea. Hurt silently acknowledged hurt, anger confronted anger, and for a brief instant, regret conceded regret. But as quickly as he'd seen those things spark from her eyes, mirroring what he knew he couldn't keep from his own, they were gone.

"Hello again," Laci said softly, breaking the stillness that seemed to hold both in its grip. He watched the corners of her lips turn upward, just slightly, in a small smile. "I didn't expect to see you here."

"The doc in the Justin Trailer was busy." Every cell in him ached to reach out to her, his body and mind in total conflict. He wanted desperately to close the distance between them, slip his hands around her waist and drag her up against his length as he used to do. But that had been a long time ago.

Steeling himself against the feeling, Brant called on all the self-control he had to keep from acting the jester yet again. The mere fact that she was so close, that it was all too possible to reach out and touch her, to draw her into his arms and press her body to his, was sweet torment to his soul, torturing him until he aborted the image in his mind with a mental threat to cut off his own arms if they so much as moved in her direction.

Laci frowned. "Are you hurt?" She hadn't wanted to ask, and she didn't want to care, but she could help neither.

He shook his head. "No, I'm okay. It's just an old break I figured I'd best get x-rayed, that's all, after Nightmare so gracefully tried to square dance on it." His mouth spoke the words, but his thoughts were elsewhere. He shifted his weight, realigning his left hip, cocking his right, and ignoring the dull pain in his leg. What did he want to say to her? He cleared his throat. What he wanted to say and what he could allow himself to say were two different things. "I heard about your folks, Laci. I'm sorry."

He saw the surprise in her eyes at his mention of her parents. Maybe she hadn't expected that he'd have heard about the accident. Or maybe she hadn't expected him to voice any compassion over the death of Ed James, who had made no secret of the fact he'd accept Brant Garrison if his daughter insisted, but he felt she could do a hell of a lot better.

A faint smile pulled at the corners of Laci's mouth. "Thank you. I still miss them."

He nodded. With the loss of his own family, Brant had known all too well the grief she'd been feeling when her parents had been killed in an automobile accident. He'd reached for the phone a dozen times the night he'd heard, but he hadn't called. He had been too afraid...sensing that just hearing her voice again would tear open all the old wounds and he'd never be able to sew them back up.

"Mom, I'm hungry."

Laci threw an apologetic look toward Brant and half turned from him to talk to her son.

She still wore her hair long, a flowing mane of dark gold that accentuated the heart-shaped face and china blue eyes he had never forgotten, no matter how hard he tried. He had gazed into other women's eyes over the years, some bluer, some paler, some not blue at all, but none had ever haunted him like Laci's. He'd seen her eyes everywhere, in his dreams, his nightmares and in his memories. A few times he'd even thought he'd seen her eyes looking at him from within another woman's face...but then he'd looked closer and realized it wasn't Laci at all, merely his longing to see her there.

But this time he wasn't dreaming or pretending, this time she was really standing in front of him, only a few feet away, and if he wanted to, if he dared, he could reach out and touch her.

At the arena he'd been caught off guard, not quite ready to face her, and he was no better prepared this time. His gaze devoured her, ravenous for the sight that had been denied him for so long. She had changed. He'd sensed and seen that earlier.

Now he saw it more distinctly. She was no longer the girl he'd left behind, she was a woman, and more breathtakingly beautiful than his memories had allowed him to imagine. Her nose still had that sassy little flare at the end, and her full, naturally pink lips still looked made for kissing, a temptation he guessed most men would find nearly irresistible. But her cheeks showed a little more hollow than they used to, and her chin a little more strength.

Brant was too afraid to let his gaze slip any lower lest he lose all control and sweep her into his arms. Instead he gave himself a mental shake, trying to push away the traitorous feelings, and found he couldn't. How many nights had he lain awake thinking about her? Remembering how it felt to hold her close and make love to her? The thought nearly brought a groan ripping from his throat.

To combat the fiery sensations that had suddenly seized his body, Brant did what he always did when his memories got too much for him...he forced himself to remember that she had refused to go with him on the circuit and three months later had married Judd McCandrick. His hands curled into fists and he clenched them tight at his sides. Three months...he'd only been gone from Reno for three months, and she'd married someone else.

The silence between them stretched endlessly, fleeting seconds that seemed like hours. For the first time in his life Brant found himself wishing he didn't always travel alone, didn't always do everything alone. He wished there was someone with him now, someone who would speak up and break the silence that hung so heavy in the air, who could say what he couldn't: that he had to go. If his brother had been there, he would have said it, but Brett was dead.

As if their previous, though brief, meeting had been merely a prelude to this one, Brant found all the old feelings of the past rushing back upon him as he looked down at Laci. Anger, desire, resentment and longing, warred with each other, battling fiercely, and offering no surrender or conquest of any one emotion.

He was torturing himself, standing before her like this, reliving a past that was better left forgotten, but it was a torture he'd waited seven and a half years to endure, and he couldn't bring himself to turn away from it.

Laci straightened and looked back to him. "Sorry," she mumbled.

Brant glanced at the boy. "Is he all right?"

She nodded. "He was thrown from his horse a few days ago and had a concussion, but he's fine now."

He heard the words she spoke, watched her lips move, even registered the concern he saw in her eyes for the child, and he responded, "Good, I'm glad." But his thoughts had remained moored in the past.

He'd stayed away from Reno ever since the day he'd walked out on her, and no one knew that had been the worst day of his life. The look in Laci's eyes when he'd told her goodbye had haunted him every minute since that day, and for years afterward he'd wanted to rip his own heart out, to stand in front of a bull and let the damned thing trample him to death. But the vow he'd made to his twin brother Brett before he'd died had kept Brant going.

A long sigh slipped from his lips. He had walked away from Laci James once and it had nearly killed him, and damn the heavens, he was going to have to do it again.

Laci was halfway across the parking lot before she realized Kit was talking to her.

"Who was that guy, Mom? Is he a friend of Dad's? Someone from the rodeo?"

Laci paused beside the Jeep Cherokee that had been part of her divorce settlement from Judd and unlocked the passenger door. "Yeah, someone from the rodeo," she mumbled absently, and bent to lower the wheelchair's leg supports. "Need me to lift you in, big guy?"

But before she was halfway through with the question, Kit had bolted from the wheelchair and scrambled into the car.

"Guess not." Laci looked around, suddenly wondering what to do with the wheelchair, and saw an orderly walking across the parking lot. He noticed her wave and moved toward her.

"Thanks," she said as he took the chair. She climbed onto the driver's seat. Her hands were still trembling and she took a deep breath in an effort to calm herself. A melange of emotions crowded in on her: gratitude, fear, longing, sadness, anger and disappointment. All battled for control and threatened to steal both her resolve and composure. She was relieved and she was frustrated, grateful that Brant hadn't shown any undue interest in Kit, and angry that he hadn't. She felt yearning toward a past that was dead, and resentment for still having such feelings.

But worst of all was the disappointment she felt that Brant hadn't swept her into his arms. Not until she'd forced herself to look into his eyes had she realized how much she wanted that, or how impossible it was.

Chapter 3

Brant strode down the corridor toward the emergency room, cursing beneath his breath each time he took a step and put weight on his left leg. It wasn't that the pain was so bad, it was the thought that if his leg had been injured again it could mean he was out of the rodeo, out of the Championships, looking at another year on the circuit and possibly losing the ranch. Yet it wasn't even just that. Pain and loss he could handle. He'd done it before. Plenty of times. The betrayal of his emotions was something else though. Ever since seeing Laci at the arena his emotions had been speeding down a course he did not want them to follow and he was having a devil of a time getting them back under control. And this latest confrontation hadn't done anything to help.

He walked into the emergency room's waiting area just as the double doors of an ambulance entry on the opposite side of the room burst open. Two paramedics raced in pushing a gurney and yelling about an accident on the freeway. Doctors and nurses hurried into the area from behind drawn curtains, desks and other rooms. Before the doors even began to swing closed another paramedic pushed another gurney through.

A woman lay on the second gurney, her blond hair spilling across the white sheets. The dark blue collar of her shirt was faintly evident through the tangles of hair, and a blood-soaked bandage covered one side of her face.

Brant stared, his heart suddenly thudding against his chest.

It couldn't be Laci.

The paramedic swung the gurney toward a nearby door and Brant caught sight of the uncovered side of the woman's face. He nearly sagged in relief.

Within seconds organized havoc had swept over the emergency room. Doctors immediately began to check injuries and yell orders while nurses, interns and orderlies rushed about trying to fulfill them. Brant stepped aside and stood near the nurses' station as a third ambulance pulled up to the entry and another paramedic wheeled a gurney past the entry doors.

"Have a seat and fill this out."

Brant turned at the calm voice. A nurse behind the station desk was holding a clipboard out toward him. A blank medical form lay on its surface.

"Might as well have a seat," she said, motioning toward some nearby chairs. "From the look of things, I'd say it's going to be awhile."

Brant shook his head. "Thanks, I think I'll pass.

Looks like those guys—'' he jerked his head toward the rooms the paramedics had wheeled the injured into ''—need the docs more than me.'' Turning, he strode back down the corridor, limping only slightly now. He'd tape up the leg himself. Or maybe he'd swing back past the arena. He should check on the next day's schedule and see when he was down to ride anyway, and maybe while he was there he'd see if things had calmed enough in the Justin Medical Trailer so that someone could look at his leg. Maybe take an X ray just to be on the safe side. Either way the leg would be fine. It had to be…he had a World Championship to win, and the leg sure as hell wasn't going to give him another year on the circuit to do it.

Brant walked out of the hospital and into the night, taking a deep breath of the balmy night air. The pain had already started to subside, which was a good sign. Once the leg was taped up he'd take a couple of aspirin and it would probably feel as good as new by morning.

A spot of gold in the parking lot caught his eye and he turned just in time to see a woman with long blond hair open her car door and disappear inside the vehicle.

The abruptly clenched fist at Brant's side relaxed. It wasn't Laci. A sigh of relief rushed from his lips. He didn't need any more encounters with her and he was going to do his best to avoid them. He only had a little over a week in Reno, then he could leave and that would be that. The past would once again be the past, dead and buried, and maybe, if he was lucky, someday it would be forgotten, too.

It took only a few minutes to drive back to the arena. He parked his pickup in the lot for contestants and rodeo personnel, which was nearly empty now, and walked toward a group of trailers clustered behind the arena office. Brant waved to one of the judges who was standing in the PR trailer near the entry gate.

"Nice ride," the man called out.

Brant nodded his thanks and continued on to the registration trailer. Near the stables a farrier was working out of the back of his truck on someone's horse, fitting a new shoe on a hoof that had obviously lost or damaged the one already there; several young boys scurried about dumping feed into the cow pens; a young girl, most likely a flag girl, was brushing down her horse, and a security guard ambled past the shadow-enshrouded chutes, walked under the stairs to the office and glanced into the arena. Other than that the entire place seemed deserted.

Brant glanced up at the office as if expecting to see Laci standing on the stairs at its entry door. His heart nearly stopped when the door swung open and someone did step from the office onto the stair landing, but it wasn't Laci, and his heart returned to its normal beat.

Turning away, and calling himself a fool for the umpteenth time since that afternoon, Brant headed for the registration trailer a few yards away. The schedule for the next day was posted on the wall next to the door and showed that he was to ride Dream Dodger the next night. Brant smiled. Dodger was a good bull, with a lot of kick. He'd ridden him before and gotten a pretty good score. He looked at the schedule for the bronc riding and saw that he wasn't posted to ride for two days. Good. One bruise at a time was getting to be all he could handle. Satisfied, Brant walked to the Justin Medical Trailer. Light poured through its windows and several golf carts, used for getting around the arena grounds, as well as a pickup truck were parked near the trailer, so Brant figured the doctor was most likely still there.

"Hey, Garrison."

He paused on the steps of the medical trailer, one hand on the doorknob, and glanced back over his shoulder.

Charley Brownning walked toward him. "Good ride."

Brant nodded. "Thanks."

"I heard you hurt your leg awhile back. Giving you some trouble?"

"Hope not. Just want to have it checked."

"Yeah, word was you woulda took the title last year if you hadn't had that bad fall."

Brant shrugged. "Maybe."

Charley stopped at the bottom of the short flight of metal stairs and looked up at Brant. "Long time since we've seen you back here in Reno, Garrison."

Brant remained silent, waiting to see exactly what it was Charley had on his mind.

"Lotsa things have changed since you were here last, you know. Lotsa things."

Brant watched as Charley allowed his gaze to move over the area, drifting past the empty chutes, the security and registration trailers then redirected his gaze back at Brant.

"You seen McCandrick?"

Brant frowned and shook his head. "No."

"Probably won't. Laci's running things now."

"So I gathered."

"You talked to her?"

"We ran into each other a little while ago."

Charley nodded, seeming pleased. "She's done a lot of growing up in the last few years. Had some tough breaks. I remember she was real upset when you left…back then, I mean. Everyone kinda thought you two was…" he shrugged "…well, you know."

Brant stiffened at Charley's reference to the past. He didn't know how much the old man really knew, but discussing his love life with Charley Brownning wasn't in Brant's plans. "Yeah, well, sometimes people just think wrong, huh? Good to see you again, Charley." He pulled open the door of the trailer and made to step over the threshold.

"She doesn't need that kind of hurt again, Garrison."

Brant paused and looked back down at the older man. "That was a long time ago."

"Time passing don't always mean things change. Especially feelings."

"In this case I think it does."

Charley shrugged but continued to look pointedly up at Brant. "Maybe—maybe not."

The older man's words followed Brant into the trailer and haunted him for hours afterward.

* * *

Brant leaned his back against the bar and settled his elbows on its curved edge. It was the opening night party for the rodeo and the place was packed. Everyone associated with the rodeo was in attendance: contestants, workers, volunteers and contractors, along with girlfriends, boyfriends, spouses and groupies. He hadn't intended to come but several of the other guys had stopped by his room at the motel and cajoled him into it, threatening to hog-tie and carry him to Hank's Corral if he didn't go on his own steam.

Brant shifted his weight. The tape the doctor had wound around his calf earlier pulled at his skin, but the leg itself didn't hurt anymore, and the X ray had shown no new damage to the break he'd sustained last year when a bull had nearly crushed it. Nevertheless the doctor had agreed with Brant's sense of caution and taped up the leg as a safeguard, just in case there was a hairline fracture that wasn't showing up on the X rays.

On the opposite side of the dance floor a local band knocked out one country melody after another but Brant was only listening with one ear, the other tuned in to the conversation of the cowboys who stood beside him. Occasionally he threw in a comment or answered a question, but what he really wished was that he could just slip away unnoticed, go back to his room and crash on the bed.

Next to him Zach Taylor and Cody Roidan laughed. They were two of the best clowns the circuit had, and both had saved Brant's rear more than once. But without their colorful costumes and painted faces they just looked like two more crazy rodeo cowboys. They were also the two who'd insisted Brant come to this shindig.

He took a sip of his soda as Cody turned to him. "Hey, Brant, that's an awful pretty little filly doing the tush-push with Mike out there."

"Yeah," Zach chimed in, "and just your type, Brant...alive!" He jabbed an elbow against Cody's ribs and the two burst out laughing again.

Cody punched Brant's arm. "Get 'er boy."

Brant smiled. His reputation as a ladies' man was still alive and well and following him around just as solidly as his shadow, even if it was no longer true. He hadn't exactly given up on women, but he had become a lot more selective in the past couple of years, to the point that he was more alone than not. He unconsciously let his gaze scan the room in search of a lithe blonde whose long curls reminded him of spun gold. Now that he was back in Reno the thought of being with any woman other than Laci James seemed unimaginable.

The music changed from a lively beat to a mellow tune and many of the couples crowding the dance floor immediately moved into each others' arms and began to two-step.

Brant spotted Laci almost immediately, dancing with Charley Browning. The urge to approach her, to weave through the maze of tables between the bar and dance floor, move old Charley aside and pull Laci into his arms was more than Brant could resist. It was crazy, but at the moment he didn't care. Here, on the dance floor, maybe only for a few minutes, he could at least hold her.

For seven and a half years he'd dreamed of having Laci in his arms again, and though it would probably do nothing more than torture his soul, he was going to do it. Setting his half-empty glass of soda on the bar, he straightened and followed his impulse, moving through the tables purposefully and easily. His eyes never left Laci as Charley guided her around the dance floor.

She commented on something Charley said, then laughed when she stepped on his toe and looked down at his feet as if to see if they were all right. Brant stopped at the edge of the dance floor and watched Laci and Charley move closer to where he stood waiting.

How many times had he wondered what it would be like to see her again? To be this close to her? His gaze moved over her slowly, appreciating the way the jeans she wore hugged her long legs and slender hips, while the blue shirt, with a striking red-and-white bolt of lightning streaking across its bodice, accentuated both her figure and the luscious mane that sprayed about her shoulders.

Someone rose from one of the chairs beside Brant and made for the bar, brushing against him while doing so. A second later a woman he didn't know moved to stand beside him. Brant stepped aside, thinking to let her pass but she didn't move. "Need a dance partner, handsome?" She smiled up at him.

Brant's gaze darted down to meet hers. The fact

that she definitely had more in mind than a dance was
clearly evident in both her tone and manner. Once,
long ago, he'd have had her crushed up against him
within seconds after an invitation like that. He'd have
used her to satisfy his own needs, and help him forget,
just for a while, the face that haunted his dreams.
"No, thanks," Brant mumbled, wanting nothing more
than for her to go away. She was pretty, her hair a
thick mass of flaming red curls, her eyes a vibrant
green, but she wasn't Laci.

The woman started, obviously surprised and hurt at
the rejection.

Brant regretted that he'd hurt her, but it couldn't
be helped. He wasn't interested.

"Your loss, handsome," she quipped coolly, then
forced a laugh, whirled and sashayed her way toward
a group of cowboys standing across the room.

He looked back at Laci. *Turn and walk away,* a
little voice in the back of his mind whispered. *She
never loved you.* Instead of heeding the warning,
Brant ignored it and moved toward Laci, his body
once again proving a traitor to the orders of his mind,
emotion overruling logical thought, desire casting
aside caution. He saw her glance up and catch sight
of him as he positioned himself to intercept her as she
and Charley danced toward him. He instantly recognized the uncertainty in her eyes, and the shadow of
reluctance that swept over her features as he stepped
forward and his intent became all too clear to her.

"Charley," Laci said, "I think we'd better stop. I
mean…" She'd been about to pull away from Charley's arms and bolt when Brant tapped the older man

on the shoulder and Laci's escape became impossible without risking a scene. Charley paused, still holding her in his arms, and turned to look over his shoulder at Brant.

Laci had seen him earlier, when he'd first entered the room, and she'd been doing her best to avoid him ever since, constantly dancing or table hopping, but never remaining in one spot for too long. They'd exchanged their greetings at the arena, and again at the hospital; now she needed to keep as much distance between them as possible.

Unable to help herself, her gaze raked over him. Unlike most of the men at the party, whose shirts sported loud colors and dangling fringe, Brant was dressed simply, and it suited, even complemented him. A pair of black jeans hugged the sinewy length of his long legs, while a white shirt gave emphasis to broad shoulders, and the customary black Stetson sat on his head, the brim riding low on his forehead. He was tall, dark and handsome, but to Laci, he was also dangerous. Lethally dangerous.

"Mind if I cut in?"

Charley stared at Brant, then turned to look back at Laci.

No, it isn't all right if he cuts in. The thought silently screamed through her mind, begging Charley to receive it. But it was clear by the look on his face that he didn't. Laci wanted to groan in frustration, shake her head in denial, stamp her foot in anger. Mental telepathy had never been an ability before, but she'd prayed that by some miracle Charley would hear her thoughts now. Or at least sense them.

Brant watched as she forced a smile to her lips, but he recognized a good front when he saw one, since he'd put on enough of them himself.

"Nah, I don't mind," Charley said, "long as you stick around 'til the end." The innuendo hung in the air between them as Charley looked at Brant pointedly, and after a few seconds turned back to Laci. "See ya back at the table, honey." He gave her a quick peck on the cheek and stepped aside. "Til the end, Garrison," Charley grumbled under his breath as he brushed past Brant.

"Some songs don't have an end, Charley," Brant said, and pulled Laci into his arms.

"Then maybe they shouldn't be played." Charley turned and walked away.

Brant watched Charley go and coerced a chuckle from his throat in an attempt to lighten the moment, but he hadn't missed the meaning in the old man's words. Charley wanted Laci to be happy, and he didn't want her hurt again by Brant. But then, wasn't that what Brant wanted, too? "Still a cantankerous old coot, isn't he?"

"He's just trying to protect me," Laci countered, her tone a bit cooler than she'd intended.

"From me?"

She didn't answer him, but she didn't have to. Brant knew exactly what she was thinking, and suddenly wished he didn't. Seven and a half years ago Laci's father and Charley had tried to protect her from him. He'd already been married and divorced twice by the time he'd met Laci, and he'd had a reputation as a real ladies' man. Love 'em and leave 'em Garrison, that's how the other cowboys following the circuit had tagged Brant back then.

But that wasn't the only worry Charley and Ed James had back then concerning Brant being involved with Laci. They hadn't viewed him as a good prospect for the future, personally or professionally. He took too many risks when he rode, didn't have a home base or anything else permanent in his life, had been crazy with competition fever ever since his twin brother had been killed riding a bull. They'd told her everything they knew about him, and his reputation, hoping to discourage her from seeing him, but Laci hadn't listened.

A sense of guilt washed over Brant. Maybe she should have listened. Maybe both of them would have been better off now if she had, because Brant had ended up doing exactly what Ed James and Charley Brownning had somehow known he would do: he'd loved Laci, and then he'd left her.

What most people didn't know, and Brant wasn't about to tell them, was that the day he'd left Laci had also been the day he'd stopped living and begun to merely exist. His heart had continued to beat, his blood persisted in running through his veins, and his mind kept working, but something inside of him died. But he'd had no choice. He'd made a promise to Brett, and it was one he had to fulfill, no matter what.

As it turned out, in the end, leaving Laci hadn't mattered. When he'd heard the news that she'd married someone else, he had felt cheated, betrayed, and then forced to the realization that she hadn't really loved him.

Propelling the memories of the past back to the shadows of his mind where they normally dwelt, and he ignored them, Brant savored the feeling of having Laci once again in his arms, if only for a few moments.

She moved with him naturally, their steps a graceful fluidity of motion as if they were of one body rather than two. He wanted to draw her closer, but was afraid if he did she would pull away, maybe even walk away, and he couldn't bear that just now. But he was also afraid that if he pulled her nearer, held her closer, he wouldn't be able to let her go. "You're more beautiful than I remembered, Laci."

The moment he said the words he knew they sounded too intimate. He'd meant to keep things on a casual level, merely friendly, but being this close to Laci, holding her in his arms, had restirred too many yearnings within him, brought back too many old memories he couldn't stave off, no matter how hard he tried.

Her heart had started pounding erratically when he'd drawn her into his arms. Now, at his words, it was thudding nearly out of control and all she could do was pray that he couldn't hear it. She tried to ignore it, and the warm flush stinging her cheeks. *Keep it light, Laci,* a little voice in the back of her mind warned. *Keep it light.* "Right, Brant, and you're just as full of bull as you ever were." She summoned a laugh from her throat that, even to herself, sounded strained.

She dropped her gaze, unable to meet his, and

turned her head to look around the floor at the other dancers.

Brant's surprise at her flip comment stopped him for a second, then he laughed, a deep, solid laugh the likes of which he hadn't done for a very long time. "You know Laci, I nearly forgot just how damned sassy you are."

At his laugh she had turned to look up at him and smiled. Now, the smile froze on her face. He could have said almost anything else, but his mention of having forgotten something about her hit a nerve, a very sensitive nerve, and one she hadn't even been aware existed. Laci felt her resolve to remain smiling instantly threaten to desert her, and scrambled to retrieve it. Whatever he said, whatever he remembered about her, about them, or had forgotten, shouldn't matter to her at all. It was the past, after all. "Well," she retorted, injecting her tone with a light sarcasm she was far from feeling, "you can't remember everything."

The music stopped but Brant didn't release her from his embrace. "I have," he said seriously. His eyes bore into hers, blue fusing with blue, and whether Laci was aware of it or not, Brant knew his eyes were asking the questions, making the statements, he was afraid to murmur aloud. For a split second no one else in the room existed. It was just him and Laci, alone, together, like he'd always wanted.

The music started up again, and people began moving around the dance floor. Laci attempted to pull away from him but Brant's arm tightened around her waist, refusing to let her leave him.

"I never thought I'd see you again, Laci."

His deep voice wrapped around her like a warm blanket of honey, seeping into her pores and sending delicious chills rippling throughout her body. It invaded her senses and left the better half of them wanting. How many times had she dreamed of being in his arms again? She stared at his shirtfront, unable to meet his gaze, and leaned toward him, feeling his strength, needing it, wanting it.

Laci felt his breath on her cheek and her skin tingled. She inhaled deeply, trying to quell the runaway pace of her heart, and managed instead to fill her senses with the redolence of him, which in turn pervaded her mind with memories of sensuous afternoons and seductive nights spent in his arms. The scent of leather, horseflesh and the outdoors that clung so naturally to Brant was as much a part of him as the faint fragrance of his after-shave, an aroma that suggested the warmth of summer, a bed of pine needles and a slowly setting sun.

Since the day she'd met him, she hadn't been able to walk into a barn and inhale the sweet fragrance of fresh hay, ride a horse, or saunter through a pine forest and luxuriate in the smell of its natural earthiness, without being reminded of him. Individually they were smells that she encountered every day in her life. Melded together they were uniquely Brant Garrison.

Looking up then, Laci felt his eyes instantly pull her into a vortex of memory and emotion, a blue sea turning into a black abyss that called to her, beckoned her to surrender to their will, while his hands moved to hold her arms and pull her closer. She felt her breasts crushed against his chest and a shock, like a bolt of electricity, charged through her body, leaving her trembling.

She had tried to forget what it felt like to be in his arms, and every day of that time waiting for the moment it would happen again. She knew she should pull away from him. He was going to kiss her, she was certain of it, yet she had no will to resist him, no desire to do anything but let it happen.

Brant's head lowered toward hers, the brim of his hat acting as a shield and cutting off what little view she had of the others in the room. Only the music flowed around them, soft and lilting now, words of love set to a tune of passion, made for the moment...their moment...taking them to a world meant only for them, where harsh realities and painful memories no longer existed, a world of sunshine and smiles, of love and laughter and happily-ever-afters.

And then the music stopped.

Laci started, the sudden silence bringing instant realization of where she was, who was holding her in his arms, and what she'd been about to do. She jerked away from Brant.

Inwardly she struggled to regain her composure. Outwardly she forced herself to at least appear calm. She couldn't let this happen, couldn't let history repeat itself. She'd been wrong then, she had known that for a very long time, maybe even from the moment she'd said no. She should have gone with him, but she'd been too scared of losing him to a raging bull. Yet in the end, she'd lost him anyway.

For what she'd done later though, she had no excuse. Laci inhaled deeply, trying to calm her runaway emotions with logical thought. It was too late for regrets, and too late for her and Brant. She had Kit to think about now, and the company, James Enterprises. Yet even if there was a chance, she knew in her heart it still wouldn't work, because the things that had torn them apart were still there, hanging over them like a black cloud. Brant was still the same: a carefree, reckless wanderer, still living out of motels and following the circuit, riding the bulls and wild broncs, still chasing a dream. And she still needed her home, its stability and security, but more than that, she was still terrified that if she watched him ride, some day, inevitably, she would be watching him die.

"Brant, I..." She glanced at the silver-and-turquoise watch on her wrist. "I really have to go." She pulled herself out of his arms, half afraid he would pull her back, half afraid he wouldn't.

He didn't try to stop her. Brant had known that dancing with Laci, having her in his arms again, would be a mistake. He had been a fool to do it, but he hadn't been able to resist. But all he'd done was frustrate himself further and obviously make her uncomfortable. Laci wasn't attracted to him anymore, that was clear as crystal. She was edgy, nervous, seemingly anxious to get out of his arms and constantly looking everywhere but at him. Each time that day they'd encountered each other and talked she'd acted in a hurry to terminate the conversation and leave. He should be thankful.

He'd believed she loved him once, and he'd learned the hard way that he'd been wrong. He didn't need that kind of grief again. Yet after holding her in his arms for only a few brief minutes, and silently reciting all the reasons he should stay as far away from her as he could get, his body was a raging inferno of desire. His hands closed into fists as he resisted the urge to go after her.

Laci paused at the crowded table where Charley sat. "Need a dance partner?" he asked, and smiled.

Laci shook her head and tried to ignore the trembling sensation coursing through her body. "No, thanks, Charley, I think I'll call it a night."

Charley's already furrowed brow pulled together in a deep frown. "Something wrong?"

She smiled and grabbed her handbag from beneath the table. "No, everything's fine, Charley, really. I'm just kind of tired and I want to get home and make sure Kit's all right, that's all."

"Ain't Clara with him?"

"Yes, but it's getting late and Mrs. Dabney is getting…" She shrugged, nearly biting off her tongue at realizing she'd been about to say "old." Her housekeeper was three years younger than Charley.

Charley touched Laci's hand. "Garrison say something to upset you?"

She shook her head. "No, really, I'm fine. I just want to check on Kit." Laci leaned over and kissed Charley's cheek. "I don't know what I'd have done if you hadn't come back to the company."

''You'd've done fine.''

She smiled. ''I'll see you tomorrow at the arena.'' Waving at several friends, Laci hurried toward the exit door and missed the scathing look Charley turned on Brant. But Brant didn't miss it.

Turning on his heel he strode toward a door at the rear of the room and walked out of Hank's Corral and into the night. ''Damn.'' The lone word snapped off his lips. He had competed too long, come too far, was too close to winning the Championships to let anything interfere now. Winning, that was all that mattered. He needed to set all of his concentration on winning, all of his attention and energy.

A car engine started up nearby and Brant glanced over to see Laci's Cherokee move through the parking lot. He stepped away from the door and its overhead light, into the shadows of the night, and watched her drive away.

He should never have come back to Reno.

Chapter 4

Brant shook his head and placed both hands, palms down, on the sink's counter. It had not proven to be a good night. He should have slept. Especially since the last forty-eight hours had afforded him little rest. He'd driven straight to Reno from Tucson, then stayed up late that night getting his equipment situated and his horse settled. Little more than a handful of hours later he'd ridden Nightmare and nearly ended up a bad imitation of Humpty Dumpty. And he'd hurt his leg, though thankfully, according to the X rays, it was only the muscles, not the bone.

He'd needed sleep, but it hadn't come. At least not restful sleep. Instead he had tossed and turned all night, drifting off from exhaustion only to be plagued by dreams of Laci that always turned into nightmares as he watched her laugh and walk away, leaving him in a cold, lonely land with no way to reach her.

Leaning forward he glared into the bathroom mirror. "I doubt you could look much worse if a truck drove over you," he told the image that stared back at him. A few minutes later, after splashing his face countless times with cold water, he felt better—somewhat.

Donning a tank top, shorts and running shoes, Brant grabbed his gym bag and left the motel room. His schedule during competition was practically a ritual and unless interrupted by an emergency or injury, he never veered from it.

The gym was practically deserted when he started his workout, and for the most part it remained that way. With grim determination he exercised every muscle in his body, including his injured leg. The hand that had been caught beneath the grip rope the day before was fine, showing no signs of injury or even bruising. There was a slight bruise on his lower right rib cage, most likely from his belly slam into Nightmare, but that was all. His leg felt fine, his hand felt fine, and he felt two hundred and fifty years old.

He loved the rodeo, loved the competition, but he'd gone nonstop on the circuit for over fourteen years and he was worn-out. He'd promised Brett the Championship, but if he didn't get it this year he didn't think he had it in him to try again. But that's exactly what he'd have to do. Brant felt as if a huge weight sat on his shoulders. He had the ranch and camp to think about now, too. If he didn't win the Championship and its purse this year the camp would be in jeopardy, which meant he had no choice. He had to win. And if he didn't, and he lost everything, he'd have to start all over, and what did he know how to do besides rodeo?

Thoughts of Laci invaded his mind, coming at him from out of nowhere, blindsiding him and taking over. But he didn't fight it. Maybe, if he won, if he retired from the circuit... Brant pushed the thoughts aside. Why did he keep playing these mind games with himself? Keep fooling himself? There was still physical desire between them, that much was clear in spite of her nervousness around him, but there was no love, at least not on her part. If she'd loved him they would have been together for the past seven and a half years.

Brant set the barbells back into their rack and grabbed his sweat towel, wiping it across his forehead. Working out gave him the strength to ride, made his body tolerant of the abuse, gave his muscles the resiliency to withstand the physical battering, and allowed him to work off frustrations that sometimes he didn't even know he had. Unfortunately this time he knew exactly what his frustrations were, and they were all named Laci James-McCandrick.

Several hours later, after returning to the motel where he showered and shaved, Brant stopped at a local restaurant for a late breakfast. He was sitting at a window booth, sipping his third cup of coffee and staring out at the passing cars when he saw Laci drive past. Brant stared after the black Cherokee, wondering where she was going, wishing he was going with her.

Brant drained his cup of the last of the coffee it held. He wasn't going to win anything if he didn't get his mind off the past, off daydreams of what could never be, and back on the rodeo where it belonged.

Paying his bill, he left the restaurant and returned

to his motel room. He had no errands to run, didn't gamble, and had no one to buy souvenirs for, so there was no reason to go downtown.

To ward off boredom, and assuage the frustration he felt roiling in his gut whenever he thought of Laci, he sat down on the bed and began to oil his chaps and polish the silver conchos that adorned its outer seams. When he finished those he polished the conchos on his black Stetson, then his spurs, Grand National belt buckle, and boots. Finally, figuring he'd wiled away enough time and had begun to feel stir crazy in the small room, Brant changed into a white shirt with red pinstripes and cord trim, and left for the arena.

It was nearing four when he arrived at the exposition center. The rodeo's first event was set to start at six, but the accompanying carnival section was already packed with people. Brant pulled his pickup into the lot reserved for rodeo personnel and contestants and grabbed his gear from the bed. It was only then that he realized he'd parked next to a black Cherokee. He stared at it as if it were about to come alive and attack him. Damn, were the powers-that-be conspiring against him or what? He slung his chaps over one shoulder, spun on his heel and stalked toward the entry gate that led to the rear of the arena. He had to forget about Laci and concentrate on his ride, otherwise he was going to end up flat on his face with an angry bull trying to turn him into hamburger. Anyway, there were thousands of Jeep Cherokees in the world, most likely hundreds in Reno, and probably several dozen in town that were black. That one wasn't necessarily hers.

But gut instinct told him that it was.

Brant walked through the backstage area of the rodeo grounds, nodding to several people he knew as he passed. The place was a bustle of activity. Horses were being brushed, washed, saddled, shod or walked. The association reps and the vet were checking the bulls and broncs, several groups of cowboys stood around comparing rides and strategies, points and positions, while others stopped by the registration office to pick up their numbers and have them pinned to the backs of their shirts. Nearer the stable area the flag girls were practicing their riding while several unattended dogs darted around and in between moving hooves and boots.

Brant turned the corner of a paddock alley. His horse was standing with his head hanging over the gate of his stall. He whinnied loudly as he saw Brant approaching. Brant smiled. He'd owned the black gelding for almost three years, since the animal had turned two, and he was proving one of the best roping horses on the circuit.

"Hey, Blackjack, how's it going?" He pulled a sugar cube from the pocket of his shirt and held it out to the horse. "Ready to do some roping tonight?"

Blackjack scooped up the sugar and nuzzled his head against Brant's shoulder.

"Little restless, huh? Want to take a spin around the arena to exercise them old bones before show time?"

The horse pawed the ground and whinnied, as if knowing exactly what Brant had said.

Brent laughed and, reaching around the doorway,

grabbed a bridle from a hook on the wall and slipped it over Blackjack's head.

"Seems like one hell of a smart horse you've got there," Charley said, coming up behind Brant.

He turned. "Yeah. I got him from old Ernie Santana, down in Texas. Proving to be a good roper. Not bad on cutting, either."

Charley nodded. "Didn't know you was doing any roping, Garrison."

"I started about a year ago." When I realized I needed more money for the ranch than I was making riding rough stock, Brant thought. "I'm going to give him a little exercise in the arena." He opened the gate and led Blackjack out, handing the reins to Charley as he walked into the paddock to retrieve his saddle and hang his chaps on a hook.

Brant stepped away from the counter of the refreshment stand, a can of soda in his hand. He tossed a couple of quarters into the donation bucket on the counter and glanced up at the raised arena office across the way. Was Laci already in there, preparing for the evening's events? Tallying up her records? Or was she down on the grounds somewhere? Would he see her before he rode?

He shook his head, disgusted with himself. Seeing Laci, even thinking about her was the last thing he needed, especially right now when he was supposed to be preparing for a ride. He had a lot to do before tonight and the first thing was to check out Dream Dodger, the bull he'd drawn to ride. The rodeo veterinarian and judges always examined the animals before each event, but Brant had made a practice of doing it himself as well. Caution had impressed itself upon him the hard way.

As always happened at this time, thoughts of his late twin brother filled Brant's mind. It had been a little over nine years, but he remembered the day as if it were only yesterday. He'd been hurrying toward the chutes, heard the crowd scream and knew in his heart that whatever horror had just happened, it had happened to his brother. As Brant ran toward the rails he'd seen Brett. He'd looked like a casually discarded rag doll, one leg bent beneath him at an awkward angle, arms flung out at his sides. But rag dolls didn't bleed.

The bull was still in the arena, prancing angrily in front of the chutes but not going in, despite the clowns' efforts to usher him through the open gate.

With tears nearly blinding him and streaming down his face Brant had run into the arena and pulled his twin brother into his arms. If he lived to be a hundred, Brant knew he would never forget that moment. Brett had smiled up at him and asked if he'd made his points—then he'd died.

But it shouldn't have happened that way, and that thought, and the guilt that had dwelt within him since that day, Brant knew, would haunt him forever. It had been his scheduled ride, not Brett's, and it should have been him on that bull's back. He's the one who should have been killed.

He glanced at his watch. Five-thirty. Still too early for the bulls to be moved to the chutes. Brant walked to the stock pens and found Dream Dodger with little problem. The animal was big and black, with a slash of white across his face and the tip of one ear cut off.

Brant ran a hand lightly over Dodger's broad back to get a feel for what his seat would be like that night. The bull, leaning against the metal rails, moved slightly, but his eyes remained closed, as if he didn't have even enough energy to raise his eyelids. Brant knew anyone who believed that was deluding himself.

The bull was wide, but not fat, his spine a high arch, his ribs broadly curved but not protruding. Brant hunkered down to look at the Brahman's legs and ran his hand slowly over one thick, short front leg, then reached past it to do the same to the other.

"I told you, Judd, no."

Brant froze, recognizing Laci's voice instantly.

"As far as I'm concerned there's nothing more to talk about."

Brant heard the anger in her tone and indecision filled him. He didn't want to sit there and eavesdrop, but he didn't exactly want to rise to his feet and announce his presence, either.

"We belong together, Laci," Judd countered, his voice dark and insistent, "and you know it."

"No, Judd, we don't, and you know that."

Brant heard Laci sigh, and her tone softened with her next words, but he remained tense because of the suggestion of a threat he'd heard in Judd's tone.

"We never really did belong together, Judd. I think you know that as well as I do. Maybe that was my fault, I don't know."

"You're wrong, Laci," Judd bellowed. "We had a good marriage, a damned good marriage, and we could have again, if that son of a…"

"Don't say it, Judd," Laci said, abruptly cutting him off. "You know it isn't true." The anger left her tone again. "We were never right for one another, no matter how much we tried to convince ourselves that we were."

"We were fine together until you found out your old boy…"

"No, that's not true and you know it, Judd," Laci retorted, her words sharp and stabbing now. "Please, I don't want to argue about this again. He has nothing to do with us."

Laci glowered at Judd, as if daring him to call her a liar again, then as quickly looked away. What he'd said, what he had always said to her when they'd argued in the past did hold some truth to it, in spite of her denials. She had never forgotten Brant Garrison, and she never would, but she had truly tried to put her love for him behind her and make her marriage to Judd work.

"He has everything to do with us," Judd sneered.

Laci continued to stare at her ex-husband. How could she call him a liar when she knew, in her heart, that he was right. She'd loved Brant more than life itself, but when he'd refused the job with her father, and asked her to go with him on the circuit all she could think of was Sonny being thrown to his death from his motorcycle, and Brant being thrown from the back of a bull. A month after he was gone she'd discovered she was pregnant with his child, but she hadn't tried to contact him. Instead, she convinced herself that he didn't love her anyway, because if he had, he would have stayed in Reno and settled down as she'd asked him to do.

But when her tears had finally dried, Judd had been there, claiming he'd always loved her and would take care of her and accept her child as his own. At first she'd resisted him, but he'd persisted, and her parents had been thrilled. They'd liked Judd. He was settled and financially comfortable.

Finally, too lonely and afraid to think for herself, she'd done what her parents had wanted, and what she'd thought best for her unborn child. She'd known from the beginning that though she could love Judd, she would never fall *in* love with him. But she'd tried to make it work. And she had stayed with him far longer than she should have because she knew he loved her, because Kit needed a stable home and a father, and because she really didn't have a reason to leave. At least not one she'd wanted to acknowledge. Judd had been a good father when Kit was a baby, but that was before Kit's features had started to really develop, before his black hair had turned curly and his eyes blue. Before he'd started to look like Brant.

Laci had seen Judd's jealousy and insecurity show itself in small ways over the years, but she'd tried to ignore it, tried to tell herself she was imagining it. But Judd's growing resentment of Kit had continued. Then he'd said he wanted them to have a child, but when she'd failed to get pregnant, he refused to be tested even after she had been. Instead he'd become sullen, angry, moody. He'd accused her of taking the Pill in order to not get pregnant, and late at night, while they were in bed, he'd accuse her of still loving Brant Garrison.

The barbeque had been her wake-up call. They'd been on the patio, she, Judd and Kit, along with some others Judd had invited over for a Sunday barbeque. Kit had misbehaved and Judd slapped him across the face, something he'd never done before. She'd been shocked and angry at her husband's action, but the jealousy and contempt she'd seen in his eyes as he looked at Kit had terrified her. Within hours she'd packed up her own clothes, as well as Kit's, and had moved into a hotel in town. The next day she'd filed for divorce and, as a Nevada resident, six weeks later the decree was final. But Judd didn't want to accept it.

"Laci, I'm warning you," Judd snapped, impatient with her silence and breaking into her thoughts. "I've just about had enough. If you..."

"No, Judd, don't warn me," she said softly, not sorry that they weren't still married, but sorry that they couldn't find a way to remain friends. "Just go. There really isn't any more to say." It hadn't been fair of her to marry him when she'd still been in love with Brant, but she'd needed someone and Judd had been there for her, strong, reliable and stable. Everything she thought she'd wanted...except that he wasn't Brant.

She looked at Judd. He was every inch as tall as Brant's six foot two, and most women would say he was just as handsome. His razor cut hair was blond, as was the mustache he sported, and the brows that curved over his intense brown eyes. But where Brant's features gave the impression of rugged strength, Judd's seemed merely hard and unyielding.

"You're my wife, Laci, damn it. Nothing's going to change that, you hear? Nothing."

"We're divorced, Judd."

"Not in my book we're not, and as far as I'm concerned, that's the only book that counts."

"Judd, please," Laci said.

"No, I don't care what those court papers say, you're my wife and you always will be. Rethink all this, Laci, I'm warning you, for your own good or I'll...I'll..."

Brant wrapped a hand around one of the metal fence rails, his fingers pressing into the cold steel. The thought of Judd McCandrick, or anyone else for that matter, threatening Laci, brought on a slow, burning anger within Brant that he had to struggle to keep under control.

"Or you'll what, Judd?" Laci challenged, sounding suddenly furious. "Hit me like you did Kit?"

"There's nothing wrong with disciplining a kid, Laci. Maybe you ought to try it, instead of spoiling him and treating him like he's some kind of..."

"I don't want to talk about this anymore," Laci said, cutting him off. "What's done is done and nothing is going to change it. I'm not coming back, Judd. We're divorced. It's final and I'm not changing my mind. Please accept that, Judd. It's over."

"You're my wife."

"Not anymore." Laci made to turn away. "Goodbye, Judd."

Suddenly Brant heard the scuffle of feet and what sounded like a soft shriek of surprise from Laci.

"Let go of me," Laci snapped, jerking her arm away from Judd's grasp. The chute rails rattled, as if someone had fallen against them. "Judd, blast it, stop, and leave before I call security and have you thrown out."

"Come back to me, Laci, or I'll make certain that James Enterprises is ruined. And you know I can do it. I'll see that this rodeo closes down and your father's precious company goes bankrupt. Then what will you do, huh?''

"You need some help, Laci?'' Brant said, walking up behind her.

Judd looked past Laci, his dark eyes meeting Brant's. "She doesn't need anything from you, Garrison,'' he sneered. "Except to be left alone.''

Laci whirled around and stared up at Brant, surprise raising her brows. He saw a flash of fear in her eyes and wondered if it was from his sudden appearance, or her physical encounter with Judd.

"No, Brant,'' Laci said, and glanced back at her ex-husband. "We're just…having a minor disagreement.''

Brant ignored Judd and looked down at Laci. "Sounded like a major one to me.''

"No one cares what it sounded like to you.'' Judd spat.

Brant allowed his gaze to graze over Judd McCandrick, making no effort to hide the disdain he felt toward the man. Brant had never liked Judd when he'd been on the circuit, or afterward when the other man had inherited his father's ranching operations and later added stock contracting to the rodeos to his investments. But from the moment he'd heard that Judd had married Laci, he'd liked him even less. Now, seeing the way Judd had tried to manhandle her and hearing how he talked to her, Brant's feelings toward him bordered on pure fury.

The two men glared at each other. Brant was fully aware of the tension hanging thick in the air and intensifying with each passing second, but he did nothing to alleviate or lessen it. Out of the corner of his eye he saw Laci look nervously from Judd to him, but he continued to let his dark gaze bore into the other man, challenging him.

Finally Judd broke both the silence and the stare. He glanced away, then snapped his gaze back to Brant's. "You make a habit of creeping about listening in on private conversations between a man and his wife, Garrison?" Judd asked, his tone derisive and somewhat accusatory. "Or just when the wife is one of your old girlfriends?"

"Seemed to me like you were about to do something more than argue," Brant drawled, his gaze darting toward Judd's closed fist.

Laci saw the rage on her ex-husband's face, and the fire of hatred that turned his eyes nearly black as he glowered at Brant. If she didn't do something quickly she knew Judd would let his anger get the better of him and start swinging. She'd seen it happen too many times before. She turned back to Brant hurriedly. "It's okay, Brant, really. There's no need for you to stay, I can handle this."

Brant looked from her to Judd, ignoring her plea for him to back off and leave. He didn't need to get involved in her problems, it was the last thing in the world he needed in his life, yet he couldn't bring himself turn away and leave her to this brute. His eyes narrowed. "The way I understand it, McCandrick, Laci's not your wife anymore," Brant said, his tone edged with a threat of its own. "And if I heard right, she asked you to leave."

Two cowboys suddenly appeared from around the corner of the stables and sauntered in the direction of the pens. One said something to the other and they both laughed.

Judd glanced their way, then looked back at Brant. "This isn't over, Garrison." His gaze moved to Laci. "Remember what I said, Laci, and consider changing your mind. Consider it real hard." Spinning on his heel, Judd strode down the dirt drive that led to the parking lot.

"Just what in the hell did you think you were doing?" Laci snapped, jamming curled fists onto her hips and turning to glare up at Brant.

He stepped back, having expected a smile and maybe even a thank you rather than a snarl and accusation.

"I don't need you starting fights around here, Brant Garrison," Laci continued before he even had a chance to think of a reply to her first comment. "And I can take care of myself and any business I might have with my ex-husband, without any help. I don't need you playing white knight and running to my rescue."

"Sorry," he mumbled.

"Well, you should be. Next time would you please just...just butt out." Whirling around, Laci stormed away in the same direction Judd had taken, but instead of heading for the parking lot she made an abrupt right and strode directly to the arena office, stomping her way up the stairs, disappearing inside and letting the door slam behind her.

Brant stared after her. He should have known better than to get involved. Whatever was going on in Laci's life was nothing but trouble, and none of his business.

The bull in the pen next to him snorted.

Brant glanced down at him. "Who the hell asked you?" he snapped.

"I heard about people talking to plants to try to get them to grow," Cody Roidan said, striding up behind Brant, "but I ain't never heard of a cowboy trying to sweet-talk a bull before his ride."

"Oh, shut up," Brant snarled, and walked toward the stables. Why had he poked his nose in where it didn't belong? That was the million dollar question. Hadn't Laci made it perfectly clear that she had no interest in him? She'd practically run away from him every time they'd encountered each other since his return to Reno. And hadn't she just told him, in no uncertain terms, that she didn't want or need his help? What more proof did he need? Anyway, he didn't need a woman in his life right now, not even Laci. He had to concentrate on winning. In two months he owed a balloon payment on the ranch. He could make it by cashing in some of the investments he'd made over the years, if he had to. But without winning the Championship purse he couldn't get the camp up and running, might even have to cancel it altogether. And without winning the World Championship title he couldn't fulfill his promise to Brett.

Brant continued to stare up at the arena office. Why in the hell did life have to be so blasted complicated? He turned around and strode back toward the stables. He was scheduled for both bull riding and calf roping this evening, but had several hours before his first event.

The tall black gelding stood with his head over the stall gate and snickered as he saw Brant walking toward him, then shook his head, sending long streams of silky black mane flying about in every direction.

"Yeah, yeah, I know, you're anxious to get out there and show off in front of everyone." He opened the stall gate and walked inside. "Not content with a few laps around an empty arena, huh?" Brant chuckled softly and slapped Blackjack's back as he reached for the bridle hanging on the wall. Hunkering down, he ran his hands over one of Blackjack's rear legs.

"We were never meant to be together."

The words Laci had said to Judd echoed in Brant's mind. He'd felt a spurt of joy upon hearing them, and as quickly had quelled it, trying not to read something into her meaning that wasn't there. But he couldn't help wondering. Had she regretted not waiting for him? He'd left town angry, he knew, but she had to have known that he'd meant to come back for her. Hadn't he told her that he loved her? That she was the only woman he'd ever truly loved?

Brant moved to examine Blackjack's other rear leg, cupping the hock with one hand and running his other lightly over the long length of the cannon.

But what did it really matter what Laci said now? She hadn't waited for him, and she wasn't interested in picking up where they'd left off. And neither was he.

"Damn him," Laci snapped. "Damn him, damn him, damn him." She stared out at the empty arena but didn't really see it. What she saw instead was Brant Garrison walking away from her. *"I'm not the settling-down type."* His words were carved into her memory and branded into her soul, never to be forgotten. He'd left her, walked out of her life as if what they'd had together hadn't matter to him at all, and she'd done her best to forget him and make a life for herself and Kit without him.

So why couldn't he have just stayed away? She didn't need this kind of problem in her life. Especially now. "Damn him." Laci slammed a fist onto the counter.

"Hope you wasn't imaginin' that was me you're hitting," Charley said, stepping into the office just as flesh connected with wood in a solid thud.

She jumped, startled and embarrassed, and tried to blink back the tears that blurred her eyes.

"Judd?"

She nodded. It was half true anyway. "We argued, out by the pens." She shook her head and brushed her fingertips over the soft skin beneath her eyes. "Heaven knows how many people overheard us. Too many, I'm afraid. He wants me to go back to him, and he's not exactly subtle about voicing his demands."

"You aren't, are you?" Charley said, riveting her with eyes that were suddenly wary and hard. "Going back to him?"

"No, but he doesn't want to believe that. He insists we belong together."

"Judd McCandrick never did like losing at anything. What else?"

Laci shrugged and picked up the evening's competition schedule. She didn't want to go into the rest of what had happened. "Nothing, that's all."

Charley didn't move, just remained standing by the door, staring at her. She glanced at him and was instantly sorry she had. He had always been able to tell her moods, especially when she was trying to hide something.

"What else, Laci?"

"Oh," she waved a hand through the air as if to dismiss her own words, "he threatened to make enough trouble to close down the rodeo and ruin James Enterprises."

"Humph! A man could find himself alone in the desert with an air tunnel ventilating his head after making threats like that."

Laci chuckled. "Judd's all bluff, Charley. Don't worry about it."

"Anything else?"

"No."

"So you were cursing out Judd when I came in? Making believe that was his head you were pounding on?"

"Yes." She looked out at the arena. The stands were already starting to fill up, people back up along the stairs and walkways waiting to find their seats. Laci kept her gaze averted from Charley's, afraid he would see the lie in her eyes if she looked at him.

"Well, I gotta go check the chutes. Just came up to get my gloves."

Laci nodded but didn't turn, even after she heard the door close. She inhaled deeply, letting the air fill her lungs and help calm the trembling that had erupted in her body the moment Brant had confronted her and Judd. She could handle Judd, at least most of the time, but being around Brant, trying to control all the old feelings his presence stirred within her, was playing havoc with both her senses and her temperament. And this was only the second day of the rodeo. How could she make it to the end?

It was a hopeless situation. Nothing between them had changed. They'd grown older, she'd taken on more responsibility, and he'd become even more devastatingly handsome than he had been. Other than that, everything was exactly the same. Rodeoing— following the circuit and winning the World Championship—was still the most important thing in Brant's life. Having a stable home and family were still the most important things in life to Laci. Even if they weren't, she didn't have that choice anymore. She had Kit to think of now, and James Enterprises to oversee. And secretly, she still had her fear to contend with every time Brant climbed up on a bull or wild bronc.

Laci straightened her shoulders and tried to command the calm she needed to get through the evening, and the rest of the week, into her system.

Brant wasn't in love with her now any more than he had been seven and a half years ago. He desired her, yes. She could see that in his eyes every time she looked into them. And if she'd let him he would have kissed her last night at the party. She almost had. She'd wanted to…desperately. But thankfully she'd come to her senses in time. There was no point to letting things get physically out of control. Brant Garrison and Laci James had no future together. She couldn't risk letting her heart get any more attached to him than it already was, because if she did, if she let him kiss her, make love to her, she would never be able to let him walk out of her life again, and she had no doubt that was exactly what he was going to do.

It took Charley ten minutes to locate Brant. He'd checked the stock pens, the association office, the registration trailer, and the parking lot. Then Cody Roidan had told him he'd seen Brant down at the stables checking over his horse.

"I see you're scheduled in the calf roping tonight."

Brant looked up at the voice. Great. He'd bet ten bucks that Charley Brownning wasn't interested in whether or not Brant was competing in calf roping or tree climbing. But he'd probably heard that Brant had stuck his nose into Laci's business and the old man was here to give him a piece of his mind and warn him not to do it again. Brant swore softly. Just what he needed. Then again, maybe that was just what he needed: a reminder to mind his own business. He finished examining Blackjack's front leg, running his fingers slowly over the horse's fetlock and pastern before finally standing and turning to face Charley.

"Yeah, I'm doing calf roping," Brant said finally, rising. "Blackjack likes the competition."

"And the money doesn't hurt, either, if you win," Charley said.

"That's a pretty big if. Harlen Kane's got a better time than me." Brant turned his back to Charley and began brushing Blackjack's mane.

"Only by a hair."

"A hair's a hair," Brant said. "That's all it takes to win first place."

"Ed James once said he knew you'd make it."

Brant's hand paused on Blackjack's neck and he twisted around to stare at Charley, surprised.

"Yep. He could usually spot them," Charley continued. "The winners. Said once he figured you had what it took to make it to the top, if you didn't let guilt over your brother's death pull you down."

"Ed James didn't like me."

"That's where you're wrong." Charley smiled at the look of surprise that swept over Brant's face. "He liked you well enough, he just didn't want to see his daughter traipsing all over the countryside after you."

"After a two-bit rodeo bum, you mean," Brant growled.

"After anyone," Charley corrected. "Ed wanted Laci to have a normal life—husband, home and kids. You know, the American dream. Wanted her to settle down here in Reno, or someplace close by so he could enjoy his grandkids. All you could think about was the rodeo."

"I loved her," Brant said.

"But not enough to quit the circuit."

He couldn't argue with that, because his love for Laci and his need to keep going on the circuit, to win the World Championship, had nothing to do with one another. But no one had ever understood that. If it had been his own choice, if his promise to Brett hadn't existed, he would have quit the rodeo and done anything Laci had wanted him to do, rather than lose her.

"But then, you never really had a choice, did you?" Charley persisted, as if able to read Brant's thoughts.

Again he found himself startled by the old man's words.

"Well, sometimes things work out for the best, you know? Like that strike down in Vegas making it so the PRCA had to move the World Championships here to Reno."

Brant's eyes narrowed. "How do you figure that worked out for the best?"

"Brought you back here, didn't it? Who knows how long you'd've stayed away otherwise. Maybe forever."

Before Brant could answer, Charley turned away.

"Well, I gotta go. Good luck tonight." He walked toward the stock pens, smiling to himself as he approached the arena office. Sometimes when cupid got derailed the little fella just needed a bit of help getting put back on the right track. And Charley wasn't above helping cupid sharpen his arrows where Laci was concerned.

Brant spent the time until his scheduled rides busying himself with a lot of nothing. He talked to several other cowboys he hadn't seen in a while, played fetch with one of the numerous dogs that ran loose around the pens, cleaned out Blackjack's stall and oiled his saddle. Then he spent over an hour working Blackjack out in the fields behind the rodeo grounds. The horse didn't really need the practice, but Brant needed something to keep his mind occupied and centered on business.

The bull riding event was split into two events tonight and he was scheduled to ride in both. The calf roping competition was in between.

Seeing Blackjack back to his stall, Brant checked his watch and walked toward the arena. It was almost time for his first ride.

Dream Dodger did his best to throw Brant from his back, but failed. The bull had started kicking and thrashing even before the chute gate opened, but Brant managed to stay seated throughout the entire ride and had even spurred the huge animal, which garnered him a few additional points. He'd gone the eight seconds, and at the sound of the buzzer, propelled himself off the animal's back and ran for the rails while the rodeo clowns did their jobs and vied for Dream Dodger's attention so Brant could get safely away.

Halfway up the rails, Brant turned and looked up at the scoreboard.

"Well, folks," the announcer said over the PA system, "you've just seen one of the best. And look at that score, ninety-one! Haven't seen one that high in a long time."

The crowd roared its approval and Brant jabbed a victory fist into the air. "Yes!" he yelled, excitement like he hadn't felt in years coursing through him. "Yes!"

"Jeff Henricks of Oklahoma City is up next on Gargantua, but Jeff's got a big task in front of him if he wants to beat Garrison's ninety-one points."

Brant climbed over the rails and walked around the back of one of the spectator stands. Ninety-one. He couldn't believe it. He'd known Dream Dodger was giving him a good ride, but ninety-one? He wanted to laugh aloud, dance a jig, shout with joy and drop to his knees in thanks and relief. Near the registration trailer, he paused and looked up at the arena office. He had the most incredible urge to run up there, grab Laci, and spin her around in his arms as he whooped with delight. It had been a great ride, his best ever, and he felt on top of the world. He wanted to share the feeling, and he wanted to share it with her.

Letting instinct and excitement rather than rational thought and common sense guide him, Brant moved toward the office stairs. He was halfway across the dirt drive that separated the registration trailer from the office and the bull chutes beneath it when he stopped cold. Judd McCandrick was headed in the same direction, a bouquet of bloodred roses in one hand. Brant felt the muscles in his jaw tighten and a cloud of blackness sweep over his good mood as he watched Judd walk past him, climb the stairs to the office, and disappear inside.

Chapter 5

"It's him, isn't it, Laci?" Judd accused. "Garrison. You're going out with him, aren't you?"

"No."

"Hah!" he snorted, trembling with rage. He stood before her, only a few inches of space separating them.

She could feel the heat of his anger threaten to envelop her.

"This whole damned divorce thing wouldn't be happening if that SOB hadn't come back to town."

"You know that's not true, Judd." Laci glanced at the counter to make certain the PA's microphone was off. The last thing she needed now was for the entire populace at the arena to overhear her in an argument with her ex-husband. The roses Judd had brought her as a peace offering lay on the floor where he'd thrown them when she'd refused his invitation to a late dinner. So much for peace. She turned back to Judd. He'd dressed up, sporting an expensively cut brown western suit, white silk shirt and bolo tie. Either he'd had business with someone at the arena, or he'd taken it for granted that she'd accept his invitation. She hoped it was the former.

"Do I?"

"Brant Garrison has nothing to do with this, Judd," she continued. "You know that. And anyway, since I filed for divorce over five months ago, and it's been final for over three, how could I have known then that Brant was coming back to Reno? You had all the rodeo records, remember?"

"Someone could have told you. Like that damned old man."

"Charley? How would he have known? He wasn't working for you, he was retired."

"He isn't now."

"No, he's working for me."

"You've been in love with Garrison the whole time, haven't you, Laci?" Judd accused, abruptly changing the course of the conversation again. "All through our marriage you kept thinking about Garrison, not giving us a chance. You never did stop loving him, did you?"

She didn't know what to say. Brant was the father of her son, the man she'd given her heart to and had been unable to forget. She had loved him when he'd left her, and knew she would probably always love him, but she'd married Judd McCandrick. And she had tried her best to make the marriage work. "It doesn't matter, Judd. I tried to make our marriage work, you know I did. It just wasn't meant to be. We weren't right for each other.''

"What I know is that you left me so you could start up with him again." Judd grabbed at the turquoise-and-silver bolo at his neck and jerked it loose, then yanked at the top button of his shirt and pulled the collar open.

"Do you really have that low of an opinion of me, Judd, to think I'd do that?" Laci demanded, shocked that Judd would think such a thing. "Do you really believe I'd fall back into Brant Garrison's arms just like that?"

"Yes," he thundered.

Yes, a little voice in the back of her mind whispered.

More startled by her own thoughts than Judd's angry accusation, Laci merely stared up at him, unable to think of a thing to say.

"You're damned right I believe that, Laci. Look at you," he bellowed, taking a threatening step toward her so that they were almost touching, "you can't even deny it." With rage twisting his features, Judd grabbed a clipboard from the desk beside him and hurled it across the room. It crashed into the wall and fell to the floor, the papers secured beneath its clip jerking free and flying everywhere.

Laci jumped, startled. "Judd…"

"You really want that SOB, Laci? A two-bit rodeo bum who never made it to the top and never will? Fine, you can have him," Judd growled. "But that's all you'll have, you hear me? That's it. Nothing else."

"Judd, please, don't talk crazy."

"Crazy? Me?" He laughed, an ugly sound that

made her shiver, and Laci realized for the first time that she was actually afraid of him. "I'm not the one who's crazy around here, Laci. I didn't break up our home and destroy our marriage. You did that. And all because Garrison's back." He glared at her.

"I'm not going to keep arguing with you about this, Judd." She glanced at her watch. Intermission had started only a minute or so before Judd had come into the office and Charley and the judges most likely wouldn't come back until the last minute.

Laci sighed. She had never wanted to hurt Judd. Even after he'd slapped Kit and she'd seen the contempt and jealousy in his eyes that had scared her half to death, she hadn't wanted to hurt him. But she couldn't have stayed married to him. Not after that. "I brought Kit home from the hospital yesterday," she said trying to keep her voice calm and change the subject. "You can come by the house tomorrow, if you'd like, and visit him."

The curve of one golden brow rose in mocking disbelief. "Why would I want to visit Kit?"

"He's your son."

The coldness in Judd's eyes suddenly seemed to intensify. "No, he's not."

Startled, Laci stepped back, feeling as if she'd just been slapped. She stared at Judd, unable to believe what he'd just said. "He believes you're his father."

"If I'm not your husband, Laci, then I'm not Kit's father." Judd turned and stormed to the door, but upon reaching it, he paused and looked back at her. "Why don't you tell Garrison the truth, Laci, see if you can get him interested in playing daddy to your little bas—"

"Judd!"

Laughing, he walked from the office, slamming the door upon his exit.

Laci slumped back into her chair. She should be relieved, and maybe she was, beneath the shock, she wasn't sure at the moment. But she would never have believed that of Judd. Though now that she thought back on the last few months of their marriage, especially that day when Kit had misbehaved and Judd slapped him, she didn't know why she hadn't expected Judd to disown Kit. His eyes had registered a contempt bordering on hatred and totally infused with jealousy. She'd been a fool not to see it before. A blind, stupid fool.

But what was she going to say to Kit when he wanted to know why Judd wasn't coming around to see him?

Before she had anymore time to dwell on the situation, the office door swung open and Charley, along with two rodeo judges, walked in. The judges nodded to her and went directly to their own stations.

Laci stood. "Charley, I'm going to get a cup of coffee. That stuff you make—" she glanced at the coffeepot and wrinkled her nose "—is strong enough to curl my toes."

He nodded and, flipping on the PA system, leaned over the microphone and announced the end of their first intermission.

So far, except for Judd's unpleasant little visit, things were going smoothly, to which Laci offered up a prayer of thanks. No unexpected crises or disasters had erupted during the earlier events other than the norm, which proved minor. One flag girl failed to show up, a dog had accidentally gotten loose in the arena just before they'd begun the steer wrestling competition, and Zach Taylor caught his arm on one of the chute doors.

On a brighter note, the arena's receipts were up, having nearly sold out for that night's rodeo.

At the canteen booth Laci doctored her coffee with a little milk and sugar, then turned and walked back toward the office. She was ascending the stairs when she heard Brant's name announced over the PA system. She paused, puzzled. She'd deliberately managed to busy herself elsewhere during the evening's first round of bull riding so that she wouldn't have to watch it, and it wasn't time for the second round. Laci hurried to the landing and looked into the lighted arena. A chute at the southern end jerked open and a calf broke out, running as if its tail were on fire. Right behind the animal was Brant Garrison whirling a rope over his head while riding a large black horse in a headlong gallop.

Laci held her breath and watched him, suddenly mesmerized. She hadn't seen his name on the schedule for the calf roping event when she'd looked it over earlier, but then she couldn't really swear that once she'd encountered it on the bull riding timetable she'd actually looked any further. "Come on, Brant," she whispered softly, unable to help herself from cheering him on, even if quietly.

To Laci, watching Brant ride a galloping horse was almost like watching a bit of magic unfold before her eyes. He was a man born to ride in a saddle, seeming to become one with his mount as they moved together. It was as if he became part of the animal, or it an extension of him, their souls melding so that man and equine were attuned to the same wavelength: thought for thought, muscle for muscle, all moving together toward one common goal.

Brant threw the rope. The looped end fell over the calf's head and Blackjack instantly skidded to a stop, shoving his forelegs into the soft earth and his weight back. At that same moment Brant swung a leg over the horse's neck, jumped to the ground and raced toward the struggling calf.

Within seconds Brant had the calf's legs tied and jumped back to his feet, raising his arms high in the air to signal that he'd finished.

The crowd cheered.

Laci glanced at the field judge and mentally ticked off the six seconds that had to pass to validate Brant's tie. The judge dropped his flag, signaling the time was up, and Laci turned her gaze to the scoreboard. Four point nine. A good time. Maybe even a winning time. She smiled absently and pulled open the door to her office.

Charley swiveled around in his chair. "You see the last roper?"

She nodded, wishing she'd waited a few more minutes to come back into the office. Then Charley would have been busy doing something else instead of bringing up the subject of Brant Garrison. But that was probably wishful thinking. Charley'd most likely have brought up the subject no matter when she reentered the office. His matchmaking comments were becoming less and less subtle.

"Damned if it doesn't look like he just might take that class, too."

"Never know," Laci said, "but we've got a ways to go before finals. Anything can happen."

"Yep." Charley eyed her pointedly. "Anything sure can happen."

Just a few more days, Laci thought, ignoring the look he threw her. Just a few more days until the World Championship Rodeo ended and Brant Garrison once again left Reno, Nevada.

She sat down at her desk and busied herself in paperwork, but an hour later, when the second round of the bull riding competition started, Laci stood. "I'm going over to the auditorium for a while."

Charley turned to look at her. "Still makes you nervous, huh? Watching him ride the bulls?"

Laci stiffened. "No, why should it? I just need to talk to a few people, that's all…about their fees, and I need to stretch my legs."

"Uh-huh."

Laci left the office, wondering whether Charley was psychic or her feelings were merely as transparent as all get out. Just because she didn't want to watch Brant ride a bull didn't mean anything other than she didn't feel like watching him get thrown, that's all.

"You sure you don't want me to stick around and help you lock up?" Charley said.

Laci smiled. "I think I can handle turning the key in the door by myself, Charley, thanks. Anyway, you've seen to most of the other stuff. I just have a vendor's report I want to go over and I want to look at tomorrow's schedule before I call it a night. Then I'll be heading home.''

"You're sure?"

"I'm sure." She waved him off. "Go on now."

"Okay, but don't stay too long. This place will be totally deserted in another hour."

"Thirty minutes," she said.

Nodding, Charley left the office.

Laci turned back to the stack of papers on her desk. She hadn't been exactly truthful with him. She had a report to go over, but not the schedule for the next day's competition. She'd checked that already, as well as the stock calendars, vet reports and even the day's receipts. What she needed to look over was the report from Ferguson, Brassea and Trammel.

Ever since her parents had been killed, Laci had been more than happy to let Judd oversee the operations of James Enterprises. But when she and Judd had divorced and she'd wanted him to turn over control of the business to her, as well as hand over all of its records, he'd stalled—right up to two days before the World Championships were scheduled to start. And he'd only given in then because she'd threatened to have the police enforce the court order she'd obtained.

By then, however, his actions had made her suspicious. Maybe unreasonably so, but suspicious all the same, and she hadn't been able to reconcile not doing something to put her mind at ease. So she'd hired the best accounting firm in Reno to go over the books.

This was only an initial report, but she was eager to see it anyway. And she didn't want anyone else to see it, not even Charley. If there was something in it there shouldn't be, it was between her and Judd, not the world.

Laci ripped open the envelope with FB and T's fancily scrolled name imprinted in gold leaf in the left-hand corner and withdrew the single sheet of paper tucked inside. Her gaze moved quickly over the explaining paragraph and few accompanying figures. Everything looked fine, but the accountant in charge of her file emphasized that this was barely an initial report, much too early to declare anything concrete.

A knock on the door startled Laci and she jumped, whirling around.

"Laci? You still in there?"

She recognized Brant's deep drawl immediately and nearly groaned. Her traitorous heart skipped a beat and her pulse instantly sped up, while her mind raced in search of an excuse for not answering him. If she remained silent would he assume she was gone and leave? She glanced at the glowing overhead light, then back at the door. It was obvious someone was in the office.

"Laci?"

She wanted to bolt for the door and let him in, and she wanted to hide until he went away.

"Laci?" He knocked again, harder this time.

She watched, mesmerized and unmoving as the door handle turned and the door swung open. Brant stepped into the office, the reflection of the overhead light sparkling off of the silver conchos attached to his hatband and settling softly upon the smooth plane of white fabric that stretched across his wide shoulders. "Charley said you were still in here."

Laci forced a smile to her lips. Thank you, Charley, she growled silently, making a mental note to kill her old friend first thing the next morning. "I...was just going over some reports."

Brant nodded while his gaze moved over her hungrily and a thousand curses danced their way through his mind. Why had he waited around for her? It had been a stupid thing to do. He didn't need any complications in his life right now, and he certainly didn't need her rejection. Not again. Once had been more than enough. Yet he couldn't seem to make himself turn around and leave. "Chris and Sherri Daniels and a couple of the guys have gone over to Hank's. They thought you might like to join them."

Laci stared at him. "Chris and Sherri?" Her mind suddenly spun with memories. Chris Daniels was a longtime friend of Brant's, and at one time they'd even traveled the circuit together. Sherri had been one of Laci's closest friends in high school and had met Chris the same time Laci met Brant. The four of them had even double-dated for a while, and Sherri and Laci had dreamed of a double wedding. But by the time Chris and Sherri got married, and took off to follow the rodeo circuit, things had already started to turn sour between Brant and Laci.

She shoved the accounting firm's report into her handbag, and looked back up at Brant. Seeing Chris and Sherri again was definitely something she'd love, but she didn't want to go to Hank's with Brant. In fact, she knew she didn't dare. She'd promised herself that she'd stay as far away from him as she could while he was in Reno, and she had every intention of doing just that. Laci shook her head. "I don't think so, Brant, thanks anyway. I'd love to see them, but I really have to get home. Kit probably..."

"Is asleep," he finished for her, then contemplated biting off his tongue. So much for being smart. She'd given him an out and he hadn't taken it. *Because you didn't really want an out,* a voice in the back of his mind taunted.

It galled him to admit that the voice of his conscience was right. He didn't want an out, he wanted Laci.

Laci glanced at the clock on the wall. "You're probably right," she said, yanking Brant's attention back to her. "But I'd really better go home anyway."

"Laci, I..." He took a step toward her, not knowing why or what he intended to do, just knowing that he desperately wanted her to come with him.

She hastily backed away as he approached, grabbing her car keys from the desk beside her and slinging the strap of her purse over one shoulder. "I really do have to get home, Brant." She stepped forward and made to brush past him but he moved into her path, blocking her escape. Laci stopped abruptly and stared up at him, realizing instantly that trying to pass him had been a mistake. His gaze caught hers and mercilessly took it his prisoner, offering no respite or deliverance. She felt herself being pulled into an eddy of emotion; memories and feelings she did not want to delve into surging up to envelop her. Yet even as she struggled to resist them, she wanted nothing more than to give in to them. She had no will of her own with which to break the spell he had cast over her, shackling her to him with its invisible bonds, neither did she care to.

As memories crashed headlong into reality, all of the dreams and longings she'd harbored over the past seven years rose up to confront her, to remind her of the loneliness her heart had endured ever since the day Brant had walked out of her life. They had plagued her cruelly, become her secret torment, and now they had a chance, if only briefly, to be vanquished.

Brant's hands moved to encircle her upper arms and draw her to him.

Laci felt the heat of his hands sear right through the thin fabric of her cotton shirt, his touch invoking a profusion of sensations within her that threatened to overwhelm her with their intensity. Longing and desire flamed to life within her blood as she struggled to fight them off. This was wrong, there could be nothing between them. Her mind knew it, even her heart knew it, but her body wasn't listening.

Brant didn't want to think about what he was doing. He didn't want to rationalize it away or pay heed to the warning that had been buzzing around in his mind ever since he'd driven into Reno three days ago. Right now all he wanted to do was give in to the hunger that had been eating at him for years. He'd thought he could come back here, see her, and still maintain control over the yearnings that had haunted him for so long. But he'd been wrong.

There had been other women during those years, usually a groupie that caught up with him in a bar, or an arena worker who wanted to catch herself a cowboy, if only for a night. But he'd never allowed himself to feel anything real for them, always making sure to keep his emotions in check, his heart securely locked away.

But now, as Laci stood only a few inches away, all of the pain and frustration of the past was forgotten. He knew it was dangerous, knew he'd most likely end up sorry he hadn't stayed away from her as he'd planned, but the need to have her in his arms again was too much to resist. How many nights had he dreamed of holding her again? Longed to know the seductive, soul-satisfying feel of her body pressed up against his just one more time? And how many nights had he gone to bed with an image of her face taunting his thoughts, and an ache of yearning in his gut that nearly tore him apart?

"I missed you, Laci." He hadn't meant to say the words aloud, but it was the truth, and they had slipped from his lips as naturally as the thought had tiptoed across his mind.

The velvet rumble of Brant's drawl wrapped around Laci like a warm cloak and sent delicious shivers rippling over every part of her body. Danger, her mind screamed, struggling to be heard over the rapid pounding of her heart. But her thoughts were already so muddled with the yearnings and desires that had lain dormant within her for so long that the warning was little more than a whisper in the back of her consciousness.

This was what she wanted, Laci thought, but it wasn't right. It could never be right between them.

Brant felt the slight resistance that swept through Laci, felt her start to pull away. "No," he said in a near breathless whisper, "don't run away from me again, Laci, please."

She felt his left hand slightly tighten its hold on her arm, while his other moved to her face, his fingers brushing lightly, sensuously, along the curve of her jaw. It was a seemingly innocent gesture, but it took Laci's breath away and left her trembling and uncertain.

The slight hint of a smile tugged at the corners of Brant's mouth at her reaction to his touch. "I've dreamed for so long of what it would be like to have you this close to me again."

She struggled to resist the temptation of him. "Brant, I really don't think…"

He pressed the pad of his index finger softly to her lips and, slipping his other hand around her waist, pulled her closer.

"That's really best for now, isn't it, Laci?" he said. "Not to think?"

For a timeless second that blended memories, dreams and reality, Brant's gaze searched her face as he compared each curve and line to the memory he had carried with him over the years. She had changed, and yet she hadn't. Passion gripped every cell of his body, firing his blood, urging his arms to tighten their hold on her, his lips to sweep down and claim hers. But he didn't move. Instead, he took his time appreciating what he hadn't seen for so long, what he'd dreamed of every night since he'd left her—golden strands of hair that spread across her shoulders like cascading waves of silk, startling blue eyes framed by long, thick lashes, high cheekbones that curved dramatically to smooth hollows now shaded with the pinkness of a blush, and finally, the irresistible curve of her lips, held open just slightly, and quivering under his inspection.

He sensed the desire his nearness invoked within her and saw it begin to cloud the dark pupils of her eyes. How many times had he stared up at a spring sky, and been reminded of Laci's eyes? He tightened his arms around her, pulling her closer, and felt a shiver ripple through her body. She was still vulnerable to his touch, in spite of the years that had passed since they'd been together. Satisfaction surged through Brant, and a kind of quiet relief. Maybe she had never truly been in love with him, but she was still physically attracted to him, and for now he would settle for that. His gaze dropped to the open V of her shirt and the soft curve of her breasts, now brushing against the wall of his chest.

With only the barest nudge of his imagination he could envision her flesh bared to him, her nipples hard and aching for his touch. He swept the long tangles of hair from her shoulder and heard her breath turn ragged as, with tormenting slowness, he lowered his head and pressed his lips to the smooth skin at the curve of her neck.

"How did we lose each other, Laci?" Brant whispered against her bared skin, and turned it to fire with another kiss. He breathed in the scent of her, tasted the honey of her flesh, and trembled from the hungers it stirred within him.

"Brant, please," Laci whispered, her tone edged with the anguish of a woman whose body and mind are at battle. She was going to lose control…she had already lost control, except for the ability to plead with him, just once. That was all she had left in her, all the resistance she could muster.

"Yes, Laci, please," he drawled huskily. But as he raised his head, instead of releasing her as she'd thought he was about to do, Brant trapped her lips with his.

Night turned into day and into night again as unbridled madness swirled through Laci's senses, tempting her, teasing her, and drawing her toward a chasm of emotions where she knew, deep within herself, she had no business being. Her universe of reason, self-denial, and common sense spun out of control as an overpowering ache of desire invaded her body, seized command and imprinted every cell and fibre with a hunger to know Brant's touch. Feelings long staved off flooded through her, yearnings long buried swept away any thought of resistance and left her with nothing but the need to give in to them. Insidious memories danced through her mind, as if teasing her, daring her to remember what it felt like to have his hands on her breasts, their bodies melded together, how that sensuously slanted mouth could ravage her lips.

Brant instantly sensed the change in her. The game had turned lethal, at least for him, but he couldn't turn back. Dragging her up against him, pulling her into his arms hadn't been the wisest move he could have made. It was the one, however, that he'd wanted to make. The one he'd been unable to resist making. He could feel his body hardening with a devastating hunger to feel her lying beneath him, naked, hot with passion, aching for his touch. What he was doing was insane. He knew he should release her, walk away, but he couldn't. Throwing caution to the winds, Brant cursed silently and deepened the kiss.

His mouth caressed hers tenderly, eliciting her acquiescence, attempting to vanquish her resistance and surrendering his own, while his tongue proved a dart of sense-routing fire, probing madly, fiercely, and burning wherever it touched.

A soft, barely audible moan escaped Laci's throat, yet even as her body betrayed her, as Brant's kiss inflamed the passions she had held in check, dormant and locked away for so long, she tried to fight him with her mind. Fire flowed through her veins while she told herself she had to pull away from him—need ignited like a tormenting ache within her as she recalled how many nights she'd cried herself to sleep after he'd left her, and want seized her soul, reminding her of how much she'd loved him—how much she still loved him.

But as Brant's mouth played delicious, mind-searing havoc with hers, the seconds ticked by, passing into oblivion even as her body strained against being conquered, and her senses, overpowered by desire, paid no heed to the faint warnings cavorting through the back of her mind. She had waited too long, dreamed too many dreams, to deny their fulfillment now.

His lips tore away from hers and Laci felt a sudden desolation. It disappeared as quickly as it had swept over her when she felt his lips glide gently down the column of her neck. His tongue traced the curve of her earlobe, then dropped to follow the frantically pounding vein in her neck that led to the bare slope of her shoulder.

Laci drew a shaky breath and pressed against Brant, leaning into him, needing to feel his length fused with her own. She wanted to resist him, wanted to scream at him for all the loneliness she had endured while he'd been gone, for the things that could have been, and weren't, but she had no resistance left in her, and nothing left with which to shield her heart from the potent magic he seemed able to create with just a look, a touch. Her senses, her body, were betraying her. With a small moan of defeat, Laci gave in to her desires. Her arms slipped around his shoulders and she pressed against him. ''Love me,'' she whispered softly, her words as much a plea as a command. She moved her head to catch his lips with hers, returning his kiss ardently, passionately, while her breasts strained against the fabric of her clothes, aching for his touch, and she reveled in the feel of her body once again being crushed to his.

Brant's kiss deepened, his arms tightening around her as his heart beat against her breast in a race with her own. He kissed her slowly, savoring every caressing movement, every response. He had endured what seemed like a lifetime without her, and if it were to be that way again, he wanted, needed, a lifetime of memories to help him get through the long, lonely years ahead. Her tongue twisted about his in a dance of seduction and Brant felt her kiss as an exquisite agony he wished never to end, her body pressed against his an exciting torment he had never dared hope to enjoy again.

A gnawing ache coiled hot and demanding deep inside of Laci. Driven by the same hungers that filled Brant, her fingers slid through his hair as her body strained to be closer to his than any two people could possibly get. Every nerve within her being seemed centered on his touch, his caresses, taking what he had to offer and craving more. The sudden need to be free of her clothes, to once again know the luscious sensation of his bare flesh against hers, the sensuous caress of his hands on her body, carried her rapidly toward wild abandon.

Somewhere outside a gate clanged shut, the sound echoing through the still night. It was a faint sound, not really enough to even take notice of, but to Laci it was like a bell of warning suddenly going off in her head. The spell she had allowed herself to slip under at Brant's touch was abruptly broken. She tore her lips from his and tried to step from his embrace, pushing against his arms. "No," she gasped, breathlessly, "I can't do this."

Puzzled, Brant stared at her. A deep frown cut into his brow, but his arms remained around her waist. "I never forgot you, Laci. Or how much I loved you."

She smiled, though her heart was filled with sadness and regret. He had never forgotten how much he loved her—and neither had she—and that was the problem. His love hadn't been deep enough all those years ago, and she knew there was no reason to think that had changed. "I never forgot you either, Brant, but this is wrong. It can't work between us. I..." She felt tears sting the back of her eyes and blinked them away, determined not to lose control in front of him. She raised her chin and met his gaze. She should tell him about Kit, but something stopped her. Fear? Defiance? Laci wasn't sure; all she knew was she wasn't ready to face that truth yet. She wasn't sure Brant was either, and maybe that's what was truly stopping her. "There's no future for you and me together, Brant. There wasn't years ago, and there isn't now."

His arms dropped away from her and he took a step back, and Laci was instantly aware of the change in him, the fact that, once more, he'd put more than mere physical distance between them.

Brant forcefully smothered the desire that had warmed him at their embrace. She'd never really loved him. She had never actually said it before, but now her words made it all too clear. He'd been wise to leave before, and wiser to stay away. What had been stupid was coming back, seeing her again, and losing control. "Yeah," he sneered, his eyes turning hard and cold, "I guess I forgot that for a few minutes."

Before she could respond, he spun on his heel and walked out of the office. Laci felt a wave of emotion surge up to engulf her as she stared at the door that he'd slammed shut on his way out. She had hoped he would tell her she was wrong, that he'd changed over the years, that he was tired of living on the road and finally wanted to settle down with her and build a future together, regardless of whether he won the title or not. An ache of loss filled her breast.

She wanted to scream at him. Force him to answer the questions he'd avoided facing for so long. But she would no more do that now than she had seven and a half years ago. It had to be Brant's decision to stay, his decision to settle down—no choices weighed, no ultimatums given. She sagged against the edge of her desk. What was the use of even thinking that might happen? They still wanted different things out of life and that, obviously, would never change.

Laci was surprised to hear the sound of the television when she walked into the house. It was well past midnight and Mrs. Dabney was usually in bed by ten. Dropping her handbag on a table in the foyer, Laci walked into the family room. The housekeeper was asleep in one of the big overstuffed chairs. The pins which held a bun that was normally arranged at her nape had come loose and allowed her silver-streaked black hair to tumble over the colorful Navajo blanket that covered the back of the chair. Laci gently shook the older woman's shoulder and smiled when she snorted loudly, shuddered, and hurriedly pushed herself to her feet.

"What...what's wrong?" She blinked several times, then stared at Laci blankly.

"Nothing," Laci said. "You fell asleep in front of the TV, that's all."

Mrs. Dabney looked toward the television set. "TV?" she echoed dumbly, and frowned. "But I wasn't watching TV, I was reading my book." She bent down and retrieved a paperback from the floor and held it up to Laci.

The couple embracing on the cover of the book reminded Laci of herself and Brant. A woman with long blond hair held securely, lovingly, within the embrace of a rugged cowboy with black hair curling out from beneath a black Stetson. Laci pushed the thought aside. "Well, I'm going to bed so..." She stopped, her gaze caught by a pair of small feet sticking out beyond the end of the sofa. Looking back at

Mrs. Dabney Laci smiled and, pursing her lips, put her index finger against them. She tiptoed toward the bare feet, stopped and, hands on hips, leaned over the end of the sofa to stare down at Kit. He was in his pajamas, white flannel imprinted with cowboys on horseback. His head was propped up on his pillow, at just the right angle to catch sight of the TV without Mrs. Dabney being able to see him, if she had been awake.

Laci stepped around the corner to stand between Kit and the television set. "Kit?"

He bolted upright, giving her a sheepish grin. "Uh, oh, hi, Mom."

She struggled not to smile. "Just what do you think you're doing, young man?"

He scrambled to his feet. "Well, uh, I couldn't sleep and, uh, I didn't feel like reading, and I, ah, didn't want to wake Mrs. Dabney to make me hot cocoa, so I, uh..."

"Decided to watch a little TV?" Laci offered.

Kit hung his head then looked up at her, waiting for her to scold him. Instead, she leaned over and kissed the top of his head, then turned him by the shoulders so that he faced the hall. "Off with you now," she ordered, giving him a light swat on the rear, "and no more midnight TV."

Kit skipped forward, smiling. "Okay. G'night, Mom."

"Good night, honey," she called after him.

"Little imp," Mrs. Dabney mumbled.

Laci smiled and dropped down onto the sofa. It had been a long day and she was tired. The problem was she wasn't sleepy. Her mind was buzzing along, replaying everything that had happened that day—especially the episodes that involved Brant Garrison.

"You want me to fix you and the imp some cocoa?"

Laci shook her head. "No, thanks, I think we'll be okay."

Mrs. Dabney nodded. "All right, I'll see you in the morning then."

"Good night."

The older woman paused at the door and looked back, the lines on her fifty-eight-year-old face deepening momentarily. "You okay?" she asked.

Laci nodded. "Yes, just tired."

"I'll have you a nice breakfast ready when you get up."

Laci lay her head back against the sofa's plush cushion and released a long sigh. She forced thoughts of Brant from her mind and was instantly sorry when they were replaced with the memory of Judd's anger and threats. Why couldn't he just accept their divorce?

"Mom?"

She opened her eyes and sat up, turning to look toward the door where Kit stood.

"You gonna come tuck me in?"

Before she answered, another thought struck her. Kit and Judd had never been extremely close, not like she'd hoped they'd become. But it suddenly occurred to her now that Kit hadn't asked after Judd even once since the day they'd hastily packed their bags and left the McCandrick ranch.

Chapter 6

Laci arrived at the arena the next afternoon much earlier than she'd intended, but then the errands she'd had to do in town hadn't taken nearly as long as she'd expected.

Brant was scheduled to compete in the saddle bronc riding competition that evening. Laci stared at the chart. He was slotted toward the end of the event, which meant if she stayed in the office with her head buried in paperwork, didn't venture out even once, and left the arena a little early, she'd avoid any chance of running into him. But since arriving at the arena an hour ago the time had seemed to drag by slowly. Charley was down at the chutes, the office was quiet as a tomb, Laci couldn't keep her mind on the ledgers spread out on the desk before her—and it was only three o'clock. The rodeo wasn't going to start for another three hours.

She sighed. Playing coward was not enjoyable, and not something she wanted to continue doing. Tossing the papers she was holding onto the desk she turned toward the door. She needed to go to the press trailer and see if they'd managed to get any more television coverage for tonight. She also needed to check with security and make sure they'd replaced the two men who had quit. The phone rang just as she reached for the door handle.

"Damn." Returning to her desk, Laci grabbed the instrument's receiver. "Arena office."

"Ms. Laci James-McCandrick, please," a cool, crisp female voice requested on the other end.

Laci frowned. "This is Laci James."

"Ms. McCandrick," the woman said, ignoring Laci's correction, "this is Miss Parsons from the Professional Rodeo Cowboys Association office in Denver."

Laci felt an unreasonable sense of foreboding sweep over her. Why was the PRCA calling? "Yes?"

"Ms. McCandrick, an allegation has been made that a contestant there is receiving favored points and..."

"What?" Laci bolted from her chair and practically shouted the word into the phone, shock and anger instantly riling for control of her senses. "Favored points? That's crazy. In fact, it's impossible."

"Nevertheless, when an allegation like this is made we must..."

"Who made it?" Laci demanded. Fury held every muscle in her body taut.

"I'm sorry, I am not at liberty to say. Now, as I was about to explain, when an allegation like this is made, especially while the World Championships are taking place, I'm sure you understand that we must act immediately.''

''Act? How?'' Laci demanded.

''A PRCA representative will be available for a hearing this evening. He's staying at the Regal Palms Hotel there in Reno and has a conference room available. We've set the time at seven.''

''But the rodeo starts at six.''

''I'm sorry, Ms. McCandrick, but this must take precedence. You will be there of course?''

''Of course,'' Laci snapped, so angry she could scream. There was only one person in the world who wanted her to fail so much that he'd pull an underhanded trick like this, only one person who wanted her to fall flat on her face so hard that she'd believe her only salvation was to go running back to him. This was Judd's doing. It could have been anyone, but it wasn't. Laci knew beyond any doubt that her ex-husband was behind the complaint.

''I have already informed the two PRCA judges in attendance there that they are also to appear.''

''Fine, but I'd really like to know who leveled this charge, Miss Parsons.''

''I'm sorry, Ms. McCandrick, but I really can't tell you. I'm certain that information will be made available to you at the hearing this evening.''

Laci fumed.

''And Ms. McCandrick?''

''Yes?''

''Please see to it that Mr. Brant Garrison is also at the meeting.''

''Brant?'' Laci echoed, then instantly realized she

shouldn't have been surprised. It made perfect sense. Judd probably figured on killing two birds with one stone. He blamed their divorce on Brant and suspected that Laci had never stopped loving him. By leveling the charge, Judd hoped that it would prevent Brant from continuing to compete in the Championships. It also besmirched Laci's name and reputation with the PRCA, enough so that her PRCA sanction was in jeopardy if they thought the allegation held even a thread of truth.

"I'll inform Mr. Begley to expect you both at seven. The Regal Palms."

Laci gently replaced the phone on its receiver, resisting the urge to slam it down as hard as she could. "Rotten snake," she cursed, thinking of Judd. She'd tried to be charitable in her attitude toward Judd, in spite of the reason she'd left him. Even when he wouldn't give up trying to talk her into returning to him, she'd tried to be nice. But this time he'd gone too far.

The door opened behind her. Laci swung around and stared at Charley.

"What's wrong?" he demanded, a frown pulling at his already deeply creased forehead as he stared at her. "You look like someone who's got an itch to murder."

"I just got through talking with a woman from the PRCA office in Denver."

"Yeah, so?"

"Someone leveled a charge against us that a certain contestant is receiving favored points."

"That's crazy. And impossible." Charley's eyes

narrowed. "A certain contestant, like Brant Garrison, maybe?"

"Yes."

"They wanna see the judges?"

"Yes. They also want to see Brant and me, tonight at seven."

"You want me to go?"

"No, someone's got to run things here, but with no judges you won't be able to hold any competitions."

"We can let the kids in for a while, let them chase some pigs."

"Yes, that's good. And offer a good prize, a couple of hundred dollars. And hold a roundup, and maybe have the flag girls do an exhibition. If we're gone too long…"

"I'll keep things going, don't worry."

"Easier said than done." Laci inhaled deeply, then released the breath in a long sigh. "I guess I'd better go find Brant." She had intended to avoid him, and here she was seeking him out. But at least it wasn't because passion had overcome her better senses again. Though at the moment that might have been preferable to the reason she was setting out to locate him. She left the office and while descending its stairs caught sight of one of the clowns who wasn't in costume yet. "Cody, where's Brant Garrison?"

The tall cowboy turned to look at her, a knowing grin pulling at his thin lips. "I saw him over by the stock pens a few minutes ago," Cody said, "checking on the bronc he's supposed to ride tonight, I think."

Laci nodded. Of course. She should have known. She stood at one end of the pens and scanned the area.

There was no one there. Frustrated, she was about to turn and go in search of him elsewhere when she suddenly saw him rise to his full height, the silver conchos on his hat catching the glow of the quickly setting sun. "Brant?"

He turned and Laci felt her heart nearly thud to a stop when a dark shadow swept over his eyes and his features took on a cold, hard slant upon his realization of who had called him. Brant didn't respond, but merely stood still and waited for her to approach.

"Someone leveled a charge with the Association that you're receiving favored points."

"What?" The rage in his voice was instant and searing. "What the hell are you talking about, Laci? Who leveled charges?"

Laci looked around quickly, hoping no one was close enough to have heard him. They didn't need this kind of publicity. Several cowboys a few yards away looked toward them curiously and her heart sank. She turned back to Brant. "We have to meet with them in an hour, at the Regal Palms Hotel."

"You didn't answer me, damn it," he growled. "Who leveled the charges?"

"They wouldn't tell me. And keep your voice down."

Brant's eyes narrowed. "Yeah? Well I've got a pretty damned good idea who it was, and I don't care much if he hears me say it."

"You will if you're wrong. Anyway, do you want *everyone* to know what's going on? I don't."

"At least they'd understand why I killed him."

Laci ignored his comment, praying he wasn't serious. "We should be back in plenty of time for tonight's events. The judges have been requested to attend, too, so Charley's going to do some special things to stall for a while. I'll meet you there.'' She turned to go and was startled when Brant reached out and grabbed her arm, forcing her to stop.

''Go with me,'' he said softly, his eyes holding hers.

Go with me. His words echoed in her mind. He'd said the same thing to her seven and a half years ago. Her answer then had been no.

''Laci?''

She nodded. They needed to make a united front. Give each other moral support. And it was only a short ride to the Regal Palms from the arena. ''Okay, I'll meet you at the office at six thirty.''

Brant turned his pickup into the drive of the Regal Palms Hotel and glanced at Laci as he reached for the ignition key and killed the motor. Last night she'd said there was no future for them, and the words had cut him to the quick. They'd also forced him to realize that ever since he'd learned she was divorced from Judd he'd been hoping, subconsciously, there was a chance, slim as it was, that she would turn to him, realize it was he she belonged with. He'd stormed out of her office, angry with both himself and her—himself for his own foolishness, and the realization of just how deeply she could still hurt him, and her for not giving them a chance, then and now.

''Ready?'' she asked.

He nodded, forcing his thoughts to the issue at hand. When this was all over he just might look up

Judd McCandrick and show the man how to fly through a wall.

The two rodeo judges were already in the room with the Association rep when Laci and Brant walked in. Judd was not there. Everyone shook hands, made introductions, and after taking their seats, the rep stated the charges and asked each to respond.

The two judges went first, denying the charge, then Laci, who did the same, indignantly, and finally Brant.

"I've spent almost my entire life with the rodeo," he said. "My father was a rodeo man, followed the circuit, with my mother, me and my brother traveling with him. Later, when we turned sixteen, my brother and I started competing."

Laci stared up at him, remembering the stories she'd heard when they'd first met. His twin brother had been killed while riding a bull. She shuddered, knowing because of her own family losses, how much that must have hurt Brant.

"Competing on the circuit is my life," Brant said, his words pulling Laci's attention back to him. "It's always been my dream, what I've always wanted to do, and I would never do anything to jeopardize my standing with the Association, not even if it meant I could win the world title. If I don't win it fair and square, in my opinion, it's a worthless win, and one I don't want."

Brant sat down and the PRCA rep, Tom Begley, thanked everyone and asked if there were any more comments.

Laci stood. "Yes, I'd like to know who leveled this

charge." She pinned her gaze on Begley, meeting his pale brown eyes and refusing to let him look away.

He nodded and a lock of thin blond hair fell onto his forehead. "I'm sorry, Ms. McCandrick, but we have determined, since arranging this meeting, that the name the caller provided to us was fictitious."

Laci's eyes widened and she had to catch her jaw as it started to fall into a gape. "Fictitious? You mean, we've been pulled into this meeting and our accuser hasn't even come forward? Obviously doesn't intend to come forward?"

"As I said, Ms. McCandrick, I'm sorry. Normally we would ignore an anonymous call, but this call wasn't placed as anonymous, and being that the staff in Denver is extremely busy this week, it took longer than it should have to check the name the caller provided."

"So now what?" Laci demanded. She didn't have proof that Judd had done this, but she didn't need it. In her heart she knew he'd made the call…just to cause her and Brant trouble.

"Well, I'm satisfied with what you've all had to say." Begley repositioned his glasses. "So, I'd say the meeting is adjourned. It's pretty obvious everything here is being handled according to proper procedure."

"Thank you," Laci said, a bit stiffly, but then she was holding in a volcanic eruption that had Judd's name imprinted all over it.

Laci stalked toward Brant's truck. "I'm going to kill him," she mumbled.

"You won't have to," Brant snapped. "I plan on beating you to it."

She stared up at Brant as he moved past her to unlock the passenger door and open it for her. Brant planned on confronting Judd, and she had no doubt the encounter would include a lot more than heated words.

She brushed past Brant and climbed onto the passenger seat. Having this thing end in a fistfight between Judd and Brant was not what she wanted. Hogtying Judd and leaving him staked out in the desert on top of an anthill was closer to what she'd like to do to him at the moment, but she couldn't do that, either. She'd be the authorities' prime suspect, along with Brant, and Judd would probably survive it anyway. The ants would most likely find him too sour to stomach.

Laci struggled a smile onto her lips. "Well, chalk up one for the good guys," she quipped, forcing a merriment into her voice she was far from feeling.

Brant paused as their eyes met. "Yeah," he said slowly, "one for the good guys." Steeling himself against the urge to pull her into his arms, he closed her door and walked around to the driver's side. He knew she was trying to make light of this thing. They'd won, it was over, but he couldn't let it go. He'd been hauled up before a PRCA rep once before—he had deserved it then, he didn't now. Brant drove in silence, his mood continuing to darken.

He had never explained to Laci why he wouldn't quit the circuit and settle down with her. But it wasn't something he could talk about, even now. He'd sworn to Brett that if it was the last thing he did, he'd win the world title, and he meant to do it. Maybe it would have made a difference for him and Laci if he'd told her about Brett, and what had happened. Then again, maybe it wouldn't have. That was something he'd never know. What he did know was that if she'd loved him enough his following the circuit wouldn't have mattered. She'd have gone with him.

But maybe he was fooling himself. Maybe he'd always been fooling himself. There weren't a whole lot of successful marriages on the circuit—and theirs probably wouldn't have lasted either.

He parked the truck near the gate.

"Thanks for the ride," Laci said, breaking the silence that had surrounded them ever since leaving the Regal Palms' parking lot. She glanced back at him as she opened her door. He didn't look furious anymore, just down, and she hated that, felt a need to reach out to him, and resisted it. "Don't worry so much, Brant, you'll have a great ride tonight."

He looked at her and nodded. Why was it so hard between them? "What are your plans after the rodeo's over?" Brant asked. He saw that the question surprised her.

Laci stared at him, her eyes wide, then she shrugged. "Run James Enterprises."

With no forewarning of his own thoughts, Brant realized he'd been kidding himself ever since leaving the hearing. He loved her too much to give up, even now, when things didn't look much better than they had years ago. "What happened between you and Judd?" He knew he had no business asking the question, no business expecting her to answer, but he needed to know. The thought of spending the rest of his life with nothing but memories of her suddenly seemed a horror he didn't want to face. He'd never stopped loving her, never stopped wanting her. But as long as she was married to someone else, as long as he hadn't put himself in a situation to see her, he'd been able to ignore those feelings, sometimes even pretend they didn't exist anymore. He could no longer do that.

Laci stared out at the parking lot, but he could tell that, for the few seconds she remained quiet, her mind was a million miles away, her eyes seeing a picture that existed only within her memories. She inhaled deeply, breaking the spell that had fallen over her, and turned to Brant. "I wasn't in love with Judd," she said simply, "and never should have married him. But after I did, I really tried to make the marriage work. It didn't, so we divorced." She sighed and shrugged again. "End of story."

"Or maybe a new beginning," Brant said softly.

Tears blurred Laci's eyes at his words. Jerking around she threw open the truck's door and jumped out.

Brant watched her as she hurried toward the arena gate. He wanted to spend his life with Laci, but he couldn't say anything like that to her now. First he had to win the title, because if he didn't... Brant forced that thought from his mind. He didn't want to think about another year on the circuit, another year of loneliness, broken bones and bruised muscles, of sleeping alone and dreaming of a woman whose memory made his body ache with need and his heart cry for her touch.

* * *

Laci hurried up the stairs to the office, threw her handbag onto a file cabinet near the door and slumped into the chair behind her desk.

Charley swiveled around to face her, ignoring the two judges who were just disappearing into their booths in the adjoining room. Within seconds one judge announced that the saddle bronc riding would begin in ten minutes. Charley eyed Laci closely. "What happened? You don't look too happy."

She shrugged. "Everything's fine, they found in our favor, but the rep couldn't tell me who leveled the charge."

"Figured we already knew that, but whatdya mean couldn't? I thought whoever done it would have to be at the hearing, too."

She shook her head. "The caller gave a fictitious name, but the rep didn't know that when the meeting was set up."

"Don't change my mind any on who done it. Something else wrong?" he persisted.

"No, I'm just tired, that's all. I didn't sleep well last night." Make that the last two nights, she amended silently, ever since Brant had come back to town. The words he'd spoken to the Association rep echoed in her mind, repeating over and over. The rodeo was his life. Why did that tear at her heart so mercilessly? It wasn't as if she'd been surprised, she'd known how important the rodeo was to him. Hadn't he proven that it was more important to him than anything?

Charley swiveled around to glance out at the arena and Laci closed her eyes. What was the matter with her? She couldn't stand to watch Brant ride, couldn't stand the thought of watching him be hurt, or killed, yet she couldn't stand the thought of losing him again. That nearly made her laugh aloud. Losing him again. How could she lose what she didn't have?

Even if she could accept his way of life, even if he did still love her enough to want to make a future together, she had Kit to think about now. How could she drag a child along on the circuit? How could she ask her son...their son...to watch his father ride...? Laci shuddered, remembering Sonny and how he'd died. She couldn't face that again, couldn't watch that happen to Brant, and she wouldn't ask it of Kit.

She heard the buzzer announcing the start of the bronc riding event, but Laci remained motionless, too weary to move, too weary to ward off the assault of her thoughts.

Brant had a right to know his son. The guilty feelings that had always haunted her conscience had intensified since Brant's return. But he'd told her once that he didn't want children, and he'd said nothing since his return to make her think he'd changed his mind. Kit had been rejected by the man he thought was his father; she couldn't risk that he might be rejected by his real father, too.

She spent the evening hassling with her conscience, struggling to concentrate on paperwork, and doing her best to ignore the announcements of who was riding what, when. But when Brant's name was announced it was like a charge of electricity sizzling through her brain. Laci jumped up from her chair and grabbed her purse. "See you in the morning, Charley," she said over her shoulder, not daring to look him in the eye as she headed for the door.

* * *

"Of course you have to go," Laci insisted, trying to reassure Mrs. Dabney. "Your sister's in the hospital."

"But what about Kit?" the older woman asked, worrying the bun at her nape with one index finger. "Who'll watch him? And who'll make your dinner? And your breakfast?"

"I'll watch him," Laci replied, urging Mrs. Dabney toward the front door. "He's come to the arena with me before, now he'll just come all the time until you get back or the rodeo's over. Whichever. And I do know how to cook. Maybe not as good as you…"

The older woman paused and gave her a stern look.

Laci laughed. "We'll manage. You just go on and make sure your sister is okay, then come back as soon as you can." She shoved one of the housekeeper's suitcases into the back seat of her car. "We'll miss you, but we'll be fine, really. Don't worry." She waved the woman off and watched as Mrs. Dabney's car disappeared down the drive and turned onto the road that led to town and the highway. "What else can go wrong?" she grumbled, then plastered a smile on her face and turned to call Kit. "Okay, big guy, it's time to go."

He bounded from the house, slamming the front door behind him. "Whoopee," he yelled, and skipped toward the Cherokee, his boots scuffing up dirt behind him and his cowboy hat flying from his head only to bounce off his back as its drawstring caught on Kit's neck and stopped the hat from going any further.

"I wish I had your energy," Laci said, helping him buckle his seat belt.

"My what?"

Laci laughed. "Never mind. Ready?"

He nodded.

"You're sure you have everything?"

He nodded again.

"Where are your comic books?"

"I left them in my room. I don't wanna read, I wanna watch the rodeo."

It was two o'clock when they walked into the arena office, an hour earlier than she normally arrived, but she was anxious to see how the day's receipts were stacking up and look over the schedule of events. She also wanted to check on Zach Taylor and make sure the arm he'd cut was okay, and ask the doctor in the medical trailer about the man who'd had a heart attack on opening night. She'd meant to do that last night but...thoughts of Brant coming to the office, holding her in his arms and claiming her lips with his, swept through her mind and left her body hot and aching.

Charley swiveled around in his chair to greet Laci and did a double take at seeing Kit. "Hey, champ, what are you doing here today?"

"Mrs. Dabney was called away on an emergency," Laci said, smiling, "so Kit's come to help us out."

He raced across the room, climbed onto the chair next to Charley and stared through the window at the empty arena. "Hey, where is everybody?" He turned and glared at Laci. "There's no one here."

"I told you," she said, "nothing's due to start for a few more hours. Here." She grabbed a pad of paper and pencil from her desk and offered them to him. "Draw for a while."

"Can I have a soda?"

"Later," Laci said, putting her handbag down and sifting through the pile of mail on her desk. There was nothing from the accounting firm.

"Can we go see the horses?"

"Later."

"What about the bulls? The big ugly ones?"

Charley chuckled.

"Later," Laci repeated.

"Can we go ride the Ferris wheel? Billy's mom took us on that, and it's real neat-o."

She looked up, about to say "later" again, and wondering why she hadn't insisted he go back into the house and get his comic books, when Charley spoke up.

"How about going with me to get an ice cream?"

"Yeah!" Kit looked at Laci. "Can I, Mom, huh?"

"Sure." But as soon as the word was out of her mouth she was sorry. What if Brant was around? "Oh, maybe you shouldn't," Laci hurriedly said as the two neared the door. "I mean, uh, you'll ruin your appetite for dinner."

"Aw, Mom."

"JM's not here," Charley said, mistaking her hesitation for fear that they'd run into Judd. "We can't keep him out when his stock is here, but I told the guard at the gate to radio me if he showed up, and I ain't heard a word."

Laci forced a smile to her lips. "Good, but I..."

"Mom, please. Charley can show me the bulls, too, I mean, if they scare you."

Only when Brant's on them, she thought silently.

"We won't go far," Charley promised. "Back in an hour."

Laci nodded and tried to swallow her fear. Brant had seen Kit in the hospital and nothing had happened. Anyway, it wasn't as if Kit looked *exactly* like him.

Forty minutes passed and Laci found she couldn't concentrate on anything. She'd read the schedule five times and still didn't know who was supposed to ride that night, or even what events were taking place. She had looked over the receipts that had come in and watched the figures swim around in front of her eyes but not register in her mind. And she'd made several phone calls which accomplished nothing since once she had the people she wanted to talk to on the other end of the line she forgot what it was she wanted to discuss with them. Frustrated and too nervous to sit still any longer, Laci left the office in search of Kit and Charley.

She wandered the grounds for ten minutes but didn't see them anywhere, then as she was passing the stable area she heard her son's voice coming from behind one of the paddocks.

"Hey, neat-o, lemme try. Please."

Laci walked around the corner of the blue paddock and stopped dead in her tracks, her heart nearly jumping into her throat.

"Hey, Mom, look what Brant's teaching me to do."

Charley turned and smiled, then waved her over. "Kid's got a real knack for roping, Laci," he said. "A natural. Look at him."

Laci tried to ignore the fact that Brant was standing only a couple of feet away from Kit. She did as Charley said and stared down at her son as he whirled a rope beside him, but if she appeared at all calm, it was a lie. Her heart was slamming against her breast as if totally out of control and ready to explode any second. "That's…great, honey," Laci finally managed to respond.

Kit tried to raise the rope and it sagged, lost momentum and collapsed to the ground. "Oh, phooey."

Brant laughed. "Hey, it takes practice to be the best," he said, hunkering down and gathering up the rope. "But you'll get there, kiddo."

Laci felt her world almost hurtle out of control as she looked down at Brant and Kit. Couldn't he see it? Couldn't he tell how much they looked alike? Her eyes darted from the curly black hair peeking out from beneath Brant's Stetson, to the crop of hair, the exact same color, that covered Kit's head. Brant looked up at her then, his eyes trying to pull her into their deep, sapphire-hued abyss but Laci resisted and turned her gaze to Kit, only to see the same deep blue in his eyes. "I…I think it's time to go, Kit," she said. "I want us to have dinner before the show starts."

"Have it with me," Brant said. "Unless you don't like pizza anymore? I was planning on going over to Mama Tia's, where we used to go. If it's still there."

Laci looked at him and felt panic erupt within her breast. Mama Tia's. He'd asked her to go on the circuit with him there. She hadn't been back to the small, family-owned pizza parlor since he'd left, though she'd driven by it hundreds of times and remembered that night. Laci shook her head. "No, we…"

"Yeah, Mom, come on," Kit said, "let's have

pizza with Brant. Please?'' He jumped up and down excitedly. ''Pretty please?''

She looked at Charley, her eyes pleading with him to rescue her.

''Sounds great,'' he said, sending Laci's heart plummeting to the depths of her toes, ''but count me out. He patted the more than generous mound of stomach protruding over his belt buckle. ''Doc's got me on a diet.''

''Me, too,'' Laci said.

Brant laughed. ''The last thing you need,'' he said, letting his gaze rake over her brazenly, ''is a diet. Now come on, how about it? Kit's all for it.''

''I don't know,'' Laci said. ''I don't really want to risk any more allegations.''

''We're old friends,'' Brant said, ''they can't fault old friends for going to dinner together.'' Even if at least one of them wants to be a whole lot more than friends, he thought to himself as he watched her. ''And we'll even be chaperoned,'' he said, smiling and nodding toward Kit.

Friends. It should have been what she wanted to hear him say. It *was* what she wanted to hear him say, so why did she suddenly feel as if a knife had been plunged into her heart? As if the future had just drawn a big blank?

''Come on, Mom, please?'' Kit begged. ''I want pizza.''

''Go on, Laci,'' Charley added. ''I'll mind the shop.''

He glanced at his watch, rather than look her in the eye when she jerked around to glare at him. Chicken, she called him silently.

"You've got a good three hours till the start of things anyway," Charley added. Without looking up he rose from his seat on a barrel, said goodbye to Kit, and turned to walk back toward the office.

Laci felt as if she were suddenly drowning and there was no life jacket within sight. She didn't want to disappoint Kit, but how was she supposed to stand being with Brant and not giving in to the yearnings gnawing away inside of her? Could she sit next to him in Mama Tia's and not reach out to touch him, not find herself overcome with memories of the past? Her mind darted about in search of an answer. Why was he doing this? What did he want from her?

An affair? a little voice in the back of her mind offered. She quickly shut out the possibility. She couldn't stand being that close to him again and then have to watch him walk out of her life a second time.

"My truck's right over here," Brant said, pointing toward the rear of the paddock area and interrupting Laci's thoughts.

Kit slipped his hand within hers. "Come on, Mom, I'm hungry."

Laci nearly groaned but allowed him to pull her toward the dark blue pickup. The same color as his eyes, she thought. Brant walked ahead of her and again she looked from him to Kit and felt a shiver of fear ripple through her. Did he really not see it? And what if he did? What if he confronted her? Demanded that she confess the truth? What would she do then?

She forced her legs to walk toward Brant's truck instead of bolting in the opposite direction. Everything would be all right. It had to be.

Just before she reached Brant's pickup, Judd

stepped into Laci's path. "Well, isn't this just the nicest picture. My wife and kid going off with a two-bit rodeo bum."

"Judd, please," Laci said, stopping several feet away from him. "Don't do this in front of..." She glanced down at Kit.

"Back off, McCandrick," Brant growled softly, stepping in front of Laci and Kit.

"Back off?" Judd echoed, feigning innocent surprise. "What do you think you're doing, Garrison, coming back to take up where you left off seven years ago?"

"That's none of your business."

Judd laughed and looked at Laci. "Have you told him the truth yet, sweetheart?"

Laci felt the blood drain from her face. "Judd, please."

"No, not yet?" He laughed again, then turned sober, his face hardening into a mask of ugly determination. "If you know what's good for you, Laci, you'll come home. Tonight."

Brant spun around and swept Kit up with one arm, then grabbed Laci's with his free hand and propelled her past Judd.

"She's not your wife anymore, McCandrick. Accept it."

"Yeah? Well, why don't you ask her how come she became my wife in the first place?" Judd called after them.

Brant pulled the pickup into the parking lot of Mama Tia's and hurried around to open Laci's door. "Place doesn't look like it's changed a bit," he said, and smiled. Laci hadn't spoken a word since they'd left the arena, but Brant wasn't going to let Judd's blustering ruin their time together. And he wasn't going to ask her what "truth" Judd had been bellowing about. If she wanted to tell him, fine. If not, that was okay, too.

Kit jumped from the truck and raced for the door of the restaurant.

"I think somebody wasn't fooling when he said he was hungry," Brant observed, and laughed.

Laci smiled. To heck with her anger at Judd for a while. "He's always hungry," she said, and stepped past the entry door as Brant held it open for her.

He nodded and followed as a waitress showed them to a table, placing a coloring book and box of crayons in front of Kit. "I guess boys are like that. I remember Brett and I were always stuffing something into our mouths, pizza, fries, burgers, you name it, we ate it. Damned wonder we didn't end up looking like blimps."

No, Laci thought, instead you have the best body I've ever seen on a man. A flush of heat swept through her and she turned to look around the room, determined not to think like that again, ever. Her gaze swept over the restaurant's small interior. Brant was right, not much had changed. Mama Tia's was still quaint, its tables covered with red-and-white checkered cloths upon which were red candles settled within a circle of fake green and purple grapes. Posters of the Leaning Tower of Pisa, St. Peter's Basilica, and several other popular tourist attractions in Italy adorned the walls.

Come with me, Laci. Promise me forever. She

jerked around and stared at Brant, wondering if she'd repeated the words aloud. But he was busy pouring wine into her glass from the decanter the waitress had left on the table.

Brant looked up at her abrupt movement, clearly puzzled.

"Something wrong?"

Laci twisted the cloth napkin on her lap and tried to smile. "No." She shrugged. "Everything's great, except we don't have any food and I'm suddenly starving."

"Me, too," Kit chirped, looking up from the picture he'd been coloring.

"Well then, pizza coming right up," Brant said, and waved to the waitress.

Later, Brant and Laci had coffee while Kit enjoyed a bowl of chocolate ice cream, and Laci found herself wishing they didn't have to return to the arena. This is the way it should have been for us, she thought to herself, looking from Brant to Kit. They belong together. We belong together. The moment the thought entered her head, a dose of fear followed, with reality swiftly pulling up the rear, and Laci stiffened. She hadn't wanted Kit and Brant to meet at all, and yet within just a few hours it seemed that they had formed a solid bond of friendship, exactly what she had feared, because there was no more hope of a solid relationship between Brant and Kit, even if they knew the truth, than there was between Brant and Laci. Within a week Brant would be back on the road, following the circuit. He might win the world title like he'd always dreamed, but she had no doubt he'd just continue on. He loved the rodeo and its way of life too much to quit. And when Brant left, Kit would be hurt.

But now Judd had given her a new worry, that he might not leave her the choice of whether Brant and Kit learned the truth.

"Hey, champ, can I have this picture?" Brant said, picking up the crayon-colored sketch Kit had done of a cowboy on a bucking horse.

Laci jerked around to stare at the picture, the sound of Brant's voice having startled her from her thoughts.

"Okay, if you really want it."

"Heck, yes. I'll frame it and hang it on my front room wall at the ranch, right next to the Remington print that's there now."

"Ranch?" Laci repeated, stunned with disbelief. "You have a ranch?"

"Yep. In Montana." Brant smiled, looking deep into her eyes. "I figured someday I was going to need a place to deposit my old broken bones. Couple of years ago I was up in Billings and got to talking to a rancher there and he put me onto this place that was for sale."

"You have a ranch?" Laci said again, unable to believe it. In spite of all the cautions she'd been reciting to herself ever since their encounter by the chutes, she felt a spark of hope ignite within her breast. He had ranch. A home. He'd put down roots.

"It's really beautiful up there," Brant was saying. "Maybe you and Kit could come up and visit me sometime."

"Yeah, Mom, that would be neat." Kit bounced in his seat. "Then Brant could teach me more rope tricks, and maybe how to rope a steer, and ride a bull and stuff.''

"Do you...work it?" Laci asked Brant, as Kit continued to rattle on, talking and coloring at the same time and not caring whether anyone was paying attention to him or not.

Brant smiled. ''We've got about five hundred head of cattle and a few horses, and we've already started supplying some of the rodeos up that way with stock.''

Laci tensed. ''We?''

"Rob Moran and I. He's my foreman. Runs the place.''

She nodded. Rob Moran runs the place because Brant was still following the circuit and obviously had no intention of quitting until he had enough ''old broken bones'' to force him into retirement. If he lived that long. She gathered up her handbag and handed Kit his jacket. Her decision to keep the truth to herself had been the right one, at least for Kit. Now all she had to do was keep Judd quiet until Brant left Reno. ''It's getting late. I think we'd better be getting back to the arena.'' She turned to rise from her seat but paused when she felt Brant's hand on her arm.

''Laci?''

She kept her gaze averted from his.

''I want to see you after the rodeo.''

She shook her head. ''That's not a good idea. Neither one of us can afford to give anyone, especially the PRCA reps, any more fuel to think you're getting favored points.''

''Laci...''

''I can't afford that kind of accusation again,

Brant," Laci said. "I have a business to run now."
She rose and without looking at him, walked toward
the door.

"I'll wait for you after the show," Brant said, stepping past her to hold the door open.

Laci didn't answer. She climbed into the pickup
and stared out the window as they drove through
town, Kit sitting between them. If the arena had been
closer she would have walked. She couldn't take being near Brant like this, not and keep her sanity and
resolve. Her body felt as if every cell were on fire,
and the ache of desire churning about in the pit of her
stomach was almost as unbearable as the sense of loss
and regret sitting like a lump around her heart.

"I wanna be a cowboy when I grow up, Mom,"
Kit said, demanding her attention.

She looked down at him and smiled. "Oh, you do,
huh?"

"Yeah." He bounced on the seat.

"Well, we'll have to see about that."

"I wanna go to the rodeo and ride the bulls and
horses." He turned to Brant. "Will you teach me,
Brant? Can Mom and me come to your ranch so you
can teach me to ride the bulls and bucking horses like
you? Then I can win the world title, too, just like
you're gonna do."

Hot tears filled Laci's eyes. She blinked rapidly in
an effort to hold them back and turned away so that
Brant and Kit wouldn't see.

Chapter 7

Laci busied herself with paperwork and refused to watch Brant ride, but she couldn't shut out the sound of the crowd cheering him on, or the announcer describing each seemingly endless second until the buzzer signaled time. Even though he was competing in saddle bronc riding again tonight, and not bull riding, she found herself holding her breath, every nerve and muscle in her body strung taut, her heart pounding madly as she waited for the disaster she couldn't help believe was sure to come.

But it didn't—this time.

Instead, the buzzer sounded, the crowd cheered wildly, and Laci went limp with relief. She stared at the papers on her desk and the seconds ticked by while her mind wondered through the past; Sonny dying after being thrown from his motorcycle, Brant stumbling and being helped out of the arena after being thrown from the back of a bull. Lost within her memories, she didn't hear the groan of the crowd when the next contestant was thrown from his bronc before the buzzer sounded. Nor did she hear their laughter at some antic of the clowns, or the applause for the night's finale.

"Well, that's it for tonight," Charley said, whirling around in his chair and looking at her.

Laci nodded, forcing the memories aside and glancing toward a couch in the corner. Kit had fallen asleep there almost an hour ago, totally exhausted.

"Can you lock up tonight, Charley?" she asked, and rose. "I think I'd better get Kit home and into bed. It's been a long day for him."

"Sure, you go on. Want me to carry him to your car?"

"No, thanks, he'll be fine. We've done this before." She bent over Kit and nudged his shoulder. "Kit, wake up, it's time to go home, honey."

He stirred, twisted around, and burrowed deeper into the couch.

"Kit, honey, wake up," Laci repeated. She shook his shoulder again.

Kit opened his eyes and looked up at her, sleep still dragging heavily on his eyelids. "Mom?"

Laci stared down at him for a moment, mesmerized by dark blue eyes ringed with a shadow of black. Sometimes it was difficult to believe she was looking into the eyes of her son, rather than into those of his father.

Kit blinked and rubbed curled fists over his eyes, breaking the momentary spell that had fallen over Laci. "Come on, tiger," she urged, helping him off the couch. "Time to go home and climb into your own bed."

He stumbled to his feet and, holding tightly to Laci's hand, shuffled toward the door. "Can I come back to the rodeo tomorrow?"

"Yes, sweetie, tomorrow," Laci said. She waved at Charley.

"G'night, Charley," Kit mumbled.

"See ya, champ."

The back area of the rodeo was still a bustle of activity as Laci and Kit made their way down the office stairs. Horses were being bathed, shod and checked, bulls were being moved, cattle examined, and contestants were checking the next day's schedules, stowing gear, congratulating each other on good rides, or commiserating over bad ones and lost points.

In spite of telling herself she didn't want to see Brant, Laci looked for him, her gaze moving slowly over the area, past the registration, security and medical trailers, beyond the chutes, paddocks and stock area. But he wasn't there. She felt a sense of disappointment and tried to shrug it away. Most likely he'd already left for the night, she told herself, and that was best. She really didn't want to see him. Laci waved to a few people she knew and urged Kit down the drive toward the parking lot.

Charley looked up at the sound of a knock on the door behind him, but before he could do little more than begin to swivel around in his seat, the door swung open and Brant walked into the office. He took one look about the room and pinned Charley with a questioning gaze.

"She left about three—four minutes ago," Charley offered.

Brant turned to go.

"Garrison?"

He looked back. "Yeah?"

Charley smiled. "How d'ya like Laci's kid?"

Brant frowned at the unusual question, somewhat taken aback by it. He'd expected Charley to warn him away from Laci, or make some other veiled but growling comment about "sticking it out to the end." He hadn't expected him to casually ask how Brant liked her kid. His eyes narrowed in suspicion. "He's a nice enough little guy. Why?"

"Yeah, nice, like his parents." Charley worried his chin between his thumb and index finger. Laci didn't know that her father, in a moment of feeling overridden with guilt and feeling partly responsible for driving Brant away from Laci, had told Charley who Kit's real father was. Charley figured if she wanted to tell him, she would. "Looks like 'em, too, don't you think?"

Brant wanted to go after Laci, not stand around debating the physical characteristics of her son with Charley. And what did it matter anyway who Kit looked like, as long as he didn't develop Judd McCandrick's personality? Though he had to admit, Kit didn't look any more like Judd McCandrick than Brant did. When he'd first seen the boy—seen his dark hair and blue eyes—he'd thought...just for a few minutes... Brant pushed the thought from his mind. It was ridiculous.

"Better hurry if you want to catch her," Charley

said, jerking Brant's thoughts back to his objective and surprising him with the encouragement.

"Yeah, right." Brant left the office and descended the metal stairs two at a time. He wasn't sure why Charley was being so nice and helpful, but he wasn't going to complain about it. Brant looked around quickly, didn't see Laci and Kit anywhere, and hastened down the dirt drive toward the parking lot. Light spilled from the windows of the trailers as well as the overhead spotlights onto the drive, but created inky shadows in between each structure. He was skirting the rear of one of the spectator stands and approaching the Cyclone fence and contestants' entry gate when he saw them.

"Come on, sweetie," Laci said, bending down to lift Kit into her arms, "you're falling asleep and trying to walk at the same time."

Brant moved up beside Laci. "Let me," he said. Bending, and with an effortless sweep of one arm, Brant scooped Kit off the ground. The child instantly curled himself into a ball and snuggled against Brant's chest.

Laci stared at him. "Brant, I..."

An area light overhead glowed down upon them, its yellow haze falling softly upon the long strands of Laci's hair. Brant yearned to reach out and run his fingers through the shimmering waves. "Where's your car?" he asked instead, knowing full well it was parked right next to his.

She pointed, and he followed her lead.

Kit was fast asleep before Brant had taken more than a half dozen steps.

Laci glanced back at them as she moved to unlock

and open the passenger door. The conchos attached to Brant's hatband danced a reflection of the parking lot's spotlight, but his face remained steeped in shadow beneath the hat's brim. She didn't need to see his rough-hewn features, however, to know their set, nor his eyes to know that his gaze was fastened upon her. She quickly pushed the front seat back and its safety belt aside.

"Just put him here."

Brant looked down at Kit as he settled the child onto the passenger seat, and felt a catch in his throat as a sense of regret washed over him. This could have been his son, if he had done things differently. His son, his wife, his family. But regrets and hindsight weren't going to get him what he wanted now, so he pushed them from his mind. He snapped the seat belt around Kit and turned back to Laci. "I'll follow you home."

She took a step back, as if retreating not only from him but from his words, and shook her head. "No, that's all right, I can get him into the house. Thanks."

"That's not the only reason I want to follow you home, Laci," Brant said. He closed the passenger door and stepped in front of Laci as she made to move past him to circle the car. There was only a few inches of space separating them. He longed to reach out and drag her into his arms but feared she would retreat all the more, both physically and emotionally, if he moved too fast. "I'm worried about you and Kit. Judd doesn't sound all that rational about your divorce, or my return to Reno. I don't like you going into an empty house alone this late at night."

She fiddled with a flap on her purse. "There's nothing to worry about. Our house has a security system."

"I'm not so sure there's nothing to worry about. And security systems can be jammed or cut off." Memory of her body pressed against his again, the warmth of it, her length melding with his like it used to, teased him from the hazy depths of thought he was trying desperately to ignore. "He threatened you, Laci, and he didn't sound rational."

Laci stiffened and met his gaze with a steady one of her own. "Judd wouldn't hurt me."

"Are you sure?"

She wanted to say yes, but suddenly, remembering the look she'd seen in Judd's eyes the day he'd slapped Kit, and just a few hours ago when he'd confronted them, and recalling how his temper had grown worse in their last year of marriage, she wasn't so sure of that answer. Her whole world had been turned upside down and she didn't have the faintest idea how to go about righting it again. Laci shook her head and moved around Brant and the car to the driver's door.

He was right behind her as she slipped the key into the door's lock.

"Laci."

"Good night, Brant."

He swore under his breath. This wasn't how it was supposed to go, not how he'd planned it. He wanted, needed to talk to her. "Laci…"

She climbed into the Cherokee, closed the door and started the engine.

Brant watched her drive from the lot, then climbed into his pickup and followed.

* * *

Laci saw him in the rearview mirror as she turned onto the drive that led to the house she'd bought immediately after leaving Judd. If not for her grandfather's trust fund, she wouldn't have been able to buy anything, since it had taken all these months to wrest James Enterprises from Judd. The house sat in the middle of twelve acres, nestled high in the hills that bordered the east side of Reno. Twenty minutes above Reno, twenty minutes below the old mining town of Virginia City and totally isolated. She felt comfortable in the ranch-style house, with its spacious rooms, large windows, rough plank walls and open-beamed ceilings. And she loved its location, surrounded by open countryside, high enough above the city so that she had a spectacular view of the valley and casinos. But most important, her home was located on the opposite side of the valley from Judd's ranch.

Laci watched the headlights of Brant's car come around a curve in the road and pull closer to her drive. She could get the automatic gate control from the glove box and shut the white wooden entry gate behind her after she passed, but she knew it wouldn't do any good. If Brant wanted to get to the house, he'd get to the house, gate or no gate.

And you do want him to come to the house, a little voice in the back of her mind whispered softly.

Laci ignored the traitorous taunting of her subconscious, not even bothering to deny it, telling herself it was because she didn't want to, rather than because she couldn't. She stopped the Cherokee on the circular drive, just before the front door, and switched off the engine. But before she could do little more than climb from the car and walk around to Kit's side, Brant was beside her.

"I told you this wasn't necessary," Laci said, trying to invoke a cold edge to her voice and realizing she'd failed miserably.

"I know, now let me carry him inside."

His deep drawl sent a wave of delicious shivers skipping up her spine in spite of her resolve to remain aloof and totally composed and cool around him. Laci walked up the shallow plank front steps, across the wide, covered veranda and opened the entry door. She swung it open, reaching in to flip on the foyer light, then stood aside so that Brant could pass. "His room's back there," she said, pointing down a long hall that led off the foyer and was softly lit by a night-light on one wall. "The last door on the right."

He nodded and walked down the hall, his steps muffled by the thick carpet beneath his feet. A subtle fragrance pervaded the house, a homey scent that impressed him as a blend of forest pines and spring flowers. Brant lay Kit down on the bed, then left the room as Laci entered, holding a clean pair of pajamas, and began to undress her son.

In the family room, Brant turned on a lamp whose light swathed the room in a soft glow. He settled onto an overstuffed chair of dull red leather and let his gaze wander over the decor. Normally he didn't take stock of such things, figuring a chair was for sitting, a TV for watching, a window for looking through and a rug for walking on. But this was Laci's house, Laci's home, and he wanted to know it all. His gaze moved over the Navajo throws that covered the twin leather overstuffed chairs, and another throw that hung on the wall. Each blazed with color—red, turquoise, white, orange, yellow, black—as did the profusion of multicolored pillows piled atop a beige sofa. But each pillow was a different pattern.

A television and stereo were set into an antique armoire of extremely simple design, while the coffee table was an old plank door, complete with black iron fittings still attached. A jumble of plants sat in one corner, a rock fireplace at one end of the room looked well used, and glass patio doors gave a view of moonlit hills and trees, and the lights of Reno far below.

The room was warm and comfortable and Brant found himself thinking that the colors and the homey decor fit Laci. Her personality was stamped all through it. He could easily imagine her in this room, curled up on the sofa with one of those romance novels or murder mysteries she had always been so fond of reading.

"Thank you for carrying Kit inside."

Brant turned at hearing Laci's voice and watched her walk into the room. Why had he ever left her? The question formed in his mind and refused to go away. But it wasn't the first time it had taken over his thoughts, and it wouldn't be the last, and he knew the answer as well as he knew his own name. He had left Laci because there'd been no other way. He hadn't wanted to, but he'd had no choice.

But she'd had a choice. He watched her as she moved to the patio doors and stood with her back to him, staring into the night. Had she loved Judd McCandrick? She'd said no, but if that was true, then why had she married him? What had Judd meant when he'd yelled at her earlier to tell the truth? When he'd told Brant to ask Laci why she'd married him?

He pushed the thoughts and questions aside, forcing them back into the shadowed regions of memory that he didn't want to dwell on right now, if ever. They were destructive, those kind of thoughts and questions, and right now, the last thing he needed was anything destructive.

"The room fits you," he said, and pushed off the sofa and crossed the room toward her.

As if sensing his approach, Laci whirled and moved to the armoire, flipping on the stereo. The soft strains of a slow country tune instantly flowed from the speakers, the artist's deep, rich voice filling the room as he sang of lost love and loneliness. Laci nearly cringed, wishing she had the nerve to flip the stereo back off and knowing she didn't. It would be too obvious. She turned and smiled at Brant. "Would you like some coffee?"

He nodded. It wasn't what he really wanted, but it would have to do, for now. "Sounds like the best offer I've had all day."

Laci walked into a kitchen the previous owner of the house had decorated in southwest tones of beige, coral and turquoise. It had been one of the reasons Laci had fallen in love with the house. She busied herself making the coffee, all the while fully, and uneasily, aware of Brant standing just a few feet away, watching her. Why had she invited him in? Why had she asked him to stay? The questions screamed through her head. She retrieved two coffee cups from a cupboard and noticed that her hands were trembling. She'd been a fool to invite him in. Asking for trouble, that's what she was doing. Unless they could just be friends. Could she do that? She set the cups on the counter and reached back into the cupboard for the sugar bowl. Why was she suddenly having such a problem breathing? She inhaled deeply. And why in blazes was her heart slamming against her chest like a jackhammer?

Laci sighed silently. She didn't need anyone to answer those questions—she already knew the answers—she just didn't like them.

Brant slid onto a stool at the bar that sliced through the center of the kitchen. He sensed her nervousness, felt his own brand of anxiety. Forcing himself to relax, he looked around the room, assessing it in the same way as he'd done to the family room. This could have been his home, he thought, torturing himself and not caring. She could have been *his* wife, Kit could have been *his* son…if Laci had loved him enough. For years he'd wondered why she hadn't, and now that she was standing before him, now that he could ask her that question, he found that he couldn't, because he was too afraid of what he'd hear. "Nice house," he said instead. "Warm. Comfortable."

Laci turned as she flipped the coffeepot on. "Thanks. We've only lived here a couple of months." She set a cup before him. "I haven't even finished decorating yet, or unpacking everything."

"You didn't live here with Judd?" The question sounded casual enough, but it wasn't, and Brant was thankful that the knife suddenly sticking in his throat hadn't evidenced itself in his voice.

"No. Judd's ranch is across town, beyond Sparks."

Brant saw the shadow that had come over her face

when he'd mentioned Judd, but they had to talk about the man. He'd threatened her today, and Brant knew, from overhearing their argument at the stock pens the other day, that this wasn't the first time. Laci might not intend to take the threats seriously, but Brant did. He watched as she poured their coffee. Her hand trembled slightly, but whether from thoughts of Judd, or nervousness at having Brant in her home, he wasn't certain. Nevertheless, he ached to hurry to her side and wrap her fingers within the warmth of his own. He steeled himself against the urge. "I'm worried about you, Laci."

She pulled the coffeepot away and stared at him, not moving, just looking deep into his eyes. How many times over the years had she dreamed about those eyes? After a moment that seemed more an eternity, she pulled her gaze from his and turned away, setting the glass pot back on its burner. "There's no need for you to worry about me, Brant," she said, her voice sounding strained. "I told you, Judd wouldn't hurt me."

"He's the one who made the accusation to the Association, isn't he?"

She turned to face him. "I don't know."

Brant's eyes bore into hers, hard and merciless. "Yes, you do. It makes too much sense to have been anyone else. Unless you have some other mighty powerful enemies." He waited for her to respond; when she didn't, he went on. "Judd lodged that accusation, Laci, and he did it as much to hurt you as me. He thinks you left him because of me, doesn't he?"

She nodded.

"Did you?"

"No." The word slipped from her lips as little more than a whisper of sound. She dropped her gaze to the counter, unable to meet his eyes. "I told you, I was never in love with Judd."

"But he thought you were still in love with me, right?"

She nodded again.

Brant felt a spurt of excitement. Maybe, just maybe, there was hope for them after all. "So, he's probably come to the conclusion that you won't go back to him, blames me, and leveled the charge with the Association to get back at both of us at the same time."

Laci stared into her coffee and remained silent. There was nothing to say. His suspicions were the same as hers, whether she wanted to believe that of Judd or not.

"I could have been disqualified from the Championships if the Association had thought I'd bribed a judge, or the rodeo sponsor, for some extra points." He reached across the counter and lay a hand atop one of hers. "But, Laci, a charge like that against you could have lost you customers, sponsors, contestants, even your PRCA standing."

She nodded again at his words, knowing the truth of them and feeling them like a weight on her shoulders.

"If that had happened it most likely wouldn't have been just for this event or this year."

"I just never thought he could be that... vindictive," Laci said softly. She pulled her hand from beneath Brant's and poured more coffee into her cup, warming what was already there. When she felt a small hint of composure return to her, she turned back to Brant and met his gaze. "Everything you say makes sense, but there's something that doesn't, and that's what's bother me."

"What?"

"Judd supplies a lot of stock for the rodeos in this region. Why would he put those contracts, as well as the one here in Reno, and his PRCA sanction, in jeopardy by making a false charge to the Association that he must have known wouldn't stand up at a hearing?

"Sometimes all you need is a hint of something wrong, something underhanded, to turn things sour." He wasn't about to tell her that this hadn't been the first time he'd been hauled before a PRCA committee to defend himself. "He probably hoped that, to play it safe, the rep would disqualify me and I'd leave town, and you'd go running back to him." He watched as Laci refilled his cup. "He does want you back, Laci, doesn't he?" It was more statement of fact than question.

"Yes, but I've already told him that's not going to happen. It's over between us."

"He obviously figures he can change your mind."

"Well, he's wrong. I could lose everything, the company, the rodeo, the house, but Kit and I are not going back to Judd, and that's final."

Brant felt like jumping for joy at her words, in spite of the insistent little voice at the back of his mind warning him that he was playing a dangerous game with himself. "How's he set financially?"

Laci shrugged. "Fine. No, better than fine really. He was an only child so when his father died Judd inherited everything, and he's made some solid investments of his own since then. If he never wanted to work at anything another day in his life, he doesn't have to.''

''So if he lost his PRCA standing and couldn't do stock contracting to the rodeos anymore, it wouldn't be a financial loss he couldn't handle?''

''No. But Judd loves the rodeo.'' She turned away to stare through the window set over the sink, unaware of the frown that pulled at her brow. Five years before she'd met Judd he'd been World Champion Steer Wrestler twice, then he'd broken his back when, during a competition, a steer fought him during the wrestle. Judd had lost his grip on the steer and one of the animal's hooves had slammed into Judd's back. That had been the end of his rodeo career even though he'd returned to full health within two years. But he'd never seemed bitter. He loved just being around the rodeo, which was the main reason he'd gone into stock contracting—to stay connected with it.

And when she'd inherited James Enterprises, he'd been more than happy to run it for her. She shook her head again. ''It's so hard to believe that he'd jeopardize his standing with the PRCA.''

''He didn't figure on anyone ever finding out who made the accusation.''

She picked up her coffee and walked into the family room, settling herself onto the heavily pillowed sofa and cradling the cup in her hands. Her gaze moved beyond the glass patio doors to the bright lights of the city and casinos that sprawled across the valley below.

Brant sat down next to her, risking that she might

move away and hoping she wouldn't. He twisted around to face her, drawing one leg up to lay across the knee of his other leg and draping an arm over the back of the sofa, though nowhere near around her shoulders. "You've changed," he said softly, studying her profile.

She turned and looked at him, her brow quirking slightly. "How?"

He shrugged. "You're more beautiful than I remembered...and stronger."

"I don't feel stronger," she said, ignoring the compliment on her looks.

"You've got a great house, a handsome son, and you're running your father's business. That takes a strong woman, Laci." He left off the fact that she also had a belligerent ex-husband. God, how he'd missed her. He felt the blood in his veins burn just at being near her again. A knot formed in his chest and twisted at his yearning to draw her into his arms. He fought against the urge to let his arm move to encircle her shoulders, to let his fingers clasp her arms and pull her toward him, but with each passing second he lost a little more of the battle.

She sipped at her coffee, then abruptly sat the cup down and rose from the sofa to walk across the room. At the patio doors she swung around to face him, the night at her back, beyond the glass, creating a halo of shimmering, silver-infused darkness about her golden hair. "Actually, you're right, Brant, I have changed."

He noticed the hard note in her tone immediately, the stiffness in her stance, the coolness that had come into her eyes, and his own body grew taut with apprehension.

"I've had to change, because a lot of things have happened in my life since you left, but then you wouldn't know that would you?"

"I've kept up," he said slowly. He leaned forward, propping his arms on his knees and studied her, trying to read the real intent behind her words.

"Really? You've kept up. I guess I should feel flattered." She stared at him, almost daring him to argue with her, and not even knowing why. She'd thought the anger and hurt were long gone. "I'm not the starry-eyed little romantic I used to be, Brant. I have responsibilities now, lots of them, and I look at life straight on, rather than through those rose-colored glasses I used to wear."

Brant pushed himself up from the sofa and moved to stand before her. He didn't understand the anger he heard in her voice, where it was coming from, but it wasn't what he'd come here to confront. Their feelings for each other, what had been and might be again, that's what he wanted to know about, talk about, act on. "I just want to talk awhile, Laci, visit, you know? Find out how you're doing." It was a lie, one of the biggest he'd ever told. He wanted to drag her into his arms, crush her lips beneath his, and bury his hands in her hair. But he sensed she wasn't ready for that, and maybe, if he was truthful with himself, he wasn't either. Not yet. Because if it ended in disaster, if he ended up taking the same road he had seven and a half years ago, they'd both be hurt again, and he wasn't sure he could survive that kind of hurt again.

"A little late to worry about how I'm doing, isn't it?" She impatiently brushed at a lock of hair that had fallen over her temple. "I mean, it's been seven and a half years, Brant, and not a word. Not a phone call, a letter, or even a blasted postcard. You just left, and now you come back and want to know how I've been doing?" She whirled away from him and walked back into the kitchen. Her hands trembled as she grabbed the coffeepot and tilted it over her cup.

"Laci, I didn't mean to..."

"To what, Brant? Walk out on me? Well, you did and it's history. So," she turned to face him again, "to answer your question, I'm doing just fine, fantastic in fact, or I was until you came back."

"Fine?" he echoed. The lone word, edged with sarcasm, challenged her stance of defiance.

"Yes, fine," Laci snapped. "As you said, I have a beautiful home, a company to run and a great son. I have it all and I'm doing just fine with it."

He took several steps toward her. "You also have an ex-husband who wants you back."

"Well, that's his problem. I want a lot of things I can't have."

Brant softened his tone and smiled. "You always did have one hell of a temper, Laci James."

Tears sprang to her eyes and with them her anger instantly disappeared. She shook her head and looked away from him. Why did it have to desert her now, when she truly needed it? "Please, Brant, don't make this any harder for me than it already is."

He moved instinctively, without thought, and drew her into his arms. She didn't resist him, but instead lay her head on his chest. "Making things hard for

you is the last thing in the world I want to do, Laci,''
Brant whispered into the golden curls of her hair. He
hadn't meant to pull her into his arms, but now that
he had, he couldn't imagine letting her go.

She was going to lose it. If she stayed within the
circle of his arms, felt the beat of his heart against
her breast, the length of his body pressed to hers for
one more second she would lose control and give in
to the desire burning within her. It was already threatening to consume her, to overwhelm rational thought
and reason. But she couldn't let that happen, because
then she'd love him again, like before, and he'd leave
again…like before. But this time she had Kit to think
of. This time she wouldn't be able to wallow in tears
and grief, and fall apart after he'd gone.

"But you are making it hard for me," she said, and
pushed herself out of his arms. She needed space,
time, to collect some composure, some calm. Moving
to the end of the counter that separated the family
room from the kitchen, she pressed a button on the
answering machine that sat next to her phone, then
nervously glanced back at Brant. "Sorry," she
shrugged, trying to act nonchalant while her insides
churned with fluttering nerves, "I forgot to listen to
my messages."

The first was from one of the concession contractors at the rodeo. He needed her signature on an in-
surance form. The second was from her cousin Trish,
saying she and her family would be at the arena Fri-
day night.

Brant crossed the room and paused before the sliding glass doors. He stared down at the city. What
would his life have been like if his brother hadn't died

and Brant hadn't made a vow that would haunt him forever if he didn't fulfill it? What would have happened if he'd accepted the job offer from Laci's father, quit the rodeo and stayed in Reno with her? His gaze moved unseeingly over the bright lights that sparkled in the distance. What would happen now if he didn't win the title, but quit anyway? Could he live with that? He'd always thought the answer was no, now he wasn't sure anymore. He pulled in a deep breath. Except that he needed the purse money for the ranch and the school, and rodeoing was the only way he knew how to earn it.

The recorder beeped and moved on to the third message.

"Laci, pick up the damned phone. I know you're there...."

Judd's demanding voice rudely jerked Brant from his musings. He turned to glare over his shoulder at the machine and saw Laci jump at hearing her ex-husband's threat. She stared at the recorder as if it had suddenly become something evil and menacing.

"Damn it Laci, you're my wife, and I'm through playing your stupid little games," Judd yelled, his voice an ugly snarl. "You pack your bags and get yourself back to the ranch or you and that damned two-bit hustler you think so highly of will be sorry." There was a short pause of silence, and then Judd spoke again, his tone dropping to a mocking growl. "Remember sweetheart, I know the truth, and you sure as hell don't want that getting out, now do you?"

Brant stared at the machine, trying to make sense of Judd's words and failing. Finally he glanced at Laci. The look on her face was one of mingled fear and anger, and she was shivering. He closed the distance between them and drew her into his arms. She didn't resist. Instead she pressed into him.

"I've never heard him like that," she whispered against his chest. Hot tears filled her eyes and dropped onto her cheeks. "He sounded so hateful."

Judd had again referred to knowing something Laci didn't want to get out. But get out to who? Brant knew he'd ask her about it, see if he could help her some way, but he also knew it could wait until later. Right now, after long years of living off memories, of trying to forget her and finding himself instead haunted both day and night by dreams of her, she was standing within the circle of his embrace again, and that's all he intended to think about.

She looked up at him, the tears that hovered upon her dark golden lashes like sparkling diamonds. Her bottom lip quivered, and Brant ached to kiss it.

He shuddered as his gaze moved over her features. The look of vulnerability on her face, the fear that caused her lips to tremble, the silent plea for help that she didn't voice, but was reflected so clearly in her eyes, was his undoing. Something ripped apart inside him. Restraint fled his mind as if having never existed, caution and fear proved a concern his heart temporarily forgot. Sensations of longing, bolts of lightning-hot desire that he had to struggle to keep under control, filled his body, and all of his self-made promises to go slow with her disappeared.

His hands slipped to her waist, drawing her closer, pressing her against him until the curves and lines of her body fused with those of his, leaving no space between them. Nothing separated them from each other but the frail barrier of their clothes.

Laci looked up at Brant. She wanted him to kiss her, to make love to her, more than she'd ever wanted anything in her life. That realization came to her without doubt or surprise, and she knew as surely as she wanted it to happen, that tonight it would. And she knew just as surely that she would regret it tomorrow, damn herself for her weakness and call herself every kind of a fool. She was setting herself up for another broken heart, and this time there would be no hope of mending it, but she didn't care. Brant had come back into her life, and if they only had tonight, then she would add remembrance of it to her other memories and hope that they could ease the loneliness she knew would haunt her after he was gone.

His head lowered and, as his mouth neared, Laci closed her eyes, waiting for what she'd dreamed of, longed after, for all the years they'd been apart.

The warmth of his breath kissed her cheek, while his mouth moved over hers, the soft caress of his lips against hers a tender and tentative brush of sensitive flesh to flesh. She felt his heart beat against her breast, its accelerating pace matching that of her own, thud for passionate thud. The unique fragrance that was him, that reminded her of high mountain springs and pine needles, filled her senses as his strength wrapped around her like a velvet cloak, holding her safe and secure within its shroud.

Welcome home, Brant. The words crept from somewhere in the back of her mind, or maybe from the fathomless depths of a heart lonely for too long. They filled her mind, repeating over and over again as he kissed her and instilled a joy within her that she hadn't felt for years, and had truly never expected to feel again.

His tongue moved between her lips and began to ravage her mouth with devastating sweetness, his kiss at once gently loving and savagely demanding. ''I want you,'' Brant whispered against her mouth. He groaned softly. ''Oh, God, Laci, I need you. I've always needed you.''

She hesitated, stiffening slightly at his words, but only for a moment. Once she'd fallen thoroughly, desperately, in love with a man she could not follow, and who would not stay. Now he had come back into her life, but nothing had changed between them except that this time she would not damn him when it came time for him to leave her again because she had finally come to understand him, and perhaps even herself. Brant was what he was, and maybe that's why she loved him so much. She had been devastated when he'd left her before, and she would be devastated this time. She would cry again, but there would be time for that later. This was their night. She wanted it, needed it, more than anything in the world. Her hands slid over his chest and, wrapping her arms around his neck, she clung to him as if clinging to life. Reclaiming his mouth with hers, she offered her acquiescence with a kiss rather than mere words.

Brant felt his mind spin. The passion that had ignited within him at her touch was threatening to consume him entirely, now reaching out to overwhelm whatever coherent thought was left him. His senses were as incited by her mere presence, as his body was intoxicated by her touch. Ever since the day he'd

walked away from her, he had denied the spark of
hope that had struggled to stay alive within him, hope
that someday, somehow, he would be with Laci again.
Now that hope burst to life in a white-hot explosion,
fusing with the desire that heated every cell, every
fibre of his body and left him with no other thought
but of the woman he held tightly within the circle of
his arms.

"You don't know how many times I've dreamed
of you, of us, together like this again," he said, his
deep voice hoarse from the intensity of emotion
coursing through him.

"No more than me," Laci whispered against his
lips.

His mouth captured hers again and he pulled her
with him to the floor. A delirious excitement stormed
his body, turning it stone hard, while his blood turned
to a seething flow of need that grew hotter and more
demanding as her tongue danced around his, teasing,
dueling and caressing. Years of longing welled up
inside of Brant. Laci was the vixen of his past, the
enchantress who haunted his dreams, the embodiment
of everything he'd ever wanted and needed in a
woman to love. For years he had fooled himself into
believing that he'd been living, but he had merely
been existing, his heart beating, his mind thinking, but
all the while the emptiness in him had been growing
deeper and more intense.

Her body lying half beside, half under him was an
ecstasy he'd thought never to experience again. For
the second time in his life, Brant made a vow to himself that he knew he had to keep, or die trying. Laci
had belonged to him once, and he would make her

his again. Somehow he would find a way to make her love him again. But this time he would find a way to make her love him *enough*.

He braced himself on one arm as the other slipped from around her and his hand moved to cup her breast. She strained to meet his touch, silently inviting it, and a surge of desire so strong it nearly stopped his heart swept over Brant. To love a woman who doesn't love you back as much is certain death, his father had once told him. But if this was death, Brant knew he welcomed it wholly.

Laci pulled her lips from his. "Brant," she gasped urgently. She moved a hand to push against his shoulder and tried to twist away from him.

No, his mind screamed. Anguish washed over him even as he found enough restraint, enough common decency and dignity within himself to move aside and allow her to rise. She hurried down the hall to the bedrooms. Brant turned to stare through the glass doors, struggling to gain control of the fiery passion that had seized his body. His gaze locked, unseeing, on the lights of the city far below. He wanted to reach for her again, to draw her back into his arms, but obviously that was not what Laci wanted. The realization brought an ache to his gut and extinguished the spark of hope that had only moments ago exploded into brightness within him.

Pushing to his feet he walked toward the hallway. He'd been a fool, and now it was time to say good-night and leave. Halfway down the hall a door stood open. He paused before it.

Chapter 8

Laci looked at him and smiled. "Sometimes Kit gets up for a glass of water." She released the pearl buttons that held the front of her western shirt secure and glanced back at Brant, her lips curving upward in a teasing smile. "You want to help me here, handsome?" she said, her voice husky with the emotions that had seized every molecule within her body.

Shock rippled through him as he watched her push the shirt from her shoulders, leaving them bare and golden in the pale glow that was a blend of lamplight and moonlight. Passion twisted like a coiled knot in his groin, and the hope that had just deserted him returned, stronger and brighter. He closed the distance between them, noticing without noticing the huge pine posts at each corner of the bed, the colorful Indian print quilt, and the array of dream catchers that hung in one corner from the ceiling. Pushing himself upright, Brant's now shaking fingers slid beneath the delicate fabric of her shirt and slipped it from her arms.

She felt him hesitate. "Don't stop," she whispered, unable to believe she could be this bold, yet wanting him so much that she had no choice.

He released the hook at the back of her brassiere and gently pushed the silky straps down over her arms. She turned to face him as the delicate white lace fell away from her.

Another wave of desire cut through Brant like the piercing slice of a razor sharp knife, the agony of his need for her suddenly a sweet torture to his soul that was almost unbearable. He sat motionless for several seconds, mesmerized by the sight of her, by what was happening, and unable to believe that what he'd prayed for, for so long, was really coming true. Tentatively, as if afraid that if he moved too fast the vision before him would disappear, he raised his hands toward her breasts, cupping them gently, reverently, one in each hand. Her flesh was warm to his touch, her skin as smooth and soft as the most luxurious silk, yet in his mind he was still unable to comprehend that she wasn't just another vision of his imagination, another dream, haunting him as she had so often over the years, only to disappear when he woke. But as his mouth closed over hers again, the loneliness of the years they'd been apart quietly drifted away from him as promise for the future unconsciously replaced it.

He felt her breasts swell with passion, felt her nipples harden into pebbled peaks of desire, her tongue dance a seductive cadence around his own, and prayed that if he was dreaming, he would never wake up.

Laci shivered at the tenderness of his kiss and gentle touches. She had been afraid to allow him back into her life, but at this moment, she couldn't remember why. She pushed lightly against his shoulders with the tips of her fingers, and once he released her, she sat on the bed, her eyes locked with his, and raised a leg toward him. "A little more help, cowboy?" she said huskily.

Passion turned the blue of his eyes to the rich darkness that hangs over the mountains at midnight, chased away the faint shadows that had lain restless beneath his eyes for so long, and softly touched upon the ruggedly cut features that had begun to turn hard and sharp from a life lived with no gentleness in it.

Laci watched the transformation sweep over him, and the last threads of doubt about what they were about to do fled her mind.

Brant smiled and grasped her foot, tugging her boot off and dropping it to the floor. Then he repeated the process with her other boot.

"That was the easy part," she teased, and unhooked the belt at her waist. Raising her hips, she watched silently as Brant pulled her jeans down and over her legs.

"Yeah, and not nearly as much fun as this part." He tossed the faded denim aside and turned back to stare at her, still unable to believe she was really there. His gaze traveled over her body, savoring every naked curve and line, and committing each to memory. He had dreamed hundreds of dreams about this, envisioned her with him, holding him, kissing him,

making love to him, but this time was different. This
time if he woke and found himself alone, he had no
doubt the searing ache that had seized every inch of
his being in its grip would worsen, until finally, un-
soothed, it would kill him.

When the minutes seemed to drag by and he didn't
move, Laci found herself assailed by thoughts of
doubt and uneasiness. "Brant?"

He heard the quaver of apprehension in her tone.
His breath was ragged now, his mouth dry, his throat
parched beyond the ability to swallow. Desire sliced
through him, no longer merely an urgent yearning,
but transformed, heightened, to a demanding, intense
hunger. She was even more beautiful, more perfect,
than his memory had allowed him to remember or
even imagine. In the glow of the fused lamp and
moonlight she appeared an illusion conjured up by
his dreams, an ethereal enchantress capable of fulfill-
ing his most desired fantasy, and instilling within him
the most desperate, unbearable, ache of loneliness.
But he didn't care. If she was nothing more than a
hallucination, a chimera his mind had presented to
both satisfy and taunt him, he would accept it, because it meant that for a little while he would hold
her in his arms and love her like he'd yearned to do
for so many years.

He let his gaze traverse her length slowly, its lei-
surely travels heightening both the hunger and anticipation swelling within him. Her skin had the faint
golden glow of being touched by the sun, except for
a triangle of white upon each breast, and a thin white
streak that crossed her hips and widened into a larger
triangle that surrounded the golden path of hair that

grew at the juncture of her thighs. A memory from years ago flit through Brant's mind, a picnic at Pyramid Lake, and Laci in a blue bikini. He remembered the tiny triangles of bright blue fabric that had been her bathing suit, and how badly he'd wanted to remove them from her body. Brant's smile widened.

"That's a pretty sly smile you've got going there," Laci said, a twinkle of mischief in her own eyes. "What are you thinking?"

"That you're beautiful," he answered. His breath caught in his throat and turned the words to a barely audible whisper. "And that I've missed you more than I can say."

But Laci heard him, saw the look of desire in his eyes, and felt her heart soar.

He moved over her then, his body stretching out beside hers, his mouth instantly capturing her lips, his hands moving over her body in a series of continual caresses that left Laci's skin aflame and the ache of need within her intensifying. Each stroke of his hands deepened her passion and the hunger growing inside her, inciting its force until her blood was like a volcanic surge seeking release and escape. As her body danced to the melody his hands played upon her flesh, Laci's senses sang his name over and over, and every cell within her hummed a chorus of need.

Once she'd thought Brant had not only stolen her heart, but also the key to her soul. Then he'd left and she'd damned him and called herself a fool, denying her love for him and banishing all thought of it to the nethermost regions of her memory where she seldom visited. It had been the safest thing to do, the only thing for her to do, in order to survive the pain of losing him. Now she knew how wrong she'd been to try to deny that she still loved him. Brant Garrison was the man she would always love, and it didn't matter whether they were together or not, or even if he loved her in return. Her love would always be there for him.

She moved her hands over the corded muscles of his shoulders and in spite of the tightly woven threads of his shirt, Laci felt the passion that heated his flesh. Bracing her hands against his upper arms she pushed, rolling Brant onto his back and herself to her knees. "My turn," she said softly, a promise in her eyes that made his senses reel with anticipation.

How—why, had he stayed away from this woman? How could he ever have found the strength to leave her? And how could he do it again—if it came to that?

Laci rose and walked to a stereo, on the small table near the dresser. Taking a CD from its cabinet, she placed it on the disk player and turned back to Brant. The CD clicked on and a soft, lilting tune filled the room. Laci retraced her steps and paused before him. A small smile tugged at the corners of her lips, and the fire of desire danced within the china blue depths of her eyes, telling him silently, lovingly, that she wanted him as much as he wanted her.

Mesmerized, Brant found himself unable to breath, unable to look away or move. The nebulous mist of night crept through the tall windows along one wall of the room, and surrounded her, gently enveloping her in a shroud of star-touched light that left her flesh burnished gold and transformed her hair to strands of shimmering honey. His fingers ached to bury themselves within that wild mane, his body throbbed with the demand to press against the tantalizing length of her naked form. For so long he had tried not to look for her in every woman he'd met, but he had never been successful.

Laci leaned over him and slipped her hand within Brant's shirt, forcing the pearl snaps that held it closed to pop open. She slid the sleeves down over his arms, slowly, relishing the feel of hard, sinewy muscle beneath her fingers. Her hands scaled his rib cage, her fingers roamed through the sprinkling of black hairs that grew on his chest, and time hurtled her into the past. She felt him tremble and she smiled as she unlatched his belt, the clasp of his jeans, and slowly pushed the zipper down. Her gaze moved up to meet his, the blue of her eyes reaching out to him, seducing him, promising fulfillment of the hopes and dreams that for too many years he'd dare not acknowledge he even harbored.

"You've got another scar," she said softly. With her index finger she lightly traced a ragged line of flesh that marred the front of his left shoulder and had not been there the last time they'd made love. How many times had he suffered an injury, and she hadn't been there to comfort him? To care for him? The question brought an ache to her heart. When her finger came to the end of the scar she leaned forward and gently pressed her lips to it.

If she had waited just a little bit longer all those years ago, would he have returned to her?

Brant inhaled sharply, want and need, passion and lust arcing through him like a shot of electricity. And just as suddenly, with no warning, a chill of fear rippled through him and settled in his blood, his mind, his heart, as stark terror. If he moved, if he dared breathe too deeply, or took just a millisecond too long to blink his eyes, would she disappear?

Laci's hands slid over his hips and pushed at the jeans that hugged his body, urging the soft denim, and black shorts underneath, downward with taunting slowness. Her fingers moving over his flesh was a physical torture more intense, more delicious, more soul stirring, than he could have imagined anything could be.

Brant allowed the breath he'd been holding to slowly slip from between his lips. She was there. His heart hammered against his chest, loud, thudding beats that felt explosive and deafening. It wasn't his imagination…or a dream, not this time. She was really there, with him, loving him, finally.

Her lips moved across the front of his collarbone to the hollow of his throat, pressing light kisses along the way and turning his flesh and blood, every cell and fiber, hot with need. Brant felt her fingers slip within the dark thatch of hairs that surrounded his arousal and he nearly groaned in sweet agony. Patience had never been a virtue with him, and what little he did possess had totally and quickly deserted him long moments ago. Tearing himself away from her he pushed to his feet, kicked off his boots, tore off his socks and shrugged the rest of the way out of his pants.

Laci stared up at him, a hint of a smile tugging at the corners of her lips, her pulse racing. She wouldn't have thought it possible, but he was more beautiful, in a rugged, almost chiseled way, than she remembered. His body seemed longer, harder and leaner, his flesh bronzed from the combination of his natural heritage of one quarter Apache and the long hours he spent in the sun competing in the rodeo. Indulging herself, bringing to fruition the dreams she had kept secret and locked away within her heart over the past years, Laci allowed her gaze to move over him with infinite slowness. She savored each swell of muscle and line of sinew, relished the look of lanky limbs, flat stomach, and a chest and shoulders that seemed as broad and strong as the mountains that rose skyward across the valley from her home.

She had seen other men naked, in magazines, movies and while married to him, Judd, but none had possessed the savage virility she sensed surrounded Brant like an invisible aura. A potent masculinity fairly exuded from every inch of him, turning her thoughts to conquering heroes, feral warriors, and dashing swashbucklers.

Brant lowered himself to the bed and reached out and drew her into the circle of his arms, crushing the breath from her lungs. "I dreamed..." He looked deep in her eyes. "I hoped...but I never believed I would ever..." His voice broke with emotion, and rather than continue to try to describe what he truly had no words for, he lowered his head and his lips captured hers in a kiss that was a command, demanding that she surrender and respond. His tongue plundered her mouth, probing and exploring, heating and inciting, and what little coherent thought he was still capable of having turned to a jumbled blend of past and present, dreams and reality.

Laci kissed him back with all the ardor within her,

releasing emotions, desires and hungers that had been locked away for years, ignored and denied, until his return forced her to take note of them, and his kisses forced her to accept them. She clung to him, her hands roaming his back, his shoulders, his arms. Tomorrow she might regret her lack of will and lament this night she was incapable of denying herself…but that was tomorrow. Tonight she would love him for all the years they'd missed, for all the years they'd been apart, and maybe for all the years in the future as well.

Brant groaned deeply, the unconscious sound ripping from his throat as he felt her hands move over his body, spreading the fire of her touch and incinerating him to the very core of his being. All of the hurts of the past faded from his mind and heart, and the worries of tomorrow ceased to exist as the taste and feel of her filled his senses, fired his blood and sent mind-numbing waves of pleasure through him. Only this night, this moment, this woman, remained alive in his awareness. She was his world, a world he never wanted to leave again.

Laci reveled in the sheer rapture of being back in Brant's arms and feeling his naked length pressed to hers, his body alive and hot beneath her hands, her own body burning with passion at his touches, some featherlight, others provocative, teasing and sensual. He was an intoxicant she had been denied for years, but tonight was for indulgence, to relish and enjoy, and there would be no holding back.

She returned his kisses and caresses with wild abandonment and an ardent recklessness that left Brant's senses reeling nearly out of control. If he was to leave her again, she wanted to make certain that he never forgot her. Her tongue dove into his mouth, dancing around his like a hot flame whose touch left him seared and wanting more.

Brant's lips moved along the slender column of her neck, over her shoulders, and finally settled upon one breast. He drew its nipple gently into his mouth, tentatively grazing its end with a brush of his teeth, laving its pebbled peak with the tip of his tongue.

A soft moan of pleasure tore from Laci's throat and her body arched up to meet his touch. He felt her hands knead into the hard plane of his shoulders, holding him to her, clutching at him, clinging to him as if in desperation or fear. It was a feeling he understood well. The desperation to have her, and the fear that she would suddenly vanish from his arms also dwelt within him, a shadow in the back of his consciousness that he was too afraid to acknowledge, yet was all too aware of its presence.

His hands moved over her hungrily, as if with a life, a need, of their own. Too long...he had been away from her too long, and now he yearned to touch every curve of her body over and over again, glide his hands down every line of her length, taste her kisses until exhaustion overcame him, feel her hot flesh pressed to his for as long as she would allow.

Like a man too long denied sustenance, Brant pillaged her mouth, drinking of her sensuality until his senses were inebriated with want of her. He had made love to more women than he could remember over the years, some before he'd met Laci, some after, but none had touched his heart like she did, not even the two women he'd married. And none had ever taken his senses, his passions, her captive. Only Laci had managed that, and he knew now, with a certainty beyond question, that he would never be free. He was her prisoner, and would remain so for the rest of his life. A smile touched his lips at the thought.

His hand slipped over the taut plane of her stomach and sought out the joining of her thighs. He felt her tighten instinctively, writhe momentarily, as the tips of his fingers brushed over the sensitive peak of flesh that harbored her most intense passions.

Laci's body exploded with sensations so severe and powerful that they left her shaking and startled at their ferocity, and with each touch of his fingers…there…a new onslaught of pleasure ripped through her, deepening her hunger, escalating her need for him to touch her again, love her more. She wanted him with an intensity that was overwhelming, needed him with a voracity that was undeniable, and perhaps, she suspected, unsatiable. His mouth, his hands, seemed everywhere, touches of searing heat, of burning fire, that left her flesh, her heart and soul, branded with his name, his mark. His hand moved over her breast, his lips pressed against the flat plane of her stomach, and his other hand moved once more over that part of her most susceptible to his touches. A kaleidoscope of brilliant colors swirled through her mind while a new wave of heat, scorching her from the inside out, swept through her body in crashing, continual waves, one after the other after the other.

"Now Brant, please," Laci gasped, her hands seeking him, pulling at his arms. "Please."

He nearly lost control at her words, and struggled to hold on to his self-restraint. Squeezing his eyes shut, he stilled instantly and reminded himself that he'd waited too long for this to lose it now—he wanted it to be perfect between them, he wanted them to reach that moment together. But first he had to calm down, just a little.

Seconds ticked by as he lay still, breathing heavily and fighting for control.

"Brant?"

"I'm here, sweetheart," he whispered, his voice a rasp of sound. "I'm here." He pressed his lips to the hollow of her neck. "Just give me a…minute."

"Are you all right?"

He chuckled softly at the concern in her tone. "I'm a lot more than all right, beautiful, I'm just a little ahead of myself, that's all."

"Ahead…?"

He inhaled deeply. "I've waited too long to be with you again, Laci…" He moved his lips down the column of her neck, dipping into the hollow of her collarbone with his tongue, then gently nipping at the curve of her shoulder. "…to lose it this soon."

Laci smiled, finally understanding what he meant. "It has been too long," she whispered. "Much too long."

Brant's heart soared at her words, and his body demanded that he do something besides just lie there. Then he remembered a caution nearly forgotten. "Are we…all right?"

Her brow furrowed as she looked up at him, puzzled by the question.

"Safe?" he added.

She nodded, and pressed her lips to his temple. "Yes, we're safe." This time, she added silently, and smiled, momentarily thinking of Kit and wishing, just for a second, that she could conceive another child with Brant.

He shifted his weight, moving over, nudging her legs part, and slid into her. Laci felt herself fill with him and once again silently welcomed him home, at the same time wishing he would stay forever, and knowing he wouldn't. A tear slipped from one corner of her eye and she quickly banished the depressing thought of his leaving. He was here now, in her arms, loving her, and that was more than she'd hoped for, more than she had dreamed could ever happen again.

She raised her hips to meet him, moaning softly as all of her hopes, dreams and fantasies forged suddenly into reality. Her body molded itself to his, hot flesh fusing with hot flesh, passion with passion, spirit with spirit. For so long she had denied that she still loved him, and she had lied the lie of a fool. He was her everything. She could live without him, she had proven that, but it was a life accompanied by a big void, a life riddled with memories and wishes. Brant Garrison was what made the air that she breathed fresh and alive, the blood that flowed through her veins warm and vivacious, the beat that made her heart continue to pump. He was every dream she had ever fantasized, every hope she had ever harbored. He was her love, and would be until the day she died.

He had walked back into her life offering no promises, no commitment, no words of love, and yet it didn't matter, because she had a part of him that would always be hers, and she would always have tonight. No one could take either of those from her. Even the pain that would undoubtedly come to her if he left again would not take the memory of tonight from her, or diminish the love she felt for this man.

Brant buried his face along the curve of her neck, nuzzled her earlobe, and breathed deeply of the sweet scent of her. The thought, the pleasure, the wonder of being inside her again was almost more than he could accept and comprehend. He had waited so long, so very long. It had been a dream he never truly expected to come true.

She moved beneath him, her legs entwined about the long length of his, the movement pulling Brant deeper inside of her. Rational thought, coherent words, even reason deserted him, leaving him only primal wonder and the physical instinct to accept and revel in the sensual and savage assault of the emotions and pleasures assailing his body.

He whispered her name, kissed her lips, caressed her breasts, and moved gently, rhythmically within her. She matched her body's responses to the cadence of his lovemaking, rising to meet his thrusts, grinding her hips to his, tightening her legs about him, brushing her lips over his neck, jaw and cheeks until finally claiming his mouth with hers.

Brant's body turned into a conflagration of desire, an inferno that knew no boundaries and burned him from both within and without. He pushed deeper into her, hearing her name echoing repeatedly through his mind, but uncertain of whether the sound left his lips or not. He felt a desperation to be as close to Laci as he could, needed to touch her heart, her soul, and steal a little bit of her for himself…just in case the morning came, and she wasn't there.

Laci had never known the depths of sexual hunger

her body could delve to, until now. Years ago she had loved Brant, emotionally and physically, and thought she had given him all of herself, but she'd been wrong. With each brush of tongue against tongue, each caress of flesh to flesh, she felt as if her world was finally becoming complete. The void that had come to life within her when he'd left all those years before was finally disappearing. She was, at last, coming to know herself, and what she truly wanted out of life.

Yearnings for his touch and love had secretly dwelt within her all through those years, buried beneath the ache of hurt he'd left behind, hiding behind a cache of memories she'd refused to recall for more than brief glimpses here and there, until his return had left her with no choice but to look closer. Now that hunger threatened to overwhelm her, and was made all the more unbearable, and delicious, with every movement of his body upon and within hers.

"Brant," she whispered, her breath frayed by the force of emotion coursing through her, "love me." A long sigh slipped from her lips. "Please, love me."

His heart lurched at her words, wishing she meant them the way he'd always dreamed she would, because he did love her. He loved her more than life, needed her more than breath, and would give anything…even his soul to the devil…if he could hear her say, just once, that she loved him—and know that she meant it.

Her hands moved over his back, like sheaths of hot satin, burning wherever they touched, igniting both his flesh and his heart. The fences he'd built around his emotions, had struggled to reinforce year after year, had begun to crumble the moment she'd welcomed his kiss. They collapsed further at the first feeling of her naked body pressed to his, and fell completely into nothingness, like wooden slats rotted by time, when she welcomed his body into hers.

Her plea for him to love her had instilled within his heart more hope, more joy, than he feared it was capable of holding. Dreams he'd dared not acknowledge, and hope he'd kept tamped and controlled, burst through him like a phoenix rising from the ashes, pouring new life into his body and soul.

"Love me, Brant," Laci gasped, pushing her hips up to meet his and throwing her head back as he thrust into her again.

Love her. Didn't she realize that he did love her? That he had always loved her. "I do," he whispered against her ear, then moved his mouth to claim hers.

Years ago she had said she loved him, but her love hadn't been strong enough to overcome her fear of leaving the safe, secure life she had in Reno. Was it enough this time? Could he make her love him enough this time?

Brant felt his body tighten with the emotions building within him, racing toward a pinnacle that promised a glimpse of heaven. Each push into her body proved a flash of erotic pleasure, each retreat a tease that lured him back.

Laci's fingers suddenly dug into his shoulders, her nails pinching into his flesh. She stiffened in his arms, threw her head back and thrust her breasts against his chest. "Brant, oh, yes, Brant."

Streaks of lightning assaulted Laci's senses, filling her mind with a hot, blinding radiance as her body

convulsed in waves of wild, exotic, shivering pleasure. Ripples of heat washed through her like tongues
of fire racing over dry grass, burning every inch of
her flesh, invading every crevice of her being, and
dancing through her body.

"Brant," Laci whispered, saying his name over
and over as if it were a spiritual chant.

"I'm here, sweetheart," he whispered, his voice
rough with passion. "I'm here."

He tightened his arms around her as she trembled
violently with the desire that filled her body and
pushed aside all other thoughts and feelings. She
clutched at his shoulders, clung to him as if in desperation, and plummeted over a zenith of desire, her
passion tumbling headlong toward the point of no return where he knew she would plunge off the precipice of ecstasy and spiral downward.

Brant thrust himself deep within her. "Wait for me,
Laci, he whispered, "wait for me." His body demanded satiation, gnawed with hunger, and shuddered
with the exhilaration that coursed through his blood.
A soft, guttural growl of completion ripped from his
throat and Brant felt love's little death surge up to
envelop him, sweeter, deeper, than he'd felt in years.

Love me. Her cry echoed through his mind and
taunted his heart.

"I do," he whispered against her neck, "I do."
Closing his eyes, Brant pushed into her one final time
and let himself fall into the infinite vortex willingly,
eagerly, giving himself up to the rapture that was Laci
James.

Brant lay beside her, his right arm resting lazily
upon his raised knee, his left arm bent so that his head

lay upon a closed fist. Only a few minutes had passed and neither had moved. He stared down at Laci, whose eyes were closed, and marveled at her beauty. Hunger to taste her passion again stirred deep inside him, and the heat of arousal began to build within his body, reigniting the fires.

"I never thought a woman could be more beautiful than my memories of you," he said softly, moving his hand to glide it lightly across the taut plane of her stomach. "But I was wrong, because you are."

She opened her eyes and looked up at him, her gaze delving into the depths of his, searching, seeking answers to questions she was still afraid to ask. He loved her, she knew that now, but did he love her enough? He hadn't before. Would this time be different? Could she make this time different?

"You're not so bad yourself, cowboy," she said softly, and ran a finger lightly down the strong curve of his jaw. "Not bad at all." She smiled, then turned to stare past the wall of windows at the bright lights of the city far below. The brilliance of the casino marquees, with their multicolored and blinking lights and moving displays was a beautiful sight, especially set against the blackness of the night and the even blacker shadows of the far-off mountains. But her eyes really didn't register the sight. Instead, they stared unseeingly while her mind replayed what had just happened between them and set it all to memory, every movement and breath, every kiss and caress, spark of passion and whisper of desire.

"Laci?" Brant moved his hand slowly over her breast and smiled when her nipple tightened into a hard peak, signaling that her passion for him was as strong as his for her, and equally renewed.

She turned her head and looked up at him. This time, she knew, there would be no hiding from her memories, from the pain his leaving would cause. And she knew he would leave. He was still after his dream…and with a certainty beyond doubt she knew that even once he got it, he wouldn't change. The rodeo had always been the most important thing in his life, still was, and it always would be. Yet she wasn't sorry she had let him back into her heart. She was only sorry that she would, in a few days, have to let him go again.

"I missed you, Laci, but I never admitted to myself how much until tonight."

"I missed you, too," she said softly, wanting to say so much more, but knowing she couldn't. Expressions of love and commitment, of tomorrow and forever, were not the kind Brant wanted to hear. *I'm not the settling-down kind.* The words he'd spoken to her years ago echoed in her mind. While she'd stayed in Reno, married, and cared for their son, trying to build a stable life, and failing miserably, he'd followed his dream. He wasn't a man who wanted roots—hadn't been then, and wasn't now, but she loved him anyway. Heaven have mercy on her, she loved him with every ounce of life in her.

"You're so beautiful," he whispered again. His kisses had left her lips slightly swollen and the veil of passion was still evident, if ever so slightly, within her eyes, but as his hand moved slowly, continually, over her breast, he saw her passion grow hotter. He leaned forward and brushed his lips across hers.

"You're more beautiful than all of my memories, more than all my dreams."

Laci turned her face away from him, her gaze resettling upon the city's lights. She wanted him to make love to her again, but she also wanted him to love her, which she knew he couldn't do, at least not the way she needed, wanted him to. A shadow of fear, the type of which she'd never really experienced before, hovered just beyond her consciousness. It was a fear borne of the thought, the certainty, that she was going to lose him again. The future yawned before her, a future without him. She was in love with a man she could never really have, never share her life with, and never tell that he had left much more behind than just her. Always before, without realizing it until now, she'd harbored a hope that he'd return, that he would realize he truly did love her, that he was the settling-down kind, and they would build a life together, she, Brant and Kit.

"I didn't know what to do when you left," she said softly. "You were so withdrawn."

A flashpoint of anger surged through him at her words. But you did know what to do a few months later, he wanted to say. You married Judd Mc-Candrick. "I intended to come back," Brant said, "but you didn't wait."

She turned to look up at him, hearing the sudden harshness and cold tone of accusation that edged his voice. "You never called."

He pulled away from her, passion quickly and thoroughly deserting him as his body filled with tension caused from the anger he had tried for years to vanquish. He pushed himself to his feet and, no more aware of his nakedness than he was of the hurt shadowing her eyes, Brant moved to stand before the windows and let his gaze roam over the sea of lights in the distance. It would most likely mean a definite end to their evening and the passion that had overcome them both, but she'd brought up the subject and he couldn't let it go, not this time. It wouldn't do either of them any good to rehash the past, to bring up old hurts and wounds, yet he couldn't help asking the question he'd been thinking of for years, the question that had haunted him mercilessly, teased his senses and tortured his soul. If nothing else, he had to know the answer to that one question. He turned to face her. "Were you happy with Judd?" he asked finally, breaking the silence that had fallen heavy between them.

Laci looked up, but kept her eyes averted from his. "For a while." It was a truthful answer, though it omitted several important things—things she did not want to talk of, did not want him to know. For the first few months of her marriage she had unwittingly called her husband Brant several times, lived in a world of depression, and cried constantly over the man who had left her.

Only with Kit's birth had she been able to force herself to put her memories of Brant aside and face life. Her son had given her a reason to smile again. His innocence had forced her to look at life through new eyes, and delight in things she'd long forgotten how to enjoy. And she had come to love Judd. She had never fallen *in* love with him, but she had loved him. He was the man who'd been there for her when she needed someone. For three years everything had seemed all right. The marriage was comfortable, she was content with her husband and happy with her son, and though she'd never forgotten Brant, she had learned how to live by ignoring her memories.

Then her parents had been killed, and a few months later Judd had started to demand that they have a child of their own. At first her failure to conceive had merely frustrated him. As the months passed and Laci failed to become pregnant, Judd's mood turned surly. His temper became worse and his patience almost nonexistent. He turned extremely possessive, and his jealousy flared almost out of control if she even looked at another man.

But when he'd lashed out and hit Kit, Laci had been terrified, and she'd known that was the end.

Laci looked back at Brant. "I was lonely." She paused when she saw his shoulders stiffen.

"And you didn't think I was?" he asked, more an accusation than a question.

His words cut into her heart like a knife, sharp and cold. She inhaled deeply, searching for strength within herself to answer, wanting to tell him the truth, and still afraid that it wasn't the right thing to do. He'd said once that he didn't want children, and he'd given her no reason to believe he'd changed his mind. "I was lonely," she said again. "Judd was there, he understood, and my parents liked him. They wanted me to marry him and…"

"And you did," Brant snapped.

Tears filled Laci's eyes. "I didn't think you were coming back. You'd asked me to go with you, I asked you to stay." She shrugged. "There was no reason to think you'd come back."

"If you'd really loved me, Laci, you would have waited."

Her head dropped and she squeezed her eyes shut in an effort to stop the tears fighting for escape. "I did love you," she whispered, so quietly that the words barely made a sound on the still air. "I always have."

Chapter 9

Laci's words echoed in Brant's mind. But the ones that kept slamming at him, torturing him, were the ones he hadn't wanted to hear, that she'd been happy—even "for a while".

He'd wanted her to say that her marriage to Judd McCandrick had been a mistake, the worse she'd ever made in her life.

He'd wanted her to say that she should have gone with Brant when he'd asked her to join him on the circuit, or that she should have waited for him to return to Reno.

He wanted—needed—her to say that she loved him, that she'd always loved him and always would. A soft curse slipped from his lips, ushered into the air beneath his breath.

Damn it.

The thought of her with Judd, in his arms, kissing

him, making love to him, tore at Brant's guts and stoked his anger and resentment. His hands clenched into fists at his sides, balls of steel that ached to smash into something, but most desirably, Judd McCandrick.

Laci rose and moved to stand beside him. "But it was a mistake, Brant," she said softly. "I never should have married Judd."

He felt the weight of his anger at her lift. It suddenly wasn't important, what had happened in the past. Only this moment, this night, and hopefully many more in the future, were important. At that minute he realized something—it wasn't really Laci he had been angry with for all those years, it wasn't even Judd McCandrick. The anger had been at himself, and the resentment at Brett. Brant had been angry with himself for leaving her, and resentful of his promise to Brett, because that's what had forced him to leave Laci.

"And I never should have left you," he said, turning to draw her into his arms. He gently lowered her onto the bed, and lay down beside her.

"You had to," she said softly, smiling when she saw the surprise that lighted his eyes at her words. "I didn't realize that then, but I do now. You have to win the Championship, catch your dream." She moved a hand lovingly, lightly, over his cheek. "And you won't be able to stop until you have."

Laci watched the look that came over his face and knew she was right, and though she tried to fight it away with acceptance, a little part of her heart began to cry when he didn't deny her words.

"But promise me something, Brant," Laci said against his lips as he rained kisses across her face.

"Umm?"

"Promise that you won't..." She hesitated, not knowing how to ask what she needed to hear him say.

Brant pulled back and looked down at her. "What?"

"I just don't want another seven years of silence between us. If you...when you have to leave, promise you'll at least say goodbye this time, and..." She felt the burning sting of tears at the back of her eyes, and a choke of emotion threatening to close her throat, and struggled to keep them at bay. She would not cry. Not this time.

He tightened his arms around her.

"Promise you'll call once in a while, Brant...and maybe even...come back from time to time."

He felt the cold, merciless fingers of fear squeeze at his heart, while pain, hot and searing, twisted his gut. He wanted to tell her that he'd never leave her again, that he loved her beyond reason and thought. Brant opened his mouth to give voice to the words, but nothing came forth. He felt his shoulders sag. She was right. He couldn't promise not to leave her, no more than he'd been able to then, because nothing had changed—yet. If he won the world title his lifestyle would change and then, maybe, there'd be a chance for them. But he couldn't say that to her, because until it happened, it might only be offering false hope.

If he won, things might work for them. If he didn't, it meant another year on the circuit, and possibly another, and another after that until he did win, or his body became so old and broken that he had no choice but to give up the dream and leave his vow to Brett unfulfilled.

He slipped a hand behind Laci's neck and pulled her to him. "I promise, Laci," he said. "I promise."

She nodded against his chest. "That's all I ask."

They came together again, each silently losing themselves in their embrace, in the passion that held them together, and the secret dreams each harbored for the future.

Afterward, Brant lay beside Laci, holding her in his arms until she drifted off to sleep. Brushing his lips lightly across her forehead, he slid quietly from the bed, figuring her son didn't need to see his mother in bed with someone just yet.

His movement, slight as it was, tugged at Laci's consciousness and she woke, though remained silent, and watched him from beneath barely parted lashes.

Brant took a blanket and pillow from the bed and silently left her room. She heard the soft padding sound of his bare feet on the carpet as he walked down the hall toward the family room. Moments later she heard the faint creaking of leather as he lay down on the sofa.

Long after he'd left her bed Laci's arms continued to feel empty, and the ache of loneliness that had invaded the euphoria his lovemaking had created within her nagged at her. She stared into the darkness, thinking of the man she loved, of their past together, and of her son lying asleep down the hall, an innocent, loving child who deserved a truth she couldn't give him.

Brant would make a wonderful father, and Kit already adored him, but she could no more use the information that Kit was Brant's son in order to hold him to her in Reno now, than she had all those years ago. He had to want to stay.

A long, soft sigh swept silently past her lips. What was it going to be like living out the rest of her life loving a man she hardly ever saw, a man who couldn't stop chasing a dream? Laci smiled into the darkness. Probably not much different than the past few years had been, except that she wouldn't be married to someone else.

Slipping from the bed she walked to the French doors and pulled one open, letting the cool night air rush in to fill the room and touch her skin. She had no doubt that a part of Brant Garrison loved her.

A star suddenly shot across the blackness of the sky. Laci's gaze followed its streaking descent. "I wish he could love me enough to stay," she said, as the dying star disappeared beyond the dark shrouded mountains in the distance.

Brant lay on the sofa and stared through the glass doors at the night, seeing the bright lights of Reno, the sparkling stars that dotted the velvet black sky, the dark silhouette of the distant mountains, and not seeing them. In spite of all of his hopes and dreams, he had never believed that Laci really loved him. Now he knew how wrong he'd been. She loved him, had most likely always loved him. The realization gave him both a sense of deep joy, and equally deep regret. "So why didn't she go with me?" he mumbled softly. "Why did she stay here in Reno and marry Judd?"

The question was like a slow torture to his heart,

but it was a question he needed to think about, a question he needed answered.

Upon his return to Reno he hadn't meant to become involved with her again. He had fully intended to stay as far from her as he could, polite if necessary, but aloof. Yet each time he'd seen her his resolve and restraint had slipped a little more, his need and want of her overcoming his better senses, and after each time he was always forced to fight an inner battle of self-reproach, and he always came out the loser.

Tonight however, was different. Tonight something within him, some little spark of defiance or lunacy, had reasoned that by making love to Laci he would finally be able to put the past behind him. He had convinced himself he would discover that the love he remembered and had thought still haunted him was actually little more than a sweet memory.

And he'd been wrong. He was as much in love with Laci James now as he had been eight years ago, but this time he didn't know if he was strong enough to leave her. But he knew that leaving her was exactly what he'd have to do, even if he won the title. He loved her more than life itself, maybe enough to finally give up the rodeo even if he didn't win the title in Brett's memory this year. He couldn't however, *wouldn't,* do that for a woman who would only love him on her terms.

His mind drifted back in time, bringing forth the bad memories along with the good, forcing him to look at the whole picture if he was going to look at all.

Laci had refused to go on the circuit with him, and even before he'd left Reno, she'd stopped coming to see him compete. Instead, she'd arranged for him to have a job with her father's company, then expected Brant to give up the rodeo and settle down to a life in Reno with her. He'd exploded when he found out about the job, especially that she'd arranged it with her father without even talking it over with Brant.

Laci had been hurt, but she'd remained staunch in her decision of the kind of life she wanted. He still remembered her words and how they'd torn him up inside, ripping at his heart. Tears had streamed down her face as she'd insisted that she truly loved him, but that she couldn't go with him. When he'd questioned her reasons, all she'd said was that she wanted a home, a real home, not a rodeo trailer or a series of hotel rooms.

He'd thought that her father had something to do with her refusal, but she'd denied that. For a while Brant considered telling her about Brett, reasoning that it might change her mind if she knew why he couldn't quit the rodeo, but he'd found himself unable to explain anything. Guilt had been his constant companion since the day he'd lost his brother, but the thought of telling the woman he loved that he was responsible for his own brother's death was more than he'd been able to handle. I'm a murderer, he'd wanted to say. My brother is dead because of me, and the only way I can live with that fact is to win the World Championship title like he dreamed of doing, like I promised him I would do in his honor as he lay dying in my arms—gored by a bull that I should have been riding.

Later he'd come to realize that even if he had told her, it wouldn't have made a difference in how things had turned out, and he knew he wouldn't tell her now for the same reason. If there was to be a life for them together it had to be because she truly loved him, enough to do what she hadn't been able to do then.

The sound of a crash penetrated Laci's slumber and brought her bolting upright in the big rough pine bed that dominated her bedroom. She frowned, listening to the silence and trying to figure out just what it was that had caused her to wake up. It certainly hadn't been her alarm clock. Another crash shattered the quiet and Laci nearly jumped from the bed, her heart settling in her throat and surrounded by fear. Was there a burglar in the house? Had Kit hurt himself somehow? Grabbing her robe, she swirled the long folds of pale blue fabric around her shoulders and slipped her arms within its sleeves even as she ran for the hall. Halfway down it she heard laughter and stopped, startled.

She doubted that burglars laughed aloud while pulling off a job.

"Mrs. Dabney's going to be real sore you put a dent in one of her pans."

Laci recognized Kit's voice and frowned. She walked down the hallway. What was he doing?

"Me?" Brant said, feigning astonished innocence. "Hey, c'mon, kiddo, I'm not the one who tossed it through the air, remember?"

Laci stopped dead in her tracks, memory of the night before flooding back to her. Brant! He was with Kit. A flutter of fear filled her breast.

"You asked for it," Kit countered.

She hurried to the doorway that led directly into the kitchen.

"Yeah, a pan. I asked for a pan, not a flying saucer."

Kit giggled. "Mrs. Dabney always catches it when I throw it to her."

"Yeah? Well, Mrs. Dabney," Brant said, chuckling in spite of the mock snarl he was trying to maintain, "has obviously had some experience with that kind of thing."

Laci stopped in the doorway and stared, totally taken aback by the scene before her. She could see now that the family room's glass doors stood open, as did the wide kitchen window over the sink. The fresh air of the morning blended with the tantalizing smell of the huge pan of potatoes, onions and peppers that were frying atop the stove. A mound of bacon was piled on the stove's grill, a bowl of cantaloupe and a pitcher of orange juice sat on the table and a fresh pot of coffee was brewing on the counter. Laci's gaze danced between Brant and Kit. Was she dreaming?

"Good morning, beautiful," Brant said.

Kit, sitting on a stool next to the island in which the stove was set, whirled around, grinning. "Hi, Mom, we're making breakfast."

"We?" Brant said, throwing him a playful glare.

Kit looked back at him and just as playfully stuck out his tongue.

"Well, I set the table."

"Oh, whoop-de-do," Brant teased. He set the pan he was holding, which Laci noticed had a slight dent on one side, onto one of the stove's burners and, picking up a bowl nearby, carefully poured a mixture of what she assumed was eggs and milk into it.

"And I made the orange juice, too, and showed you where the muffin mix stuff was," Kit said. "And I gave Bear a doggy biscuit so he'd quit bothering you."

"Yes, you did." Brant smiled, and offered a mock bow. "I owe you an apology. You've been a terrific help. Couldn't have done any of this without you, Chef Kit, but you're not finished, kiddo."

Bear barked. Brant glanced down at the small golden Pekingese sitting in front of the patio doors.

Kit frowned. "Whatdya mean, I'm not finished?"

"First, let Bear out, I think he has business outside. Then kindly show your mom to her chair and give her our present."

Kit smiled and jumped down from the stool. "Oh, yeah, I forgot." He took Laci by the hand and dragged her across the room, then spun around and ran for the patio doors. "Come on, Bear," he yelled, and disappeared.

Laci laughed, momentarily forgetting her uneasiness at the situation. "Can I help?"

"Nope, we've got everything under control," Brant said.

"Okay." She began to rise from her chair. "I'll just get myself a cup of coffee?"

"No, you won't, I'll get it for you in a minute," Brant said. "You just sit yourself down, beautiful, and enjoy this."

He opened the oven door and, grabbing a dish towel to use as a pot holder, removed a tray of steaming hot muffins. Their tangy smell instantly filled the kitchen and Laci felt her mouth water. She loved blueberry muffins.

A few seconds later Brant placed a cup of coffee before her, complete with her usual cream and sugar already added, and set the food on the table.

He walked to the open patio door. "Hey, Kit, get in here, breakfast is on the table and you're late." Moving back to the table he settled onto a chair across from Laci. "And I don't promise to leave you a muffin if you take much longer," he called over his shoulder to Kit.

"Jeez," Kit said, skipping in from the patio, "you said to get her the surprise."

"Yeah, but I didn't tell you to examine every rock and grain of sand along the way."

Kit giggled. "I didn't. Bear just wanted a hug."

"Well then, I hope you gave him one," Brant said, "and don't forget to wash your hands before you sit down."

Laci looked from Brant to Kit, waiting for her son to whine about washing his hands. She was mildly surprised when he said "Okay," and walked toward her holding out a bouquet of wildflowers. "Here Mom, me and Brant went out while you were still sleeping and picked these for you."

"You picked them?" she asked, staring at the multicolored arrangement of flowers. Some were probably weeds but she didn't care. It was the most beautiful bouquet she'd ever seen.

"Yeah, up on the hill." Kit pointed at the hills behind the house. "Out there. You said I can't go that far from the house, but Brant was with me and we didn't go too far, so I figured you wouldn't get mad."

Laci turned her gaze toward where he pointed, but her mind was on something else. How long had they been alone together? What had they been talking about? The questions screamed through her mind, bringing the uneasiness and fear back to her breast.

"We been up for a long time," Kit said, as if reading her thoughts, "but Brant said to let you sleep. We watched some cartoons, then went to pick the flowers." A slight pout pulled at his bottom lip. "You aren't mad, are you? 'Cause I went out there?"

Laci smiled. "No, I'm not mad. The flowers are beautiful." She leaned over and kissed his cheek. "Now, wash your hands and come sit down."

"So, I hope you woke up with an appetite." Brant took the flowers from her and plopped them in a vase she hadn't noticed he'd put on the table.

She watched Kit climb onto his chair and begin plucking pieces of bacon from the huge platter Brant had placed on the table.

"Actually, I'm ravenous," Laci said, and laughed after realizing it was true. Amazing how much of an appetite a person can work up while... She felt a blush warm her cheeks and glanced from beneath lowered lashes at Brant.

He was ladling eggs onto Kit's plate.

"Thank you for the flowers," Laci said, looking at Kit. She turned her gaze to Brant, "and the breakfast."

"You're welcome," they said in unison. Brant held up a hand and Kit slapped it, and both laughed.

A tremor of unease rippled through Laci again and

she forced her attention to the food on her plate. It's okay, she tried to tell herself as she ate. It doesn't mean anything. He doesn't suspect. She'd given him no reason. Her eyes darted to Kit.

But Judd had. The words whispered at the back of her mind, increasing her uneasiness.

"Taste okay?" Brant asked, breaking into her thoughts.

Laci jumped, startled, and turned to him. "Oh, ah, yes, delicious."

"Where were you? A million miles from here?"

"If she was a million miles away," Kit piped up, looking at Brant as if he was crazy, "she wouldn't be sitting here at the table."

"Up here," Brant said, smiling as he touched a finger to his head.

Kit frowned. "How could her head be a million miles away?"

Laci smiled, trying to suppress the nervous twitter still fluttering about her breast. "I was just thinking," she said to Brant, "about tonight, the events and things, and some of the paperwork I have to get done this afternoon."

Kit scooped a forkful of eggs into his mouth. "I like these potatoes," he said, looking at Brant, "but Mrs. Dabney will still be mad you put a dent in her pan."

Brant laughed. *"We,"* he said, "put a dent in her pan. And maybe she won't notice if *we* don't tell her."

Laci stared at Brant. Maybe she should tell him the truth. Wasn't it the right thing to do? *I don't want kids.* The words he'd spoken to her years before echoed through her mind. They'd been talking about a future together and she'd asked him how many children he wanted. It had been an innocent question, a normal question, but she hadn't expected the hard look that had come over his face, or the answer that she'd gotten. He'd never explained why he didn't want children, and she hadn't asked, thinking it better left to another time.

But that time had never come, because shortly after that he'd left.

Brant rose, walked to the counter and poured himself another cup of coffee. "More?" he asked, raising the pot toward Laci. She shook her head. He set the pot back on its burner and resettled himself at the table.

"Brant said he's gonna try to win the world title this year," Kit said, and smiled. "Then he'd be a rodeo champ, like Dad was."

Laci cringed at Kit's reference to Judd. Suddenly she didn't want her son to call her ex-husband *Dad* anymore. She clamped her teeth together and hurriedly counted to ten, then smiled. That was a problem for another day. "He won World Champion Steer Wrestling," Laci said. "Brant is trying to win World Champion All-Around Cowboy."

Kit's face screwed into a wrinkle of confusion. "What's the difference?"

She smiled. "Steer wrestling is one category of the rodeo, honey, but to win All-Around Cowboy you have to win the most money in two or more categories in one year." She smiled at the way he screwed up his face. "Understand?"

"No."

''Well, let's see. To win All-Around Cowboy Brant has to win two categories, like say, bull riding and steer wrestling, and make more money than anyone else who won two other categories, and then he'd win All-Around Cowboy. Get it now?''

''Yeah, I think so.'' Kit smiled. ''Dad only won steer wrestling, but he could have been All-Around Cowboy if he'd won something else, too, right?''

''And made more money than anyone else that year.''

''Yeah.'' Kit looked at Brant with wide eyes. ''You really gonna do it? Win more money than anyone else and be All-Around Cowboy?''

Brant smiled. ''I'm sure going to try my best.''

''But what if you don't?'' Kit asked.

Brant looked at Laci. This was his chance to find out what lay ahead for them, if anything. ''Well, if I don't win this year, then I guess I'll just have to try again next year.'' He saw the look that appeared in her eyes at his words, the same one he'd seen there years ago, and his heart almost stopped beating. His newborn hopes threatened to die, his dreams came close to dissipating. Yet something in him refused to let him give up entirely, something said keep trying, Brant, maybe you're wrong, maybe that look doesn't really mean what it did before.

But how much hope could he hold on to? How much hope could his heart stand to believe in—especially if it proved to be false?

Laci stared at him. Next year. She'd thought that she'd accepted the idea that he was going to leave, that he was going to continue on rodeoing, when they had talked last night. Now she knew she hadn't. And she hadn't realized how much she'd dreaded hearing those words, hearing her fears vocalized. She picked up her cup and sipped at what was left of her coffee, more to have something to do than because she was thirsty. History was repeating itself, playing out almost exactly as it had years ago, and there was nothing she could do about it.

Squaring her shoulders, Laci rose, gathered up her plate and utensils, and walked to the sink, rinsing her things off and loading them into the dishwasher. She busied herself clearing the table, all the while fighting the tears hovering at the back of her eyes, and avoiding Brant's gaze.

He remained seated, finishing his coffee and watching her.

"Hey, Mom, can I take an apple out to Buster?" Kit said. "Please?"

Laci nodded, not trusting her voice to answer.

Kit jumped from his chair, grabbed an apple from the bowl of fresh fruit that sat on the counter, and ran outside, disappearing around the corner of the house.

Laci heard Brant's chair scrape the floor as he pushed away from the table and rose. She stiffened at the sound of his approaching footsteps on the polished slate floor.

He stopped only a few inches behind her, wanting desperately to reach out to her, pull her into his arms. "Laci?"

She didn't turn around. Didn't move at all.

He didn't want to do this, but he didn't have a choice. There was no future if there was no compromise between them. "You could come with me," he said softly. "On the circuit. I could arrange for Kit to have a tutor."

Laci shook her head, swallowed hard and ordered herself not to cry. "I'm going to take a shower." She turned without looking at him and hurried toward the doorway to the hall, then paused and looked back at him.

He saw her heart in her eyes, saying the same thing it had only a few hours ago when he'd made love to her. She did love him, but she couldn't go on the circuit with him.

He smiled, and tried to make his voice sound teasing. "I'll tell you my secrets if you tell me yours?"

Laci started. Her heart crashed against her breast. Panic threatened the tenuous hold she had on her composure. She swallowed hard before quipping, a little too lightly, "What makes you think I have any?"

He knew he should press it, make her acknowledge what he'd said, and what she hadn't, but he was suddenly afraid. If her answer was no, he didn't want to hear it, and if it had been yes, she would have said so. But he wasn't giving up, not yet. He shrugged, striving for a nonchalance he was far from feeling. "Doesn't everyone?"

"You're welcome to use the guest bath if you'd like. It's off the bedroom next to Kit's."

"Thanks, I already did." He rose from the stool he'd propped a hip onto after she'd walked away from him, the graceful, easy movement reminding her of a large cat uncurling, the look of natural grace and fluidity masking a nature that could be, to the unwary watcher, lethally dangerous.

"I've got a few things to do before I go to the arena today," Brant said, "but I could take Kit along with me, if you need some time." He didn't know why he'd offered to baby-sit; it wasn't something he would normally do. In fact he'd never done it, but he liked the kid, felt a special kind of bond with him, and he wanted to do whatever he had to do to be near Laci. It was the only way he could think of to get her to love him enough, or convince himself that it was hopeless.

Laci stared at him, suddenly unnerved. "Take Kit?" She frowned and felt a tremble rush through her body. "Why would you want to do that? I mean, I never quite thought of you as the baby-sitting type, and you said…" She nearly bit off her tongue at realizing she'd been about to say *and you said you didn't want kids*.

Brant shrugged. "I thought you might need some time, that's all. You said you had a lot of paperwork and stuff to do at the office. Anyway, I like him. He's a good kid. Spunky."

She shook her head. "No…uh, thanks anyway. He'll be all right with me. He, uh, has some chores to do around here before we leave anyway and I've… uh…got some shopping to do downtown, clothes for him, things he'll need to try on. You know, shoes, jeans." She was babbling, but she couldn't help it.

Several minutes later she heard Brant's truck start up. She peeked past the sheer curtains that covered her bedroom window and saw him pulling out of the drive. Laci watched until the pickup slowed as it neared the road, then pulled onto it and disappeared from view. Kit suddenly streaked past the window, chasing Bear. She let the curtains fall back into place and walked into the bathroom. Why had he offered to take Kit with him? The question nagged at her and did nothing to calm her nerves. It was one thing to risk her heart again, which she'd foolishly done. And look what had happened—exactly what she should have expected. Brant Garrison was no more ready to settle down now than ever. But she was not going to risk Kit's heart and feelings.

She plopped down on her bed and stared into the mirror above her dresser. Who was she kidding. She'd already let Brant get too close to Kit. Pushing herself up she stormed into the bathroom and flipped on the shower, then turned and pulled her hair dryer from the cupboard beneath the sink. Rising she caught her reflection in the mirror and threw it a glare. It glared back. "You're a fool," she snapped at her reflection. "A first-class, silly, lamebrained fool and you'd better straighten yourself up, right now!"

"I wanna find Brant and have him show me more rope tricks," Kit said, skipping alongside Laci as they walked toward the arena office.

"I think you'd better stay with me, honey." She nodded acknowledgement to several people they passed.

"Why? I don't wanna stay up in the office. It's boring. There's nothing to do. And Brant said he'd teach me how to spin a loopy doo."

"Kit, I…"

"Laci."

She turned, having recognized Charley's voice in-

stantly and taken aback by his abrupt tone. She stiffened at seeing his features set in anger, alarm instantly sweeping through her. "What's wrong?" she
demanded as he neared.

Charley paused before her, reaching into his pocket
and drawing out some change. He handed Kit a quarter. "Here, champ, go buy yourself a soda, huh?"

Laci frowned. "I don't allow him to drink so…"

"Fine, water, whatever," Charley snapped, cutting
her off. "Just go get it, champ, then come up to the
office."

Laci started in surprise at Charley's brusqueness
but nodded to Kit and watched him skip toward the
refreshment stand a few feet away.

"Don't forget to put your quarter in the box," she
called after him. There was no charge for refresh-
ments to the people who worked behind the scenes at
the rodeo, or to the contestants, but there was a donation box for charity set on the booth's counter. Kit
had used it before, but she wanted to make sure he
remembered.

She looked back at Charley. "Now what was that
all about?"

"Sorry," Charley muttered, "but I didn't want the
kid to hear this." He turned toward the stairs to the
office, motioning with a wave of his hand for Laci to
follow.

She grabbed his arm as fear rippled through her
body, the look on his face telling her that something
was definitely wrong. Brant! Her heart lurched in terror. He was gone—or hurt. Her imagination immediately began to torture her with visions she didn't
want to see, memories of Sonny crashing, dying,

melding with the years-old fear that the same would happen to Brant. "What is it, Charley? Tell me, now, what's happened?"

He paused and turned back to face her. Anger blazed from his eyes. "I…" Charley stopped abruptly as a cowboy passed. "Some SOB broke into the arena last night," he said, his voice barely above a whisper.

"What?" she shrieked.

"Shhh." He waved a hand before her face. "Keep your voice down." He looked around furtively. "We don't need this getting out and making people nervous."

"Fine. What do you mean someone broke in? What did they do?"

"Ripped open all the feed sacks and threw the stuff everywhere. It's a mess. Then they poured oil on the bales of hay we got set aside for the stock. Damned good thing that feed shed we set up ain't in the thick of things or everybody and their brother would have seen that stuff and been talking."

Relief that Brant was all right was almost instantly overwhelmed by a surge of anger. "Wasn't it locked? Where was security?"

"Lock was busted. And as far as security—" he shrugged "—it could have been done anytime, Laci. Even this morning. Security makes rounds, but they can't watch every foot of this place every minute, and when the gates are open you know as well as I do that there's several hundred people coming and going around here at any given time."

"But who would do such a thing?"

His gray brows rose even as his age-weary eyes narrowed. The look she saw in them conveyed that she knew as well as Charley did who he believed was responsible.

"You don't think Judd did this?"

"Yeah," Charley snapped, "that's exactly what I think. In fact, it's just his style, underhanded."

"But why?" Laci said. "Why would he do something like this?"

"Why d'you think?" Charley said, but he wasn't looking at her anymore. Laci followed the direction of his gaze.

Kit was still standing in front of the refreshment stand, but he wasn't alone. Brant stood next to him, leaning a hip lazily against the stand, one arm resting on the booth's counter as he looked down at Kit. They were talking earnestly, as if sharing some big secret. Laci felt her heart skip a beat, but she wasn't quite certain if it was from the fear mounting over the bond that seemed to be all too easily forming between Kit and Brant, or nostalgia for what might have been, and wasn't.

"Judd wants you to fail, Laci," Charley said, pulling her attention back to the matter at hand, "and I think he'll do just about anything to make sure that happens, like poison the feed to throw off the schedule, which wouldn't make you look too good an operator to the local association or the PRCA. Especially after the way we lobbied to get the Championships held here when they couldn't do 'em in Vegas."

She tore her gaze from Kit and Brant and looked back at Charley. "I may not want to be married to him anymore, Charley, and part of me may not even like Judd anymore, but—" she shook her head "—he's the stock contractor for a good part of the

Wilderness and Mountain Pro Rodeo circuits. If he did something to sabotage us and it was discovered, he'd lose his Professional Rodeo Cowboy Association sanction, and that would finish him as a contractor.''

"Yeah, and you know as well as I do that Judd don't need the money from his contracting, Laci. He only contracts 'cause he likes staying around the rodeo. Makes him feel like a big man, wearing that Championship buckle and strutting around like a damned Banty rooster. But I don't much think the business end of things matters to him one way or the other.''

Laci began to pace, worrying the bridge of her nose with thumb and index fingers as she walked. "I don't know, Charley.''

"Colin Price seen him here last night.''

Laci felt her heart plunge to her toes and stopped her pacing to stare at Charley. "Colin, the maintenance man? He saw Judd here last night?''

Charley nodded. "Ain't proof, but it's something. Colin was late checking the paddocks. He'd had to take care of his little girl's mare after she hurt her leg kicking around in her stall. Anyway, Colin said he saw Judd's truck parked out near the entry when he left, but he didn't think nothing of it. Says he figured Judd just rode home with someone else.''

"Except Judd wouldn't leave that truck anywhere if he didn't have to. It's his baby.''

"Yep, that's what I figured.''

Laci felt anger sweep through her, overtaking the shock at having to admit to herself not only that Judd really did want her to fail, but that he'd stoop so low in an effort to have it happen. She would never have believed he could be so mean in his determination to get her to go back to him, but obviously she'd underestimated him. Or maybe he didn't want her back anymore, maybe he just wanted revenge against a woman who'd married him, promised to love and honor him, but had never loved him at all. And then she'd made matters worse: she'd left him. "Well, it's not going to work. If he thinks by doing things like this he can scare me, or ruin me into going back to him, or into bankruptcy, he's wrong. I'm not going back, and his schemes aren't going to slow us down or break us." Laci practically strangled her purse. "And I'm not going to fly into a rage, either, because he wants that, too."

"So, just what are you gonna do, missy?"

Laci smiled at Charley's use of her childhood pet name. "I'm going to clean up the mess and get new feed and hay in here before the animals get hungry, if I have to call every feed store or farmer between here and Sacramento." She turned toward the stairs, then paused and looked back at Kit. Her brow instantly furrowed into a frown.

Spinning on her heel Laci retraced her steps and approached Kit and Brant.

"Kit, I have to go up to the office, so you'd better come with me now."

Kit's smile disappeared instantly. "But, Mom…"

"Don't argue with me."

"He can stay with me for a while," Brant said. "I don't ride for hours yet."

Laci looked at Brant. *I don't want kids.* The words echoed through her mind again as he waited for her to respond. Had he changed? She didn't know, and she couldn't risk Kit's feelings. He'd already become too fond of Brant. "No, I don't think that's a good idea," she said finally. Laci looked down at Kit to see his eyes fill with tears. She felt like a louse, but it was better he be hurt now than later, when it could be much worse.

"I don't wanna go up there," Kit said, and kicked his booted toe in the dirt. A small plume of dust rose up from the ground. "I don't wanna."

"I'll watch him," Charley said, coming up behind her. "You go on and call Johnson, and tell him to pronto it with that feed and hay. After these animals get done tonight they're gonna be wanting some food."

Chapter 10

"Something wrong, Charley?" Brant stared after Laci as she climbed the stairs to the arena office.

"Yep."

He looked sharply at the older man. "What? What's wrong?"

Charley's brow remained furrowed. "Nothing Laci can't handle." He resettled his hat on his head and smiled, his thick gray mustache curving up at each end. "So, anyway, I thought I heard Kit say you were going to teach him some roping. Mind if I come along and watch?"

"Yeah!" Kit whooped. "Let's rope."

"Sure," Brant drawled hesitantly, "but Laci said…"

"Laci agreed that I'd watch the kid," Charley interrupted, "and I want to watch him learn some roping." He grabbed a soda from the counter of the refreshment stand and tossed a couple of coins into the donation bucket.

Kit giggled as the collie who belonged to the woman operating the refreshment stand walked up and rubbed against him, then licked his face. "Hey, no kisses, Lady," he protested, laughing again and rubbing the dog's ear.

"Kid sure looks like his pa, don't you think?" Charley said, eyeing Brant while taking a long swallow of soda.

"No, I don't," Kit snapped a bit peevishly. "I look like my Mom except I got black hair. She told me so. See," he said as he stuck his face out toward Charley, "she said I got her nose."

Charley laughed. "Yep, that's her sassy little nose all right."

Kit grabbed Brant's hand and tugged him toward the paddocks. "Come on, Brant, let's go rope."

Charley slapped his thigh and the barrel he was sitting on rocked slightly. "You know, champ," he said, chuckling, "you're getting so good with that lariat that by the time you're old enough to rodeo, there won't be a cowboy who can handle a rope better'n you."

Kit grinned. "I'm gonna be Champion All-Around Cowboy just like Brant. I'm gonna ride bulls, and broncs and rope steers and everything and beat everyone and win the titles and all the money, too."

Brant chuckled and corrected Kit's grip on the rope. "I haven't got the title yet, kiddo."

"Yeah, but you will," Kit quipped. "Hey, look at this, Charley." He twirled the rope in front of himself like Brant had taught him to do. "Pretty good, huh? And I can go faster, too. And hop."

"Jeez, move over Roy Rogers, here comes Kit Mc…" Charley cut himself off as he started to say McCandrick and thought better of it. He looked up at Brant.

"Who's Roy Rogers?" Kit asked. He stopped twirling and began to draw his rope into a tight coil.

"Who's…?" Charley looked down at Kit, clearly surprised. "You mean, you don't know who Roy Rogers is? Jeez, I don't believe it. Why, he's just one of the best cowboys there ever was, that's all."

"A little before our time," Brant added, and laughed.

"Watch it," Charley said with a mock snarl. "Before the kid's time maybe, but I ain't so sure about yours, Garrison."

"I like Wyatt Earp," Kit said. "He was really neat. And all his brothers. And Doc Holliday, too, but he was kinda sick. Mom bought the movie. She wasn't gonna let me see it…" A pout screwed up his face, then he laughed. "But I sneaked into the family room one night when she was watching it and hid by the couch and watched, too."

Brant tried to look impressed. "Boy, that was brave. Did you get caught?"

"Yeah, I didn't get to watch TV for a long time after that. But Mom let me watch the movie again 'cause I already saw it, so she says its okay." He grabbed Brant's sleeve. "*Tombstone*'s really neat-o. Wanna come over and watch it? Mom'll fix us popcorn."

"Yeah?" Brant hunkered down before him. "Wyatt Earp, huh?"

Kit nodded. "And I got lotsa other cowboy movies, too." He began describing them.

"You know," Brant said, when Kit finally ran down, "watching cowboy movies used to be one of my favorite things to do, when I was a kid. And it sounds like you've got a whole lot I've haven't seen."

"Maybe you could come over and we could watch some together and then you could cook Mom breakfast again."

Brant looked sheepishly at Charley. "Uh, yeah, right. Maybe I could."

"Breakfast, huh?" Charley said. He slapped his thighs and stood. He nodded to himself. "Breakfast. Well, I guess the song ain't over yet." He pulled a pocket watch from his vest pocket, flipped it open and glanced at it, then looked back at Brant. "About time you started getting ready for your ride, ain't it?"

"Can we go, too?" Kit asked. "To the chutes and watch him get on the bull?"

"Yeah, right," Charley sneered, "and then you could watch your mother tan my hide." He laughed. "No, I think we'd best watch from the office, champ. Better view from there anyway," Charley said. He stuck his hand out to Kit. "Come on, kid, we'd better get a move on before a posse comes looking for us."

Kit giggled and took Charley's hand.

"He'll be going with me," Judd said, sauntering up behind Charley.

Kit and Charley both turned.

Charley cursed silently at the entry gate's guard,

who was supposed to radio Charley a warning if Judd showed up. He glanced at the Rodeo badge on Judd's shirt that identified him as a stock contractor, and wished he could revoke it.

"Hi, Dad."

Brant stiffened. If there was one person in the world he could have happily gone through the rest of his life without seeing, it was Judd McCandrick.

"Come on, Kit." Judd reached for Kit's hand. "We're going to the ranch.

Kit jumped back, jerking his hand away.

"But I want to watch Brant ride. Mom said I could. He's gonna ride a bull and win Champion All-Around Cowboy, and I wanna see."

Judd sneered. "Is that so?"

Brant forced himself to remain silent. Kit didn't need to see him lose control, and Laci would not be exactly appreciative if Brant made a scene. And putting a fist into her ex-husband's mouth would definitely cause a scene.

"Yeah," Kit said. "He's gonna win more categories than you did, Dad, and money, too, then he'll be Champion All-Around Cowboy of the whole rodeo. Mom said so, she told me."

Judd's features tightened.

"Leave it alone, Judd," Charley said under his breath.

Judd threw Brant a murderous glare, then turned and pinned it on Charley. "Stay out of this, old man. Me and mine aren't any of your business."

"You're wrong there."

Judd grabbed the front of Charley's shirt and pulled him forward, their faces ending up only inches apart,

Charley forced to look up, Judd glaring down like a crazed giant.

Brant stepped forward, knowing he couldn't let this go any further. "You want to try that on someone your own age and size?" he said, more threat instilled within the softly spoken words than if he'd have snarled or yelled them.

Judd released Charley with a shove and turned to glower at Brant. "Maybe another time, Garrison," he growled. "I don't have any to waste right now." He turned to Kit. "Come on, Kit, we're going home."

"No." Kit spun around and grabbed Brant's leg, wrapping his small arms around it and hugging tightly. "I don't wanna go with you, I wanna stay here."

"Damn it, quit acting like a baby," Judd snapped. He made a grab for Kit. "Now come on."

"No." Kit shied away but didn't release his hold on Brant's leg.

"Why, you little brat!" Judd lunged forward again.

Brant grabbed Kit and stepped in front of him, shielding him from Judd. Something was wrong here, and he sensed it was a hell of a lot more than a kid just not wanting to go home and miss the rodeo. "He doesn't want to go with you, McCandrick."

Judd's face, already colored with rage, twisted into a ugly sneer and his gaze spit hatred. "Yeah, well as long as he's got my name, Garrison, he'll do what I want him to do. Now get the hell out of the way."

"No, I don't wanna go," Kit screamed. "I don't wanna go."

Spinning on his heel, Charley ran toward the office.

"Maybe I should just call the police," Judd said.

"Have you arrested for refusing to hand over my kid."

"Go ahead," Brant dared back, calling Judd's bluff. "If Laci wants him to go with you, fine. But she left him in my and Charley's care, and until she says different Kit isn't going anywhere with you or anyone else."

Judd lunged again. "Get the hell out of the way, Garrison, or I'll beat the crap out of both of you."

Brant caught Judd by the shirt collar and swung him around. "I don't think so, McCandrick," he snarled softly.

Kit tore away from Brant and ran toward the office. "Mom! Mom!"

Laci and Charley were already halfway down the stairs. She bent down and grabbed Kit as he nearly propelled himself into her arms.

"Mom, Mom, Dad and Brant are fighting." He spun around and charged back down the stairs, waving at her. "Come on, hurry, Mom."

She ran toward the paddocks, Charley nearly on her heels.

Brant's fist smashed into Judd's cheekbone just as Laci rounded a corner of the paddock. Judd stumbled back and crashed into the gate of one of the horse stalls. The animal inside whinnied loudly and thrashed about, startled. Judd pushed himself up and charged Brant.

"Judd, stop!" Laci screamed.

He swung, hard and fast.

Brant ducked, but Laci's scream had distracted him and he didn't duck quite enough. Judd's fist connected with Brant's shoulder. Pain shot through his collarbone and arm. He cursed and swung his own fist. It connected with Judd's jaw and sent him flying back against the paddock wall again.

A thin trickle of blood snaked its way down Judd's chin from the corner of his mouth. He wiped it off with the back of his hand and pushed away from the wall, turning his glare on first Brant, then Laci, and back to Brant. "Hope you liked throwing that punch, buddy-boy, 'cause it just cost you your career in rodeo. By the time I get through, you won't be riding anywhere ever again."

"Judd, please," Laci said, thinking to reason him into leaving.

He shot forward, startling her with the abrupt speed of his steps, and grabbed her arm. "Please, what?" His black gaze bore into hers. "Please leave my lover alone? Is that what you wanted to say?"

"Leave her alone, McCandrick," Brant ordered, and moved up behind him.

Judd swung his arm out, pushing Brant away. Brant stumbled backward into a stack of crates and lost his footing. His elbow smashed into the paddock wall.

Laci jerked free of Judd.

Kit ran up to Brant, excitedly jumping about. "Are you okay, Brant? Your elbow's bleeding."

Brant tried to push himself off the broken grates, ignoring the pain in his arm.

Judd glowered at Laci. "Please what, Laci? Just forget that I married you, kept you respectable, after lover boy here ran off?"

Brant froze in his struggle to get to his feet, and stared at Laci. *Kept her respectable?* What the hell did he mean by that? He looked at Laci, then his gaze darted to Kit, and the thought he'd had the other day, the one he'd shrugged away as a ridiculous one, filled his mind.

"Judd, stop," she yelled.

"I gave you a home, Laci. I gave you love, took care of your old man's business, and gave that bratty little snot-nosed kid everything you wanted him to have! I gave you everything Garrison wouldn't, but you still always loved him, didn't you?"

He could have said anything he'd wanted about her, she probably deserved it, but it had been just plan cruel to pick on Kit. Any warm feelings she'd had left toward Judd were gone.

Laci tore her gaze from his and glanced at Charley. "Take Kit to the office."

Charley grabbed Kit's hand. "Come on, champ."

"No, I wanna stay."

Brant moved to stand beside Laci. Blood trickled down his arm, staining his shirt, but he didn't notice. "Leave it be, McCandrick," he said, his words low and hard.

Judd laughed. "You'd like that, wouldn't you, Garrison?

"What's the matter, finally come to realize that you're just not good enough to win the big money? Figured that since Laci inherited James Enterprises you'd just waltz back in her and pick up where you left off and start living the easy life, off her?"

Laci turned a hard look on her son. "Kit, do as I say. Go to the office with Charley. Now!" She whirled back on Judd the moment Charley and Kit were out of hearing range. "You snake!" she raged, angrier than she'd ever been in her life. "How could you say those things in front of Kit? How could you...?"

"You belong to me," Judd snarled. "I married you, gave you everything. You belong to me, Laci."

"No."

"She doesn't belong *to* anyone," Brant said.

Judd's eyes narrowed. He glanced at Brant, then turned a cold glare back on Laci. "You ungrateful bitch."

"Judd, don't."

"You'll be sorry for this, Laci," Judd said. The soft, dead tone his voice had dropped to was almost more menacing and unnerving than his bellowing had been. His eyes narrowed and his handsome face took on a diabolic slant as he scowled down at her. "You're going to be more sorry than you've ever thought you could be, sweetheart."

"I already am," Laci said, thinking of all the things she'd done in the past that had been wrong. If only she could go back in time. She never should have said no to Brant when he'd asked her to go on the circuit with him all those years ago. She never should have kept the fact that she was carrying his child from him, and she never should have married Judd. But most of all she should never have denied to herself how much she loved Brant Garrison, then and now.

She had been so afraid of losing him to a horrible death, like Sonny, that she'd let Brant walk out of her life and had lost him anyway. She'd tried to console herself with the belief that the fear for him hadn't been the only reason she'd said no to going with him. All her life, all she'd ever wanted was marriage, a home, a stable life in one place, one town—but what good was having all of that if she couldn't share it, and her life, with the man she loved?

Judd turned his ugly glare on Brant and laughed. "Take the slut, Garrison. I don't want her anymore."

Brant's temper snapped. "You rotten son of a…"

Judd's arm snapped up just as Brant's swung out, his hand clenched into a fist.

A second later three cowboys came around the far corner of the paddocks, saw the scuffle, and rushed forward to break Brant and Judd apart.

Snarling another threat, Judd pulled free and stalked toward the entry gate.

Laci turned to walk to the office. She'd had enough. She was shaking with rage and nerves, and about the only thing she wanted right now was a quiet corner where she could sit for the next hundred years and pretend none of this had happened. But after taking only a few steps she paused and looked back at Brant. She had to tell him the truth.

He shrugged off the cowboys who'd pulled him away from Judd. "I'm all right, let me go." He curled his shoulders and straightened his shirt, then scooped his Stetson up from the ground and slammed it down on his head. It was then that he noticed Laci hadn't left, but was standing only a few yards away, watching him. He stalked to where she stood. "Damn bas— Are you all right?"

She nodded. "I need to talk to you," she said, the words barely offered above a whisper.

He nodded. It was time to find out what Judd McCandrick had meant about knowing a truth Laci didn't want out. And that he'd kept her respectable by marrying her. Brant took her arm and led her away from the paddocks to a row of trailers parked at the rear of the grounds. Weaving about several, he finally stopped at one, opened the door and motioned for her to enter. "Welcome to my humble abode. Nothing fancy, but a place we can talk."

She stepped past him, instilled with a sudden lightheartedness at finally having decided to tell him the truth, yet at the same time dreading it and feeling as if she were walking toward her own doom.

The interior of the trailer was small, compact. Everything neat and clean, but old and worn. All the necessities were crammed into one tiny package, with no frills or extras. Laci sat on the only chair, a dropdown seat beside a drop down table no more than two feet by two feet.

Brant sat on the built-in bed beyond her.

She didn't turn to look at him. Instead, Laci sucked in a deep breath and turned to look out through the tiny window set over the table. "Seven and a half years ago I refused to go on the circuit with you."

"I know."

"What you don't know is why."

Brant felt a chill of fear. Did he want to hear this?

"A few years before I met you I thought I was in love with a boy I'd gone to school with. His name was Sonny."

"What happened?" Brant asked, still not certain he wanted to know. Would this help to abolish the problems that still existed between them, still kept them apart, or only make them worse?

"He was racing his motorcycle one night. His front tire blew, the bike jackknifed, and Sonny flew over the handlebars. He died instantly." She turned and looked at Brant. "Then I met and fell in love with you. But that time I watched you ride, and the bull threw you off I remembered Sonny. After that, every time I tried to watch you ride, I remembered the crash, remembered watching Sonny die, and I was terrified the same thing was going to happen to you." Tears streamed down her cheeks. "I couldn't bring myself to watch you die."

Brant reached out and took one of her hands in his. "Why didn't you tell me?"

She shook her head. "I don't know." She shrugged. "I guess I thought you'd stay after you knew you could work for my father. When you said no, I figured you just didn't love me."

"You couldn't have been farther from the truth," Brant whispered.

Laci didn't pause at his words, she couldn't, because she knew if she did, if she stopped talking, she'd never be able to confess the rest—the part she feared he'd hate her for.

"After you left, I was devastated, but then a month later I discovered I was pregnant."

Her last word went through him like an electrical shock, jarring every cell in his body, slamming against his brain like a freight train into a brick wall. "Pregnant?" he muttered.

She nodded.

"I didn't know what to do. You were gone, my parents were furious. Judd had already started coming over to the house a lot, supposedly talking stock contracting with my father. My father told him I was pregnant and Judd offered to marry me."

Brant felt himself stiffen. God, what had he done?

"I didn't want to marry him, but he kept coming over. My parents really liked him, and he kept saying he'd always been in love with me. I kept waiting for you to come back, to call...." A sigh ripped from her throat. "But you didn't, and I began to tell myself I hated you. I was almost four months pregnant when Judd and I got married."

"Why didn't you try to contact me?" Brant said. He was still holding her hand, but his grip had tightened. "You could have called any number of people. Someone would have been able to locate me, tell you where I was. Even the PRCA."

She shrugged. "Everyone said you hadn't really loved me." She looked into his eyes then. "I was nineteen, Brant. I loved you, desperately, and you'd left me. You wouldn't quit rodeoing for me. Judd offered me everything you wouldn't, and my parents were so happy, they liked him, so I finally said okay to his proposal."

He dropped his head, silently damning himself, damning her.

"But I never did fall in love with Judd, because I never stopped loving you."

He looked back at her. "You had my son, and you never even tried to find me, to tell me." He struggled to contain the anger and frustration roiling inside of him. "I had a right to know, Laci."

"I know."

"Why didn't you tell me when I came back?"

Tears clogged her throat. "I...I wanted to, but...I was afraid...you wouldn't stay and Kit..." She choked back a sob. "I..."

Brant rose and stalked to the opposite end of the

trailer, all of about six feet from Laci. He yanked off his hat, instantly slammed it back onto his head, and whirled around. "He's my son, Laci. You had no right not to tell me."

"I had every right," Laci snapped back, hurt and anger melding within her and pulling the words from her heart. "You said you didn't want children."

His eyes darkened as a frown drew on his brow. "What?"

"We talked once, about our plans, about having a life together, and you said you didn't want children. *That's* what I remembered when I found out I was pregnant."

"But, Laci, I..."

"You didn't love me enough to stay when I asked you to, Brant," Laci said, hurrying on before the courage to say the words that needed to be said deserted her. "So why should I have believed you would come back for a child you'd said you didn't even want?"

The love, forgiveness, and understanding she'd hoped to see on his face, in his eyes, wasn't there. She shivered. His every feature had turned rigid, hard and cold, his eyes dark with black, smoldering rage. She watched as he drew himself inward again, reining in his emotions so tightly that the blaze of anger that shadowed his face paled beneath the chill she felt emanating from his body. Her heart cried out to him, begged him not to go, not to leave her again, but it was too late.

He stared at her for what seemed an eternity, his very stance questioning and accusing. She'd always heard there was a fine line between love and hate, and

Laci felt certain that she had pushed him too far. Whatever love Brant Garrison had felt for her was gone.

He opened his mouth to say something, then clamped it shut again. There was nothing more to say, not now. Later maybe, but not now. He walked to the door, kicked it open, and left the trailer, striding past the paddocks to the chutes. He had a ride scheduled, then he was going to... He slammed a fist against one of the chute rails. The bull standing on the other side snorted loudly and shook its head. Brant grabbed his gloves from his back pocket and tugged them on. He was going to finish his ride and then what? He didn't know. Maybe he'd find a bar and get drunk. Or drive into the mountains until he got lost. Maybe he'd find Judd again and beat his ugly face to a pulp. Or confront Laci again, demand to know how she could possibly say she loved him, and yet keep the fact that they had a son from him. All four options sounded good, but they'd have to wait. Right now he had a job to do.

His ride was a good one. Maybe the fury filling his chest had helped. It didn't matter how high the bull kicked, how fast or abruptly he spun and writhed, Brant rode him, and the crowd loved it.

As the clowns ushered the bull back to the pens, Brant jumped down from the rails he'd leapt onto when the Brahma had charged around looking for a target to attack after Brant slid off his back. Pulling his gloves off, he walked toward the gate. He didn't want to look up at the windows of the office, damned himself for even thinking of it, and found himself unable to resist the urge. But it didn't matter. All he saw was the silver glass reflecting the lights of the arena and an image of the people in the stands.

On the scoreboard the lights lit up and the spectators cheered even louder. Brant stopped at the gate and glanced back. Ninety-four. He smiled and waved to the crowd. It was the highest score so far, and the highest he'd ever gotten for bull riding. He knew he should feel good. He was going to make it. Unless one of the other contestants pulled a rabbit from his hat, Brant had the Championship, and at the moment he didn't give a damn.

Several cowboys came up and slapped him on the back, congratulating him on his ride. Brant forced himself to smile and laugh with them, but kept on walking away from the chutes. For the first time in his life he wanted nothing more than to get away from the rodeo, away from everyone he knew, and just be alone.

He left his pickup in the parking lot and walked toward downtown. He didn't have a particular destination in mind, or even a specific direction, it just happened to be the way he turned upon leaving the fairgrounds.

Hours later he was still walking, paying no attention to the casinos or people he passed. The streets could have been deserted or crowded, Brant wouldn't have noticed. His thoughts traveled through the past in an effort to make sense of the present, but it didn't help. No matter how he looked at it, she had lied to him. Laci had purposely not told him that Kit was his son.

Brant slammed a fist against the concrete wall at

his side, as if the physical pain the impact brought might take his mind off the thoughts tormenting him. It didn't.

Hours later Brant was still walking. He'd passed every downtown casino at least three times, drawing suspicious looks from some of the hawkers and security guards. But he neither cared nor noticed. The heat of the day had cooled with the onset of evening, and with the passing of evening into night the air had chilled further, the coldness of it cutting through the threads of his cotton shirt, but he didn't notice that either. He was too lost in thought, too mired in memories of the past and present, betrayals and lies.

All the things he'd said to her so long ago came back to haunt him. Maybe if they had talked then none of this would have happened—maybe she would have told him she was pregnant, or gone on the circuit with him. And maybe things would have turned out just the same.

"Maybe," Brant growled, drawing the startled stare of the hawker he strode past.

Thinking of all the things he should have done, should have said, all the things that could have been but weren't, was not going to change what the situation was now. And all the maybes in the world weren't going to help, either.

Laci had given birth to his child, but she'd married Judd McCandrick. She'd given Brant's son McCandrick's last name, and she'd let Kit think McCandrick was his father.

Brant felt as if he could explode with the rage and frustration churning about inside him.

* * *

Laci sat in the dark family room, nestled into one corner of the sofa, and stared through the patio doors. A panorama of scenery spread out before her, partly shadowed by the cloak of darkness, partly illuminated by the moon's light. But she wasn't really conscious of any of it, not the bright lights of the casinos in the valley far below, the stars dotting the sky above, or the golden sliver of moon hanging just above the ragged mountaintops in the distance. Instead she saw Brant's face, and remembered the hard, cold set of his features as he'd looked at her after she'd told him that Kit was his son.

Tears slipped from her eyes. If there had been a chance for them, it was gone now. If he had loved her at all, the truth had killed it. She'd tried to protect their son the best she knew how—but she didn't need to hear Brant say the words to know that he viewed what she'd done as a betrayal. She had seen that in his eyes, heard it in his voice, but worst of all, she now felt it in her own heart. "How could I have been so blind?" she mumbled into the dark room. "So wrong?"

She pushed off the sofa and walked across the room, stopping in front of the sliding glass doors. For years she'd done what she'd thought was best for her son. Now she was consumed with the horrible thought that everything she'd done had been wrong. She'd hurt Judd, she'd hurt Brant, and in the end she'd hurt her own child.

"Mom?"

Laci turned at hearing Kit's voice.

"Mom?"

She hurried down the hallway to his room, softly

lit by the night-light beside his bed. Judd had hated the idea of Kit being afraid of the dark, always yelling about how Laci giving him a night-light was only spoiling him and turning him into a sissy. "What's wrong, honey?" She moved to his bed and sat on the edge of the mattress. Light from the hallway shone into the room through the now open doorway and cut a path across his bed.

"Why were Dad and Brant fighting today?"

She reached out and smoothed the hair back from his forehead. "Kit, I have something to tell you that I should have told you a long time ago."

"A story?"

Laci smiled. "Kind of, yes, but this one is true."

He folded his arms over the blanket that covered his chest. "Good, that's the best kind. What's it about?"

She took a deep breath and plunged in. "A long time ago Brant was my boyfriend."

"You mean like Chrissy Parks is my friend Billy's girlfriend?"

Laci laughed. "Well, kind of yes. But we were a lot older than Chrissy and Billy, and Brant had to go away...."

"To follow the rodeo?"

"Yes."

"How come you didn't go with him? Did your mom say no?"

"No, she didn't say no, but I was afraid. Anyway, a few weeks later I found out I was going to have you.

"Dad...Judd and I got married a little after that. But what I'm trying to say is..." Laci inhaled deeply as her mind searched for just the right words. "What I'm trying to say is that when Judd and I married I was already pregnant, Kit, with you."

"Oh." He smiled. "You mean I was already inside your tummy like you told me before?"

"Yes."

He nodded. "Okay. But where was Brant then? At the rodeo?"

"Yes, far away at the rodeo."

"And you and Dad had me."

He didn't understand. She felt like a knife was twisting inside of her heart at just the thought that what she was trying to get him to understand would hurt him. "Honey, we had you but," she paused again, closing her eyes and praying for the strength to do what she knew she had to do.

"Is Brant my real dad?"

Laci felt a start of surprise. Kit had always been a very wise child, mature beyond his years, but she hadn't really expected him to jump to that conclusion, even if it was the right one. She took his small hand in hers. "Yes, honey, Brant is your real dad."

Kit smiled. "Good."

"You're okay with that?"

"Yeah, I think it's neat. And now I look like my dad, huh?"

Laci frowned. "What?"

"Well, Billy looks like his dad, and so does Tommy Harkins. And Chrissy looks like her mom."

"Yes?" Laci said, somewhat confused.

"See, Mom, me and Mrs. Dabney was talking one day about babies, after her cat had kittens, remember?"

Laci nodded.

"And she told me…"

"The cat?" Laci asked.

Kit laughed. "No, Mrs. Dabney. She told me that the kitties were black and white 'cause that's what their mom and dad were, and she said it was the same with kids, that we always have the same color hair and eyes that our moms and dads have. But you've got yellow hair and Dad…I mean…" He frowned.

"Judd?" Laci supplied.

"Yeah, Judd, he's got brown hair. But my hair is black, like Brant's, so now I look like my dad, too, huh?"

He'd sensed something was wrong and never said anything. Laci's eyes filled with tears. "How in heaven's name did I ever have such a smart little boy?" She ruffled his hair with her fingers.

Kit giggled. "You were lucky."

Laci laughed, then leaned over and kissed his cheek. "Yes, I am. Very lucky."

"I'm glad Brant's my real dad, Mom. I like him. Is he gonna come live with us now?"

She smiled. "I don't think so, honey. Brant is still a rodeo cowboy, which means he has to go where the rodeo goes."

"But doesn't he have to live somewhere sometime? Like a headquarters or something? Like soldiers and stuff have?"

Laci thought about that for a few seconds. "He said he had a ranch in Montana, I think. Remember? He mentioned it when we were at the pizza parlor."

Kit smiled. "Oh, yeah. But, why can't he come live

with us, I mean, if he's my real dad!'' He sat up. ''Are we gonna go live on his ranch?''

''He has his own way of life, Kit, and this is our home, but I'm sure he'll come visit often.''

''Do I half to keep calling Dad…ah, Judd, Dad? Can I call Brant Dad now? I don't have to go to Dad's…Judd's ranch anymore, do I? 'Cause I don't want to. He always yells at me, especially about being afraid of the dark. Is Brant gonna yell at me, Mom, for being afraid of the dark? Do you think he's ever afraid of anything? I bet not. I…''

''Kit, slow down,'' Laci said, laughing. ''You're supposed to be going to sleep.''

He looked at her solemnly. ''Okay, but do I have to keep calling him Dad?''

She shook her head. ''No, you can call him Judd, and you don't have to go to his ranch anymore if you don't want to.'' She smiled. ''And I'm sure Brant won't yell at you because you're afraid of the dark.''

A frown cut across his brow. ''Should I call him Dad?''

Laci wished with all her heart she could change this entire situation—go back to the beginning and do it all over again—differently. ''I think you'd better just keep calling him Brant, honey, unless he asks you to call him Dad. Okay?''

He nodded. ''Okay. Are you mad at him, Mom?''

''No, honey, I'm not mad at Brant. Why?''

He settled back upon his pillow, looking very thoughtful and suddenly very grown-up. '''Cause he got into a fight, and you always told me it was wrong to fight.''

''Yes, but sometimes you have to do things that are

wrong even if you don't want to.'' She saw his face screw into an expression of puzzlement.

"You mean he didn't want to fight?"

"No, I don't think he did, but Judd was mad."

"So Judd was wrong. He started the fight, huh?"

Laci sighed. She didn't want Kit to think ill of Judd, but she couldn't pretend that what had happened tonight hadn't. "Yes," she said finally, "he was wrong. Now," she leaned over and gave him another kiss, "I want you to forget about all of that and go to sleep, okay?"

He smiled and yawned, raising a curled hand to rub at one eye. "Okay. But are you mad at Dad…I mean Judd, 'cause he started a fight?"

Laci smiled. "Yes, and I'll be mad at you, too, if you don't go to sleep right now."

He snuggled beneath the covers. "Okay. G'night."

She walked back into the family room, glancing at the kitchen table as she passed it, then at the sofa, and finally at the spot on the floor where she'd lain with Brant, where they had held each other. Had that only been last night? A mere handful of hours ago? At the moment it seemed like ages. She wanted him with her so badly she could feel the ache of need gnawing at her insides. But that was something she was going to have to learn to live with…again.

Then I'll have to try again next year. The words Brant had spoken that morning at the kitchen table, in answer to Kit's question about what he'd do if he didn't win the Championship this year, had been haunting her all day. She'd tried not to think about what he'd said, about how his words had nearly cut her heart in two and once again shattered dreams she been afraid to admit she even had. But not thinking about it was impossible. His words were always there, in her mind, blending with those he'd said all those years ago. *I'm not the settling-down kind. I don't want kids. I'll have to try again next year.* They were like a tormenting echo in her head, whispering through her mind repeatedly when she was thinking of Brant, screaming at her when she tried to concentrate on anything else.

She moved to stand before the window again. Brant was no nearer quitting the rodeo and settling down to a normal life now than he had ever been. He hadn't wanted that life then, hadn't wanted her or children, so why should she think he'd want those things now? He was angry because she hadn't told him he had a son, but that didn't mean he was ready to accept the day-to-day responsibility of having a son.

Tears stung her eyes and fell over her lashes, streaming down her cheeks.

Chapter 11

Brant walked past the Cyclone fence and onto the rodeo grounds, his back ramrod straight, shoulders stiffer than the arena fencing. He didn't look up at the office to his left, or even in that direction. Instead he walked directly to the registration trailer, re-checked the scheduled times for his rides, and got his number pinned to the back of his shirt. He'd dressed in all black. Silver conchos lined the outer seams of his chaps and the leather band on his hat, and he wore the silver buckle he'd won for World Champion Saddle Bronc Rider two years ago. But as far as color went that was it, except for the large white square of paper with its black number forty-nine pinned to the back of his shirt. It hadn't been a conscious thing, dressing in all black, but at seeing his reflection in the trailer's window as he passed, Brant figured it was probably appropriate, a reflection of his mood and temper.

He tried to push those thoughts from his mind. Concentration on riding was what he needed tonight. He walked up the steps of the Justin Medical Trailer. His leg had been throbbing all afternoon, most likely as a result of walking over half the city's concrete last night, like a fool.

The nurse inside the trailer smiled and waved him to a chair. "The leg?" she asked.

"Yeah. I want to have it wrapped," Brant said. "Just to be on the safe side."

She nodded and grabbed a roll of elastic bandage.

Brant sat on the examining table and swung his leg up onto it, pushing his fringed chaps aside, kicking off his boot, and pulling up his pant leg. He was too close to winning to blow it now by taking any stupid chances.

While the nurse worked on wrapping his leg, he stared at the skylight overhead. He'd known, deep down, that coming back to Reno and seeing Laci again would tear into his gut and open old wounds that had never really healed. He'd known, somehow, that his life would change, with or without winning the World Championship, and he'd been right. He just hadn't expected it to change the way it had. That he'd see her again, have to face the fact that he still loved her but she didn't love him, or at least not enough to accept him for who and what he was—all of that he'd expected. He'd dreaded it, but he'd expected it.

What he hadn't expected, what he never would have guessed in a million years, was that he had a son. He never would have believed that she would carry their child inside of her, that she would give birth to their child, without even trying to find him and tell him. Or that she could marry Judd Mc-Candrick and let Brant's son, and the rest of the world, believe that McCandrick was his real father. Even now, after Brant had come back, after she'd made love to him, she still hadn't planned to tell him.

That knowledge cut into him like a knife slicing slowly, cruelly, through his heart. He felt the anger, the rage and frustration of all those lost years burn inside him. He had missed seeing his own son as a baby, missed seeing him learn to walk and talk, missed his first tooth, his first day of school, his first time on a horse.

Thanking the nurse when she finished, Brant shoved his foot back into his boot, straightened his pant leg, and left the trailer.

"Hey, Garrison."

He turned at hearing Charley's voice, and watched the older man stride hurriedly toward him. "Yeah, what?"

"Look, kid, I know it ain't any of my business, but I gotta tell you, Laci didn't..."

"That's right, Charley," Brant said, cutting him off. "What's between Laci and me isn't any of your business, so let's just keep it that way, huh?" He turned and strode away. His ride was scheduled to take place in half an hour, and that didn't give him a whole lot of time to look over the bull he'd drawn and get himself psyched up.

"Garrison."

Brant stopped and spun around. "Charley, I don't have time for this," he snapped, biting each word off curtly.

"What happened, back then, years ago, I mean, it

wasn't her fault, Garrison. She was young and scared and…''.

"Yeah, well so was I, Charley, but everybody damns me just the same.'' Suddenly he didn't care who heard. He was no longer aware of the others standing nearby who'd turned to look at him. "I'm the one who wouldn't give up the rodeo and stay here and work for her old man, but nobody ever asked my reasons, or even if I had any. Not even Laci. I'm just the SOB who got her pregnant, left her and didn't come back. Me. Brant Garrison. I did that, but nobody gives a royal damn that I didn't know she was pregnant, that she didn't even have the decency to tell me.''

Laci stood at the door of the office, each word Brant spoke like a slap to her face. He was right. Everything he said was true, but she couldn't do anything about the past. It was over. All she could do was plan for the future, and protect Kit.

"What ya gonna do?'' Charley asked.

"I'm going to ride, Charley. I'm going to win my points, win that damned Championship buckle, collect my money and get the hell out of Reno, Nevada. Satisfied now?''

"No.''

Brant spun on his heel. "Tough,'' he yelled back over his shoulder. Every muscle in his body was tight with tension, every nerve as taut as a stretched rubber band. He'd hold it together just long enough to finish this thing, then he was out of here. It had to be that way, because it was the only way he'd be able to survive. In a few months, maybe, he'd come back and establish a permanent relationship with Kit, the kind they should have had all along. He had a son, and by all that was saintly his son was going to know his real father. But Brant wasn't going to be able to accomplish that until he found a way to deal with the anger he felt toward Laci.

Twenty minutes later, after prowling the grounds like a dog in desperate need of someone to bite, he strode through the chute area, grabbed a top railing and climbed up. "Bodacious ready?" he asked one of the chute hands.

"Ready and in one helluva bad temper," the man answered.

"Good. That makes two of us." Brant dropped down onto the bull's back and slipped his hand under the grip rope. "We oughta get along just fine." He tightened his grip and pounded on his bent and gloved fingers with his other hand, as if to settle them in place. His name was announced over the loudspeaker.

Brant tugged on the front of his hat's brim, held his left arm up in the air and nodded to the gate man. "Let's go."

The gate swung open and Bodacious charged into the arena.

Laci stood behind the silver window and looked down into the arena, watching Brant ride. Her heart was in her throat, but she wouldn't look away. She would watch him ride no matter how terrified she was. He'd be gone soon, this time most likely forever, so she had to store up all the memories she could before then.

"Wow, Mom, look at him go," Kit said, jumping up and down beside her.

She looked down at her son. There was a new tone to his voice, to his excitement now. Before, when he'd watch the contestants, they were just strangers or acquaintances riding the bulls and broncs. But this time it was his own father atop that one-ton mass of angry, dangerous animal.

The buzzer blared. Brant swung a leg hastily over Bodacious's shoulder hump and jumped from the animal's back. The clowns ran toward the bull. Brant's bad leg gave out as he hit the ground and he stumbled, but regained his footing quickly and ran to the rails as Bodacious pranced haughtily back toward the pens.

Brant turned toward the scoreboard. Laci and Kit did the same. It lit up and the crowd roared their approval and Brant waved to them.

"A hundred! Mom, wow, look, he got a hundred."

The deep, blaring honk of a truck horn drew her attention. Laci frowned. There were no deliveries expected this late, and that sounded like a big rig, which definitely shouldn't be on the grounds at this time. "Kit, stay here. I'll be right back."

Brant stood at the end of the cattle chutes and watched as several large cattle trucks pulled past the Cyclone fence. He frowned as the one in the lead drove directly toward where he stood. "What the…?"

"Hey, get those things outta here," Charley yelled, running out of the registration trailer and waving at the approaching trucks.

The drivers ignored him and kept the trucks rolling forward.

Laci ran down the office stairs. "What's going on?" She looked up at the cab of the first truck and her heart thudded madly against her breast. Judd sat in the passenger seat, a nasty grin on his face.

"Hey, Mom." Kit scooted down the stairs. "Billy's mom just called the office to see if I could go over to the carnival with them. Could I, huh? Please? She said they'd meet me at the crossing gate. Please?"

Laci glanced down at him. "Okay," she said hurriedly, sensing what was about to happen and not wanting him anywhere around to hear. "But be back in an hour, okay? And don't talk to any strangers." She handed him the change from her pocket. "Remember our secret word if anyone tries to say I sent them."

"Okay." He skipped away.

The truck stopped a few yards from the cattle pens. Laci, along with everyone else who'd seen them enter, stalked toward the huge vehicle. The driver climbed down and began opening the trailer's loading chutes. Judd sauntered around the front of the cab, then stopped to lean on its red fender, waiting for Laci.

"What are you doing?" she demanded, stopping a few feet from him and not wanting to get any closer.

"I've come to get my cattle," he said easily.

Laci felt dumbstruck. "Get your cattle? You can't take the cattle now. We're in the middle of the rodeo."

"Yeah? Well, sorry, but I was looking at these pens this morning and, frankly, they look pretty unsafe to me." He grinned nastily. "And I heard a rumor there was oil in some of the hay the other day.'' He shook his head. ''Can't take chances on my animals getting sick or hurt from things like that, Laci. They're too valuable.''

''Judd, you know that's not true. The pens are safe, and the food is, too. There's nothing wrong.''

''I don't agree. I'm breaking my contract and taking my stock.''

''You can't.''

''Watch me,'' Judd growled.

''You'll ruin the Championships. You'll lose your PRCA standing. They'll sue you.''

He shrugged. ''I'm getting tired of playing around with the rodeo anyway. I can make more money selling this beef off as hamburger and playing the stock market.''

''But you love the rodeo,'' Laci said, trying to reason with him. ''You've always loved it.''

''Yeah,'' his gaze turned ugly, black and mean. ''I used to love you, too. So what? Things change.''

Twenty minutes later his trucks pulled out of the rodeo grounds and rumbled down the street toward the highway, along with all of the contracted stock. Laci looked at the crowd milling about. ''I guess we're canceled,'' she said, feeling suddenly like a balloon that had just been popped.

''Like hell!'' Brant roared, pushing his way through the crowd. ''I didn't come all this way, ride all year, and get my first perfect score, just to have the damned World Championships cancelled before I win the blasted thing.''

The others murmured and nodded in agreement. Several cowboys shouted out their support.

Charley pushed his way to her side. "I called some of the other contractors in the area. California, Oregon, Utah. They're all booked up. Can't supply us much of anything. I called the PRCA to see if they could help." He shook his head. "No dice, but they are going to pull his sanction. Too bad they can't hang him."

Laci looked at Brant, then at the others all looking at her, waiting for her to say something, come up with some way to fix what had just happened. But how was she supposed to do that? The only thing that might change Judd's mind was if she ran after him and said she'd go back to him, be his wife again—and she couldn't do that. She took a deep breath. "Then there's nothing else we can do," she said, forcing herself to look into the eyes of each person surrounding her and face their disappointment.

"And I said, like hell!" Brant snapped again. Turning away abruptly he stormed toward the office. Halfway up the stairs he turned and looked down at the gathered contestants. "Don't you go anywhere, any of you! We've all come too far to give up now. The rest of tonight's rides may be postponed, but this damned rodeo sure as hell isn't canceled."

Stalking into the office, he straddled a chair, picked up the phone and dialed. "Losing his sanction isn't enough," Brant muttered, listening to the phone ring. "He should be tarred and feathered and run out of town. Stripped naked and staked out in the desert, with wet leather thongs around his head and chest and honey poured all over him."

Laci ran up the stairs with Charley right behind her. "What are you doing?" she asked Brant.

He glanced over his shoulder. "You want this rodeo to go on?" He practically snarled the question at her, his eyes so dark from the anger exploding within him she'd swear there wasn't a hint of blue left, merely fathomless black.

Laci jammed clenched fists onto her hips. "Of course I want the rodeo to go on, but I don't see how…"

A voice said hello in Brant's ear.

Brant turned his attention back to the phone. "Yeah, is Chuck Lynch there? This is Brant Garrison."

Laci walked to the desk and sat on the chair set at its end, since Brant was sitting in hers. She needed to call her attorney, she knew that, and dreaded it. But she had to take steps to protect James Enterprises from whatever repercussions Judd's actions might cause. First though, she wanted to know what Brant was doing.

"Yeah, Chuck, listen, we've got a problem at the Championships, the contractor pulled his cattle. No, there's no disease, unless it's in his brain."

Laci watched Brant smile at whatever the person on the other end of the phone said.

"Yeah. Listen, can you help us out? Great, what have you got available?" He grabbed a pencil and a scratch pad and began jotting down numbers and words. "Terrific. No, transport's no problem, I'll arrange it. How fast can you have them ready? I need them here by tomorrow." He nodded. "Good. I owe you one, buddy. Yeah, I'll put in a word for you with the owner here. She'll be looking for a new contractor."

The minute he hung the phone up, Laci tried again. "What are you doing?"

He looked up and met her gaze. "I thought it was obvious. I'm trying to get us some stock so we can keep this thing going. Want to help?"

"You think you can really do it?"

His gaze bore into hers. Judd McCandrick had married the woman Brant should have married, and for seven years Judd had raised the son that Brant should have been raising. However it had come about— through Brant's own stubbornness and stupidity, or Laci's betrayal and silence—Judd McCandrick had stolen Brant's family from him. He wasn't about to let the man steal his chance to fulfill Brett's dream, too. "I can do it," he said, his voice hard and determined. "If you'll help me."

Laci felt a spurt of renewed hope and excitement. Maybe if this worked and he won the Championship, maybe then they could talk and she could explain. They might never have a life together, he might not love her the way she needed him to love her, but maybe he could at least forgive her. She rose. "Okay, but I've got a couple of other phone calls to make first." She walked to another desk and sat down.

"Charley, you got a list of stock contractors sanctioned by the PRCA around here anywhere?" Brant asked.

"Yeah." He pulled a book from his desk drawer and handed it to Brant.

"Good." Brant immediately began checking off certain names, then tore the sheets from the book and divided them into three piles. He kept one, handed one to Charley and shoved the other on the desk where Laci sat. "Start calling the ones I marked. They're not going to like getting a late-night call, but we don't have a choice. Apologize, mention my name, say it's a personal favor to me, but we need whatever stock they've got."

Laci dialed the number of her attorney. She'd never thought it would come to this, but what Judd had done was unforgivable. If it had been something that only hurt her, maybe she would have just turned the other cheek. After all, marrying him when she knew she didn't love him hadn't exactly been the most fair thing she'd ever done. But pulling his stock out of the Championships could have repercussions on too many people.

Laci hung up the phone and drained what had to be her twelfth cup of coffee. Her shoulders ached, her ear felt as if it had swollen to the size of a cabbage, and the fingers on her right hand were sore from scribbling arrangements and times for pickups and deliveries.

Brant swung around in his chair to face her. "What have you got?"

She looked at her list. "Barnes, Hemsted, Donovan and Bowers came through. Hawkins and Dellos couldn't help us."

"You got the pickups arranged?"

"Yes."

Brant looked at Charley. "What about you?"

"All set. Connors, Sinclaire, Toomes and Kirby's animals will be here tomorrow."

"Good." He turned back to his desk and wrote something on his own pad, made another phone call, then tossed his pencil down, leaned back in his chair and stretched his arms wide. "I'm bushed."

They'd worked through the night. He rose and walked to the window, looking out at the empty arena. The sun had risen beyond the roof of the spectator stand opposite the office. He glanced at his watch and turned to look at Laci. They'd barely spoken to each other all night, except to relay names, numbers and status of who was supplying what, or who couldn't do a thing for them. Strictly business.

When Kit had returned to the office an hour after Judd's stunt, Laci had sent him home with Billy and his mom.

In the few minutes that Brant stood at the window, Charley had left his seat at his desk and moved to the couch in the corner of the office. The soft sound of his snores echoed through the room like the faint, rhythmic rumbles of a far-off but steadily approaching steam train.

Brant looked at Laci. She was still sitting at her desk, but had folded her arms atop the papers strewn before her and laid her head down.

He wanted to pull her into his arms worse than he'd ever wanted to do anything in his life. For years he'd tried to convince himself he didn't need anyone, especially her, fooling himself into believing that the only reason he avoided returning to Reno was to keep from dredging up old memories. But he needed her, wanted her, as much now as he had then. Maybe more. She was a part of him, a fire within his heart that neither distance nor time had quite managed to extinguish.

At the same time he wanted to pound his fist on

the desk and demand to know why she hadn't told
him about Kit. He wanted to know how she could
have let him walk away when she was carrying his
child. Why she hadn't told him.

She raised her head and looked up at him. "Are
we okay?" she asked softly. "Through?"

He nodded, steeling himself against the surge of
desire that had gripped him as he'd stood watching
her. "We should have enough stock here for tonight's
show," he said. "And more will arrive tomorrow."

"I owe you a lot for this, Brant."

He took a step toward her, his gaze locked with
hers. "All I want is to know is why you didn't..."

The door flew open, banging against the inside wall
with a loud crash.

Brant jerked around, expecting to see Judd.

Kit burst into the room like a miniature cyclone.
"Hey, Mom, look what Billy's mom bought me." He
ran around Laci's desk, a toy airplane made out of
red-and-silver Coke cans held high in the air, its pro-
peller rotating as he moved.

Charley snorted and sat up, blinking rapidly.

"Kit," Laci said, "come here."

He whirled around and ran to her. "Isn't it neat-o,
Mom? She bought Billy one, too, but his is green."

"Yes, it's neat-o." She brushed a hand over a way-
ward curl that dangled onto his forehead. "Did you
remember to thank Mrs. Olsen for taking you to the
carnival, and letting you spend the night at her
house?"

"Yep, I did. She let me and Billy sleep in sleeping
bags out on her patio. It was neat-o. We had flash-
lights and shined them up in the sky."

Laci turned to Brant. "Thank you for all your help."

His gaze held hers, refusing to let her look away. Talk to me, his eyes said, tell me why.

Kit hopped over to Brant. "Hi."

He tore his gaze from Laci, not realizing how hard it would be to do until he was forced, and looked into a pair of eyes the same color as his own. Brant frowned. Funny, how he hadn't noticed that before. Or the fact that they both had the same black, wavy and slightly unruly hair. He smiled. "Hi, kiddo."

"Mom said you're my real dad."

Laci felt an unreasonable fear seize her heart and the words Brant had spoken so long ago once again screamed through her mind: *I don't want any kids.*

Brant sat down and pulled Kit onto his knee. "Yep, kinda looks that way."

Kit looked at him.

"Is it okay with you, that I'm your real father?" Brant asked when Kit didn't say anything.

Kit screwed his face into a thoughtful frown. "Are you afraid of the dark?"

Brant laughed. "No, actually, I kind of like it. Why?"

"I am. It scares me, kinda, when it's so dark I can't see anything, and my da...I mean Judd, used to yell at me and say I was a sissy."

A flash of anger wiped the smile from Brant's face, but as quickly as it came over him, it was gone. "Come to think of it, kiddo, when I was your age, I was scared of the dark, too."

"Did you have a night-light in you room like me?"

"No, I had a brother and a teddy bear."

"What was his name?"

"Buddy Bear."

"No, silly." Kit laughed. "Your brother. Is he in the rodeo, too?"

Laci watched as a shadow of sadness fell over Brant's features and she felt a tug at her heart. He'd told her once that he'd had a twin brother who'd died, but when she'd asked him what happened he'd just shook his head and said he didn't want to talk about it.

"His name was Brett," Brant said, "and he used to be in the rodeo, we were a team. But he lives in heaven now."

"He's an angel?" Kit asked, his brows soaring.

Brant nodded. "Yeah."

Laci had never asked Brant about his brother again, but she had asked her father. One night, at a rodeo down in Oklahoma, Brant had been late for his ride. Rumors said he'd been with a girl. Brett took his place so Brant wouldn't lose his point standing. The Garrisons were identical twins, so no one knew it was Brett on the bull instead of Brant, until he'd been thrown. The bull had gored him and Brant had gotten to the arena just in time to pull his dying brother into his arms.

An investigation cleared Brant of any wrongdoing, and since Brett was dead nothing further came of the situation. The cowboys, PRCA, even the spectators, soon forgot about it.

"But I don't have a brother or a teddy bear," Kit said, drawing Laci's attention back to the conversation.

"No teddy bear?" Brant echoed, as if aghast.

Kit shook his head.

Brant chuckled, leaned over and whispered into Kit's ear.

His eyes lit up and a wide smile split his face. "Really?"

Brant nodded. "Really."

"Okay." Kit slid from Brant's knee and began to run around the room with his airplane again.

Laci looked at Brant. There was so much she wanted to say, but she didn't know where to start, or even if he'd want to hear it.

Brant pushed out of his chair and strode to the door. "The first trucks ought to be arriving about three or so. I'll be back before then."

She watched him walk through the doorway and disappear. In a few days he would be walking out of her life again and she couldn't think of a thing to do to stop him, just like the last time. She ran to the door and stepped out onto the stair landing. He was moving around the corner of the office toward the parking lot. She had to stop him, she couldn't let him go, not again. Laci opened her mouth to call to him.

"Mom, Brant said he'd bring me Buddy Bear tonight so that I wouldn't have to be afraid of the dark anymore."

Laci looked down at Kit, relief sweeping through her and tears filling her eyes. He wouldn't make a promise to a little boy, his own son, and not keep it. Brant wouldn't do that.

"Whoa, that was really a long night," Charley said, coming to stand behind her and stretching his arms wide. "Want to go have some coffee, missy?"

She shook her head. "I don't think so, Charley,

thanks. I've had enough coffee in the past several hours to last me a few years. What I need is a hot shower and a few hours sleep.'' She grabbed her handbag from the table near the door and walked back outside. ''I'll see you back here tonight.''

''This afternoon,'' Charley said. ''Those trucks will be arriving about three, like Brant said, and someone has to be here to see to their unloading.''

She nodded. ''About three. Come on, Kit, we're going home.''

The sound of Kit tapping on his computer keys and talking back to the figures on his screen drifted down the hall and into Laci's room. She lay on her bed and stared up at the ceiling. The soft strains of some classical tune or other filtered through the speakers of the radio on her nightstand, supposedly to soothe her into sleep, but it wasn't working. Nothing was. She'd counted several hundred sheep, taken an aspirin, made herself some hot decaf cocoa, counted cows jumping over the moon, and ordered each part of her body to relax. But she was still awake and bone tired. A hot shower had relaxed her, soothed her tired muscles and drawn her into a delicious languor, but her mind wouldn't shut down long enough for her to fall asleep.

How had her life turned into such a mess? Once she'd thought everything was roses and sunshine and always would be. So what had happened? Where had all the black clouds come from?

Laci rolled over, pounded a fist into the pillow, and stared at the wall. She'd fallen in love, that's what had happened. Or at least, that's where it had all started. Brant Garrison had walked into her life and stolen her heart. She'd thought, years later, that she'd finally gotten it back, but she had only been fooling herself.

Laci sighed deeply. If she thought about it logically, she could even tell herself it was better that things had turned out the way they had. If she'd gone with Brant on the circuit when he'd asked her it would have meant hauling Kit from city to city, rodeo to rodeo, which was no way for a child to grow up. And she would have hated it, hiding in their trailer or a motel room and cringing every time he went out to compete, wondering if he'd come back horribly injured, or not come back at all. Eventually she might even have left Brant and come home to Reno, to her parents. At least Kit had enjoyed a stable home and family for the first six years of his life, and Brant had been able to chase his dream without worrying about feeding and supporting a wife and child.

"Right, and I love going to the dentist, too."

"Hey, Mommm, telephone."

Laci forced her eyes opened, groaned, closed them again, and tried to burrow her head into her pillow.

"Mommm."

She pushed up from the pillow. Her head throbbed, her body felt as if every muscle had turned to lead and her blood had been replaced by some kind of sluggish moving goop. She'd never been drunk, but she imagined this was probably pretty close to what the morning after tying one on felt like.

"Mommm."

Good lord, was the house on fire? "What?" she

yelled, then immediately winced as pain shot through her temples. What in blazes had she done to deserve this?

"Boom. Wow, gotcha." Kit ran into the room, Bear romping alongside of him. "Guess what, Mom? I won Supercruncher. Isn't that great? First time ever, too. I crunched him." Kit jumped onto her bed. Bear followed suit.

The mattress bounced and Laci's head throbbed. She grabbed it between both hands, as if holding it would make the pain go away. It didn't. "Wonderful. You won a computer game. Congratulations." She ruffled the hair on Bear's head and flopped back down onto her pillow. "Is that what you were yelling about?"

"No. Mrs. Dabney's on the phone. You were sleeping so when I heard her voice on the machine I answered it, but she wants to talk to you."

Laci glanced at the clock as she reached for the phone on her nightstand. Two o'clock. She bolted upright. Two o'clock? She only had an hour before she was due back at the arena. She grabbed the receiver, riffling through the drawer with her other hand in search of some aspirin. She came up with an empty bottle. "Mrs. Dabney? Are you back?"

"She can't come back for three more days," Kit said, at the same time the housekeeper said it over the phone.

"All right, yes, I understand. Yes, we'll see you then." Laci hung up the phone and threw back the covers. "I need coffee and aspirin, and we need to hurry."

"I cleaned up already," Kit said, bouncing on the bed. "Did I do okay?"

Laci glanced at his jeans, T-shirt and cowboy boots.

"Absolutely perfect." She grabbed a pair of designer jeans from her closet along with a blue-and-red plaid, western-cut blouse. "Are you hungry, sweetie?"

"Nah, I made myself a peanut butter and jelly sandwich a little while ago. I even toasted the bread. And I put everything away, too, just like Mrs. Dabney always says to do." He bounced again and Bear momentarily flew into the air.

"Terrific," she grumbled. "Next thing I know some know-it-all social worker will be pounding on the front door wanting to know why I let my kid live on junk food."

"What's a social worker?"

"A busy bod—" She caught herself. "A nice person who likes to make sure that little kids don't live on peanut butter and jelly sandwiches."

Kit bounded from the bed. "Oh. Can I go give Buster a carrot before we leave?"

Bear belly flopped onto the floor.

"Sure, but don't get dirty, okay? And come right back. While you're at it, give Bear a couple of biscuit bones."

Kit paused at the door. "Mom, if Brant, I mean, my real dad, doesn't want to come live here with us, could we go live with him on his ranch?"

She suddenly felt like crying. Why did children have such a simple way of looking at things? "I don't know, Kit," she said softly. "We'll see, okay?"

"Okay. But Brant said it's real nice up there. He said they've got lots of trees and grass and his ranch even has a lake on it where we could go swimming in the summer and if the ice gets thick enough he said you can skate on it during the winter and…"

"Kit." Laci stared at him, frowning and confused. "When did Brant tell you all this?"

"Just a little while ago."

"A little while ago?" She clutched the doorjamb. "He's here?"

Kit shook his head. "No, he phoned, but he said not to wake you up." He smiled widely. "Anyway, he said he just wanted to talk to me."

"What did he want?"

Kit shrugged. "Nothing. We just talked. But he said he's got horses on his ranch, and cows and chickens and he's got a lady living there who's got a little boy, too, and Brant, I mean, my real dad, he said me and Jeffrey could play together. That's the other little boy's name, Jeffrey."

A lady. Brant had a woman living on his ranch. Laci felt her heart plummet to her toes and stay there. She moved to the bed and sat down. A woman and a little boy. The implications of Kit's words weighed down on her, making her think things she didn't want to think.

"Come on, Mom, hurry up or we'll be late. Brant said he'd teach me more rope tricks before he rides tonight, if we have time. And after the rodeo he's going to give me Buddy Bear so I don't have to be afraid of the dark anymore. He says I'm not a sissy if I have a teddy bear 'cause he's had one all his life and he's not a sissy."

Laci walked into the bathroom, moving in a daze. She ran a brush through her hair. A lady—on Brant's ranch. She couldn't get the thought of it out of her mind.

Fifteen minutes later she was ready to leave, at least physically. Mentally she was a mess. Jealousy had edged its way into her heart and she couldn't seem to get rid of it, even if she did know it was ridiculous. Brant wouldn't have made love to her if he was living with someone else. He wouldn't.

Her mind whirled back to that night he'd followed her home after the rodeo. He'd been afraid for her, worried that Judd might do something to harm her or Kit. They'd made love in her bedroom.

Laci closed her eyes, remembering. She had said "love me," and he'd said "I do."

But he hadn't actually said he loved her, and he'd never made any mention of a future for them together, even after she'd told him about Kit.

Chapter 12

Laci gripped the steering wheel tightly. She'd once let Brant walk out of her life without trying to stop him. This time, if he was going to leave they were going to talk first.

Kit bounced on the seat and chattered nonstop all during the ride into town, too excited to sit still and totally unaware of the fact that Laci was so deep in thought she barely answered him.

As she pulled the Cherokee into the parking lot, Kit jerked off his seat belt and threw open his door. "Come on, Mom, look, there's already trucks here." He ran toward the gate.

"Kit," Laci yelled, "wait!"

He skidded to a stop and turned back to her, looking sheepish.

"You know you're not supposed to run off like that." Her voice was sterner than she'd meant it to be. Laci chided herself. She had no business taking her foul mood out on him. He'd only been the messenger. And an innocent one at that. "I don't want you around when the cattle are being unloaded. It's dangerous."

"Aw, Mom."

"Sit on the steps to the office. You can see from there and I won't have to worry about you getting trampled."

Kit brightened. "Okay." He scrambled halfway up the stairs.

Laci saw Charley supervising the unloading of one truck, but she didn't see Brant and in spite of herself, felt a wave of disappointment.

"Hey, just in time," Charley called out. "We could use some help."

"Fine, what do you want me to do?"

"Take down the chutes on that other truck so we can start unloading. I'll be over in a minute."

"Right." Laci walked to the rear of the truck parked just behind the one Charley was unloading. She looked it over as she walked past the cab and proceeded toward the rear of the trailer. It was old and badly in need of paint. Probably closer to retirement than Charley, she mused. At the rear gates she reached up for the lock latch, but it was a few inches higher than she could manage. "Damn." She looked around for something to stand on, saw nothing, and looked back at the truck. There was what looked like a toehold, or foot bar, running beneath the battered and half-rusted license plate. She stepped on it and holding onto the door handle, hoisted herself up and grabbed for the lock latch.

Brant was just walking past the entry gate when he spotted Laci. For only the second time in his life he felt his breath stall in his lungs. Fear, like icy cold tentacles, viciously gripped his heart and threatened to squeeze the life out of it, while allowing him to watch another person he loved die. Though his legs suddenly felt like rubber he forced them to move and ran toward her, but when he needed speed, it seemed that his body was only willing to move in agonizingly slow motion.

"Laci, no," he screamed.

He saw several others start and jerk around at hearing him, saw Kit jump up from his seat on the stairs, and even caught, out of the corner of his eye, the scared look that instantly came over the child's face. But most of all Brant saw Laci, saw her fingers wrap around the handle of the trailer's gate lock.

She pulled down on it at almost the exact second Brant screamed her name.

He swerved to the right, just a little, then swerved back toward her, his arms outstretched.

A startled shriek flew from Laci's lips as Brant smashed into her side just as the gate began to drop away from its frame. She flew sideways and slammed to the ground. Brant landed on top of her, his weight forcing the air from her lungs.

The loading chute crashed to the ground with a deafening thud, its metal end plunging into the hard-packed earthen drive and sending a cloud of dust, dirt and bits of gravel flying upward.

Stars whirled in front of Laci's eyes, every bone in her body felt jarred or broken, and she couldn't catch her breath. She was going to die. Dust clogged her nose and throat and swirled in front of her eyes.

Brant pushed himself off her, then grabbed her arms and hauled her to him. "Are you all right? Laci, talk to me! Are you all right?" One hand held onto her arm while the other moved over her lightly. "Are you hurt?"

"I'm..." She inhaled deeply, needing the air. "I'm okay." She coughed raggedly on the dust that had invaded her throat along with the air she'd sucked into her lungs. "What happened?"

Brant dragged her into his arms and crushed her against his chest, holding her tighter than he'd ever dared before, needing to feel the warmth of her against him, as if to verify that she truly was still alive. "You could have been killed." Tears suddenly filled his eyes. "God, I could have really lost you."

"Wow, Dad, I mean Brant, that was neat-o," Kit said, running up to them.

Charley shooed Kit aside. "C'mon champ, before you get trampled by cattle eager to get themselves outta that truck."

The others who'd been helping with the unloading merely stared, unable to comprehend what had happened.

Brant pulled away from Laci finally and sat back. He touched a hand to her face, tentatively caressing her cheek. "I could have really lost you this time," he whispered again.

Laci frowned. "I don't understand. What happened?"

He closed his eyes, summoning his composure back, then opened them again to meet her gaze. "The gates on some of these older model trucks don't have safety bars or latches. I recognized this truck as Ted Barnes's truck. I've helped him unload before and knew there was no safety. When I saw you unlatching the lock, I knew you didn't know the chute was going to come flying down. If you had been struck by it..." He shook his head.

Laci felt herself start to tremble.

He pulled her back into his arms. Years ago he'd been late to another arena, and because of that his brother had died. This time however, being late had been a godsend. Otherwise he'd have been elsewhere, maybe up in front helping Charley, and wouldn't have seen her reach for that latch.

"You okay?" Charley asked, coming up beside them.

Laci looked up and nodded, and with Brant's help, got to her feet.

Charley hurried off to supervise the unloading of another truck.

"We need to talk," Brant said, as if reading her mind.

Her eyes met his, china blue fusing with black-touched sapphire blue, like the melding of a spring day with the coming of night. This man had stolen her heart years before, and she knew now she would never get it back, nor did she want to. Brant Garrison was everything she wanted in a man, everything she had ever hoped and dreamed. She could only pray that he wanted her, too.

Laci nodded. "Yes, we do."

"When we get done unloading I'll come to the

office and we'll go have dinner somewhere before tonight's events start. Okay?''

''Yes,'' she whispered.

An hour and a half later Brant walked into the arena office. He looked at Laci, then at Kit. ''So, you two ready for some of Mama Tia's pizza?''

''Yeah!'' Kit yelled, jumping up from the floor where he'd been playing with a plastic fort surrounded by tiny plastic soldiers.

''I thought maybe Kit should stay here with Charley,'' Laci said. She tried to ignore the pout that instantly came to her son's face at her words.

Brant frowned. ''Why?''

She shrugged, unable to voice the thoughts running through her mind. *Because I'm afraid you're going to walk away like you did seven and a half years ago. Because you told me once that you didn't want kids and I'm not sure you've changed your mind enough to really accept the responsibility of a son, but most of all because I love you, but I don't know if you love me enough to stay.* ''I just thought it might be better,'' she said finally.

''I think he should come,'' Brant said, surprising her.

''Whoopee,'' Kit said. ''Can I have ice cream for dessert again? And play the video games?''

''Sure.''

Kit ran out the door ahead of them and scooted down the stairs.

''Ready?'' Brant asked Laci.

No, she wanted to scream. *I've waited for this day for years, but I'm not ready. I'm afraid of what you're* going to say. I love you. I can't lose you again. But I don't know how to hold on to you. She nodded and walked past him to the door. Suddenly she remembered what Kit had told her about a lady living at Brant's ranch and felt an urge to run, to flee this confrontation and just find somewhere to hide. She didn't want to hear him say goodbye again, or tell her he was in love with someone else. Or maybe he was married, maybe his making love to her hadn't meant anything more to him than reliving old times. Was the child Kit had mentioned—Jeffrey—was he Brant's son?

Steeling herself against the questions parading through her mind, she forced herself to walk calmly toward his pickup, while her insides churned in panic. She was being silly. Brant had been outraged to learn he had a son that she hadn't told him about. He wanted Kit. But who was the woman at Brant's ranch? The question continued to nag at her.

If it hadn't been for Kit's constant chatter on the way to the pizza parlor, the ride would have been made in total silence. Brant concentrated on driving and answering Kit's questions and comments, while Laci concentrated on staring out through the passenger window at scenery she'd seen a hundred thousand times.

Brant parked the pickup beside the restaurant and Mama's son Peter welcomed them enthusiastically, showed them to a window table and took their order.

"I guess Kit told you I called earlier today."

Laci nodded and glanced across the room at Kit, who was playing a video game. "He said you told him all about your ranch in Montana."

"Yeah. I think he'd like it there."

She bit her lip, not certain how to ask what she needed to know. "He...he said there was a little boy there named Jeffrey."

Brant smiled. "Yeah, Jeffrey. He's a good kid. His mom's my housekeeper and cooks for the hands. Her husband was a rodeo clown. He died a few years ago." He saw the haunted look that came into Laci's eyes, the fear. "His car blew a tire on the freeway, he lost control."

"Oh."

"Shelly's one of a kind."

Laci's feelings had momentarily soared at learning the "other" woman was Brant's housekeeper. Now, hearing the way he'd said she was *one of a kind,* they took a nosedive.

Brant caught her gaze. "Now she's in love with my partner, most likely be marrying him next year."

Laci couldn't help the smile that split her lips.

Brant leaned forward and grabbed her hand, holding it cradled within both of his. "I never forgot you, Laci, and I never stopped loving you."

Her heart sighed in relief, and swelled with joy. "And I never stopped loving you," she said softly.

"Then why?" he asked, his gaze penetrating hers, searching.

She pulled away from him, needing to call on all her reserves, all her strength to answer him. "I didn't know until almost a month after you'd left."

"But why didn't you try to contact me?"

She shook her head, looking everywhere but at him. He wasn't going to understand. She'd known he wouldn't, and she couldn't blame him, not really.

What she'd done had been wrong, but she hadn't thought so at the time.

"Hey, Brant, look, I won."

He glanced at Kit and smiled. "That's great, kiddo. Now see if you can top your own score."

"Okay." Kit plunked another quarter into the machine and began working its dials furiously.

Brant turned back to Laci. "Why, Laci? Why didn't you find me and tell me?"

"Because by that time I was sure you didn't really love me, and I didn't want you to come back just because I was pregnant with your child." There, she'd said it, finally, and it sounded so impotent, so shallow, but back then, with her parents echoing her own feelings, insisting that she didn't want to be married to a man who'd only married her because she had his child, it had felt right.

Brant's hands clenched into fists. "But I'd planned on coming back, Laci. You had to have known that."

She shook her head. "No, I didn't know that. You didn't say that. You said you weren't the settling-down kind, remember? You were so angry when you left, infuriated that I had tried to get you a job with my father, and that I didn't want to go on the circuit with you."

"But I loved you," Brant said. "You knew that. You knew I would have come back."

"I waited three months, Brant, and there was no word from you. Not a call, a letter, nothing." She shrugged. "Judd was there. He wanted to marry me, and my parents wanted me to marry him." Laci looked up then, meeting his gaze. "I didn't want my child not to have a father."

"But he had a father."

"Not one who was around. Not one who had given him his name. I'm not the settling-down kind—I don't want children, those were the things you said, and I had to believe you'd meant them. I did what I thought was best, for all of us."

Brant clenched and unclenched his hands. "I would have been around, would have given Kit my name, Laci, if I had known."

Tears filled her eyes. "Don't you see, that's exactly why I didn't try to find you. I didn't want you to come back to me and Kit because you felt obligated."

"Damn it, Laci, I loved you. I still do."

"But not enough," she whispered. "You love the rodeo more. You always have."

"What?" He leaned forward across the table. "Is that what you think?"

She couldn't answer. The words had dried up in her throat. What was the use of this arguing? Neither of them had changed. Brant had a ranch now, but it wasn't a home. His home was still the road, the circuit. Laci still wanted stability, a home, family, and she was still terrified whenever he rode. They still wanted the same things out of life they'd wanted years ago, and the two weren't compatible.

Brant leaned forward again, taking her hands in his and drawing her toward him. "That's what you thought? What you think now? That I love the rodeo more than I love you?"

She sighed. "Yes."

"That's why you weren't going to tell me, even now, that Kit is my son?"

"Yes."

"Damn it, Laci." The words were little more than whispered anguish. He dropped his head, sitting hunched over for several long seconds, holding tightly to her hands.

Laci stared at the top of his hat. She'd been wrong. She knew that now. Whether he had decided to stay or not, she should never have kept the knowledge from him that he had a son. They may only have seen each other a few times a year, but she'd had no right to keep Brant and Kit apart.

Brant looked back up at her. "I love the rodeo, Laci, that's true, but I love you more than anything in the world." He sighed and sat back. "And I guess I always have. Even when I was cursing you for refusing to go with me on the circuit, even when I thought I hated you after hearing that you'd married Judd, I still loved you. I've tried for years to forget you, to fall in love with someone else, or convince myself I didn't need anyone at all, but it didn't work. I couldn't forget you Laci, or stop loving you, that's why I never came back to Reno. I was afraid to see you again, afraid it would only make the ache in my gut and the loneliness worse."

She stared at him, unable to believe what he was saying. "Then why'd you leave? Why was it so important that you follow the circuit even when I said I couldn't go with you?"

"I had to."

Laci frowned. "Had to?"

He released her hands and sat back. Suddenly his shoulders seemed to sag. He rubbed his eyes with his fingers, then looked out through the restaurant's bay window, staring at the street. He had never told another soul about what had happened and why, or about the feelings of guilt that ate at him every day, every second. And now he had to tell her. "Two years before I met you my brother died."

She nodded. "I'd heard that."

"Did you hear that it was my fault?"

Laci stared at him, but remained silent.

"We were going to win the Championships, that was our dream. Together. Then we were going to buy a ranch and operate a rodeo school for kids. City kids and disabled kids who dream of being cowboys."

"So, you're trying to fulfill that dream alone?"

"Yes, but not for myself. It was my fault Brett died. It should have been me on that damned bull."

Laci saw the hurt that crept into his features, and shadowed his eyes. She wanted to reach out to him, comfort him, but hesitated, not certain he would want her sympathy.

"But I was too busy playing around to worry about the time. I was off in our trailer with a woman."

He looked up at her then, waiting for her condemnation, for the look of disgust to come into her eyes that he'd seen so often in his own when he looked into the mirror and remembered that day. But it wasn't there.

"You had no way of knowing Brett would take your place," Laci said.

"Yes, I did. I should have. We were twins. We looked alike, thought alike. If the situation had been reversed, I would have ridden for him. I should have known he'd do it for me." A long sigh slipped past his lips. "We were on top then. We would have made the Championships that year, easy. I should have known he'd take my ride because he didn't want to win the world title without me, and not taking the ride, not making those points, would have most likely dropped me down to second place.'' He felt as if he were reliving the whole thing all over again, the ache of loss ripping at his heart, tearing at his insides.

He looked back up at Laci. ''That's why I couldn't quit the circuit when you asked me to. I had to go on. The day Brett died, I held him in my arms and promised that I'd win the World Championship for him, and I'd start that school for kids.'' Tears filled Brant's eyes. ''It had always been more his dream than mine, and I knew then that no matter what, I had to do it for him. I had to.''

Laci reached across the table for his hand. ''Why didn't you tell me?''

Brant shrugged. ''I never talked about it with anyone, but I especially couldn't with you. How does a man tell the woman he loves that he's responsible for the death of his own brother?''

Laci held his hand and stared into his eyes. They'd both hidden behind their fears, and because of that, they'd lost seven and a half years together, and they'd almost lost forever.

''It wasn't your fault, '' she said softly. ''Brett knew what he was doing, what the risks were.''

''Yeah, but if I...''

''You had no way of knowing what would happen.'' She reached to him and pressed a finger to his lips.

''Hey, Brant,'' Kit said, running up to them, ''it's...''

Brant turned to Kit. ''Hey, kiddo, I'm your father.

Think you can call me Dad?'' He looked back at Laci. ''If it's okay with your mom?''

She smiled.

''Okay, *Dad*, but look,'' he held up his arm and shoved his cowboy watch in front of Brant's face, ''it's almost time for your ride.

''Well, the Association's suing Judd,'' Charley said the minute Laci walked into the office.

She turned back to Kit. ''I saw Billy down by the wash stalls. You want to go on down and play with him outside for a while?''

He surprised her by shaking his head. ''No, I want to watch the bull riders!''

She smiled. ''Okay.'' Laci turned back to Charley and threw him a warning look. Kit might know now that Judd wasn't his father, but he had been for almost seven years.

Charley nodded. ''They took away his sanction so he won't be stock contracting anymore, not that it'll hurt his pocketbook much anyway, but at least it's something. Be interesting to see what happens with the suit though.''

''He just wanted his family back, Charley,'' Laci said.

''Yeah, well, that was the wrong way to go about it. Anyway, I figure to try contracting through some of the ones who came through for us today, if that's okay with you.''

''Fine.''

''I got the final report back from the accounting firm on the books, too.''

Laci stiffened. She hadn't wanted anyone to see

that until after she had, but she hadn't told Charley not to open it if it came. She'd never thought to. No more bad news, she prayed. Please.

"Everything's fine. Judd had some of the figures screwed up a bit, but nothing's missing or anything."

She breathed a sigh of relief. She might not feel real fond of her ex-husband right now, but she didn't want to discover that he'd done anything while managing James Enterprises to jeopardize its financial standing.

"Brant Garrison's up next folks, riding Midnight Fever, a young bull, new to the circuit, with a lot of energy."

Laci felt her insides cringe.

"Come on, Mom," Kit called, and raced to the window, "let's watch Dad ride."

Charley looked up at Laci, a wide grin splitting his face. "Dad?" he mouthed, and grinned.

She smiled, realizing then that Charley had known the truth all along. "He knows. They both know. I'll fill you in later."

She sat down at her desk, memories of Sonny flying from his motorcycle and hitting the hard pavement flashing through her mind. She grabbed a folder full of papers from her In basket and shuffled through them.

"Mommm."

"Garrison's a contender for World Champion All-Around Cowboy tonight folks, and if he can lead on this one, he'll have it."

The sound of the bull chute gate opening echoed into the office.

"Good start. Over a ton of angry animal…" the announcer said.

Laci felt every muscle in her body tense and tried to block the announcer's voice from her consciousness.

"Wow! Ohhh, Wow," Kit shouted, jumping up and down in front of the window.

"Excellent form," the announcer continued. "Brody, see the way Garrison spurs?" he asked the other announcer.

"Perfection," Brody Dunn said.

"Whoa, Midnight's pitch is high but Garrison's hanging in there. Keeping his arm clear."

Laci closed her eyes. The buzzer blared and she jumped slightly in her chair.

"Yeah!" Kit yelled, jumping about and clapping his hands.

"Clean dismount," Brody Dunn announced.

"Well, I'll be damned," Charley said. "Will you look at that scoreboard."

Laci opened her eyes and ran to the window.

Brant stared unbelievingly at the scoreboard.

The crowd erupted into an earsplitting cheer, standing on their seats and waving their hands.

Picking up his hat from the ground, where it had fallen during his ride, Brant waved to the spectators, then turned to look up at the office window. He couldn't see Laci behind the silver glass, but he knew she was there. She and Kit. He waved his hat toward them and smiled, then was instantly surrounded by a crowd of whooping cowboys, all laughing, congratulating him and slapping him on the back.

He looked around for Laci, his gaze continually

moving toward the stairs leading up to the office, but she didn't come. Brant took a swallow from the bottle of water someone had shoved into his hand. He should be elated, he knew that. He'd finally done it: gotten the Championship, the silver buckle, the money for the school. Everything he'd promised Brett was coming true, but it wasn't enough. His gaze moved toward the office stairs again.

Laci returned to her desk and sat down. Relief that Brant was all right coursed through her system, while remembrance of Sonny's death was tucked back into the recesses of her memory where it belonged.

"Mom, Mom, let's go see Dad," Kit said excitedly. He buzzed around her desk, jumping up and down.

"Not yet," she murmured softly. What was she afraid of now? He was safe. Yet her nerves were abuzz and her heart was beating at an incredibly fast pace. "In a little while, honey."

"Aw, Mom," Kit whined. "I wanna go now."

"In a little while," she repeated, a bit more sternly.

"Okay, folks, we've got Tim Hallert up next," the announcer said, "riding Red Eye."

Kit ran back to the window.

"He made it," Charley informed her, swiveling around in his chair to face Laci. "He's won the title. No one can come close to his point and money spread."

She nodded. "I know."

An hour later the announcer called everyone's attention to the east side of the arena, "...where we'll be presenting the World Championship titles and buckles,'' he declared.

Laci pushed away from her desk. He loved her, he'd said that. And she loved him. But there was still a problem, still a question, unanswered, gnawing at her mind, and it wasn't going to let her rest until she put it to him. Then she'd know if there was any possibility of a future together for them. ''Kit, stay here,'' she said over her shoulder and hurried toward the door.

''Ah, Mommm.''

''Brant Garrison, World Champion All-Around Cowboy.''

Laci heard the announcement just as she descended the office stairs. Pride for him swelled within her breast. He really had done it, finally. She walked past the chutes, arriving at the gate just in time to see the PRCA rep hand Brant his silver World Champion buckle.

The spectators erupted into a roaring cheer.

Now, Laci thought, as tears filled her eyes, maybe Brett can rest in peace, and Brant can begin to live his life for himself. She clutched the chute rails and watched as cowboy after cowboy congratulated him, hugged him, slapped him on the back, and shook his hand.

Brant looked up and saw Laci. ''Excuse me, guys,'' he said to the crowd around him, ''but there's something I've got to do that I should have done a long time ago.'' He broke away from the laughing group and walked to Laci.

''Congratulations, cowboy,'' she whispered.

He drew her into his arms, crushing her against him.

"Dad, Dad," Kit yelled. "You did it! You won!" He threw himself against Brant's legs, wrapping his arms around them and jumping up and down. "You're the best cowboy ever!"

Laughing, and pulling away from Laci, Brant hunkered down in front of Kit. "You liked that, huh?"

"Yeah, it was great. Can I see your buckle?"

"How about if you wear it for me?" Brant said.

"Really?"

Brant quickly unbuckled Kit's belt and attached the silver buckle to it. He refastened it and leaned back slightly, as if to get a better look.

"Wow, you mean it? I can wear your Championship buckle?"

"Can't think of anyone I'd rather see wear it."

"Neat-o! Look, Mom," Kit said, spinning toward Laci.

Wrapping an arm around Kit's legs, Brant scooped him up from the ground, then, holding Kit against his chest, stood and wrapped his other arm around Laci.

"It's over," he said, his deep voice rich and full of life. "Now it's time to go home."

Laci looked up at him, happy and scared at the same time. She didn't know what he was saying.

"I want to go home, Laci," Brant said, as if reading her mind and confusion, "I want to settle down on the ranch, raise cattle, run the school Brett and I always dreamed of, and contract a little stock to the rodeos."

"That…sounds wonderful," she said, her fear mounting. Was this his way of saying goodbye again?

"But only if you'll come with me," he added, and smiled.

In spite of the way her heart leapt with joy at his words, Laci hesitated.

Brant saw the shadow in her eyes, sensed her indecision, and felt his own heart falter in its beat. He couldn't lose her now. He wouldn't. "Talk to me, Laci," Brant pleaded softly.

She looked at Kit. "Honey, could you go up and ask Charley if he'd mind closing up for me tonight?"

Brant frowned. What was she going to say that she didn't want their son to hear? He felt the blood in his veins chill. Goodbye was the worst word that came to his mind.

"Okay, Mom. Then can we go for pizza?"

Laci smiled. "We just had pizza a few hours ago. Don't you ever get tired of it?"

"Nope."

"Okay, we'll see."

"Neat-o."

Brant set Kit down on the ground and watched him skip toward the stairs. He turned back to Laci, truly terrified for the very first time in his life.

"Brant..."

"Don't say no, Laci," he said suddenly, cutting her off. "I love you, I need you with me."

She reached up and touched his cheek lightly with the tips of her fingers. "And I love you," she said softly, "but it's not just the two of us this time."

He frowned. "Kit doesn't want to go? He doesn't want me for a father?"

Laci smiled. "Kit adores you."

"Then, what? What is it?" He felt as if ready to

explode from the fear that had gripped every nerve cell in his body. Unable to help himself, Brant grabbed her and dragged her into his embrace, crushing her against his chest. "What?" he breathed into the long, silky strands of her hair. "What's wrong?"

She pushed against his chest, moving away from him slightly. "You told me once that you didn't want children."

"I didn't want..." He stared at her, his mouth agape as he tried to come to grips with her implication.

"You refused to explain to me then, but you were adamant," Laci said. Maybe after everything he'd already said, after seeing the way he and Kit had bonded to each other, she was being foolish, but she had to hear him say he really wanted Kit, and she had to know why he'd thought he never wanted children at all.

His laugh startled her. "At that time I was, and I was a fool for saying it to you. But now I can't think of anything I want more than for you and Kit to come to Montana with me, forever. He's my son."

"But you said..."

He suddenly sobered and looked into her eyes, holding her gaze with his, letting the shutters he'd always hidden his emotions behind open. "I was still eaten up with grief over Brett's death then, Laci. I felt responsible for it, and in spite of what you say, or what I do, a part of me probably always will. But back then, when I said that to you, I figured if I couldn't handle being responsible toward my own brother and his safety, then I couldn't handle the responsibility of a kid. But I was wrong not to talk to you. I shut you out, and because of that I cost us seven and a half years together. But I never stopped loving you Laci, and now I love Kit, too.''

''Are you sure?'' she whispered, afraid to believe him, afraid to hope.

''Marry me, Laci,'' Brant said, the deep drawl of his voice heavy with the emotions churning through him. ''Marry me and let me prove to you, and Kit, every day for the rest of my life, how much I love you both.'' He brushed his lips tenderly across hers. ''Marry me, and maybe, if you want, we can even see about getting Kit a little brother or sister. Or,'' he smiled wickedly, ''maybe more, since twins run in my family.''

Laci looked up at him, into the eyes that had haunted her every dream and waking moment. In all that time she had tried to convince herself that she had stopped loving this man, but her heart had always known the truth: she would never stop loving him. No matter the pain of the past, or the uncertainties of the future, she would never stop loving Brant Garrison.

Sweeping the black Stetson from his head, Brant caught Laci's lips with his own, his kiss warm and exquisitely gentle in its taking, yet the heat of his passion, the fire of his desire for her, hovered just beyond the regions of that tender assault. ''Marry me, Laci,'' he said against her lips, his own moving to caress the delicate curve of her cheek. He pulled back slightly and looked down at her, reaching up to run the fingers of one hand through her hair. ''Make me the happiest man in the world, Laci, and marry me. Let's have a dozen more wonderful children like Kit, let's watch the sun come up every morning together, and hold each other every night when it goes down." He caressed her cheek. "Marry me, Laci," he said softly again, "and let me love you forever."

His mouth captured hers again, his tongue diving between her lips to probe the honey-sweet softness there, stroking flame upon flame wherever it touched.

"Mom, Charley said okay," Kit yelled. He jumped off of the next to last stair and ran past the chutes toward them. "Now can we go get pizza?"

Brant reluctantly tore his lips from Laci's and they both turned to watch their son skid to a halt in front of them.

"Yes," Laci said, "but first I have a question for you."

"Okay, what? But hurry up, 'cause I'm hungry."

"How would you like to go live on Brant's ranch in Montana?"

"Are you coming?"

She laughed softly. "Yes."

"Does that mean he's really going to be my dad all the time then?"

Tears stung the back of Brant's eyes, and emotion clogged his throat, but he pushed both aside. Taking Laci's hand in his, he hunkered down before Kit. "Would you like that, kiddo? For me to be your dad all the time?"

Kit frowned. "Would you?"

Brant nodded. "Very much."

A wide smile pulled at Kit's lips. "Neat-o." He jumped forward and threw his arms around Brant's neck. "Can Buster and Bear go, too?"

Brant laughed and straightened, holding Kit firmly

against his chest with one arm, and wrapping the other around Laci to pull her close. "Buster, Bear, Buddy Bear, Blackjack, you, me, Mom and…" He turned a devilish eye on Laci. "Maybe we can even see about getting a little brother or sister to make an appearance here pretty soon."

"Really, Mom?" Kit asked excitedly.

Laci tried to look at Brant through the tears of happiness that filled her eyes. How could she have ever been so wrong about him?

Epilogue

Two days after Brant won the World Championship and proposed to Laci, they were married in a quaint little chapel on the Bonanza ranch, just outside of Lake Tahoe, where the television show used to be filmed. Charley gave Laci away and her cousin Trish was her maid of honor. Brant's partner on the ranch flew in to be his best man, and Kit carried the rings.

It took almost another month to pack up everything and transfer the management of James Enterprises into Charley's more than capable hands, though Laci put a condition on handing over the reins to him. For at least one month every summer, as well as at Christmas, he had to come and live with them on the ranch in Montana. It was a condition he readily and happily agreed to.

Brant hired a moving company to pick up all of Laci's furniture, packed her and Kit's suitcases in the back of his pickup, sold his single-wide horse trailer and rented a double-wide horse trailer to accommodate Buster and Blackjack on the trip to Montana. Bear was riding in the back seat of the pickup with Kit.

"You okay back there?" Brant asked over his shoulder, glancing in the rearview mirror at Kit at the same time.

"Yep, 'cept I'm getting hungry."

Laci moaned softly.

"I'm beginning to think you've got a tapeworm hidden in that stomach of yours," Brant said.

"Stop the truck," Laci snapped suddenly. "Now."

Frowning, Brant pulled over to the side of the winding road. "What's the ma—"

Laci threw her door open and jumped out, gulping in huge swallows of air and clinging to the bed's railing.

Brant hurried around the truck and grabbed her arms. She was suddenly too pale. "What's wrong?" he growled, half scared out of his wits now. They were in the middle of nowhere, miles from any major town, and Laci looked about ready to faint.

She held up a hand and took a deep breath. Straightening, she shook her head and after a few seconds, smiled. "Well, I had planned on waiting until we got to the ranch, then I was hoping to have a romantic evening in front of that rock fireplace you were telling me about and..."

"Laci, damn it," Brant thundered, "what's wrong?"

"Nothing."

"Nothing?" he fairly shouted. "You yell at me to

stop the truck, for several minutes you look about ready to faint, or gag, or whatever, and now you say nothing's wrong?''

''Nothing's wrong, except…well, you've been busy packing my things up and helping us to sell the house and—'' she threw a hand through the air ''—didn't notice, which was fine with me. I mean, this isn't exactly the best time of the day for me.''

Brant didn't know what she was babbling about, or what he should do. He only knew she looked sick, and that was scaring the hell out of him. ''Laci, honey, what's wrong? Come on, get back in the truck and I'll turn around. Maybe there's a doctor in that town we went through aways back.''

Laci laughed. It was a weak laugh, but it was a laugh, and that gave him hope.

''I've already seen the doctor,'' Laci said, and slipped her arms around Brant's waist. ''It started about two days after our wedding night.''

Brant frowned. ''Started? What started?''

''The morning sickness.''

Brant stared at her, eyes wide, mouth agape in surprise.

Laci laughed softly. ''Shut your mouth, handsome, before you catch a fly.''

He snapped his mouth shut. ''Are you…are you really…?''

She smiled. ''Yes, I am, really.''

Laci felt certain the whoop of joy that ripped from Brant's mouth startled every living creature for several hundred miles around.

*   *   *   *   *

Harlequin® Historical

From rugged lawmen and valiant knights to defiant heiresses and spirited frontierswomen, Harlequin Historicals will capture your imagination with their dramatic scope, passion and adventure.

Harlequin Historicals...
they're too good to miss!

Silhouette®

Where love comes alive™

SILHOUETTE *Romance*

From first love to forever, these love stories are
for today's woman with traditional values.

Silhouette® *Desire*

A highly passionate, emotionally powerful
and always provocative read.

Silhouette®

SPECIAL EDITION™

Emotional, compelling stories that capture the
intensity of living, loving and creating a family in
today's world.

Silhouette®

INTIMATE MOMENTS™

A roller-coaster read that delivers romantic thrills
in a world of suspense, adventure and more.